Andreas de Harcla

NORTHERN WARRIOR

~~~~~~~~~~~~~~~~~~~

A story of the English borderlands
at the time of Robert the Bruce

~~~~~~~~~~~~~~~~~

by Adrian Rogan

HAYLOFT

NORTHERN WARRIOR

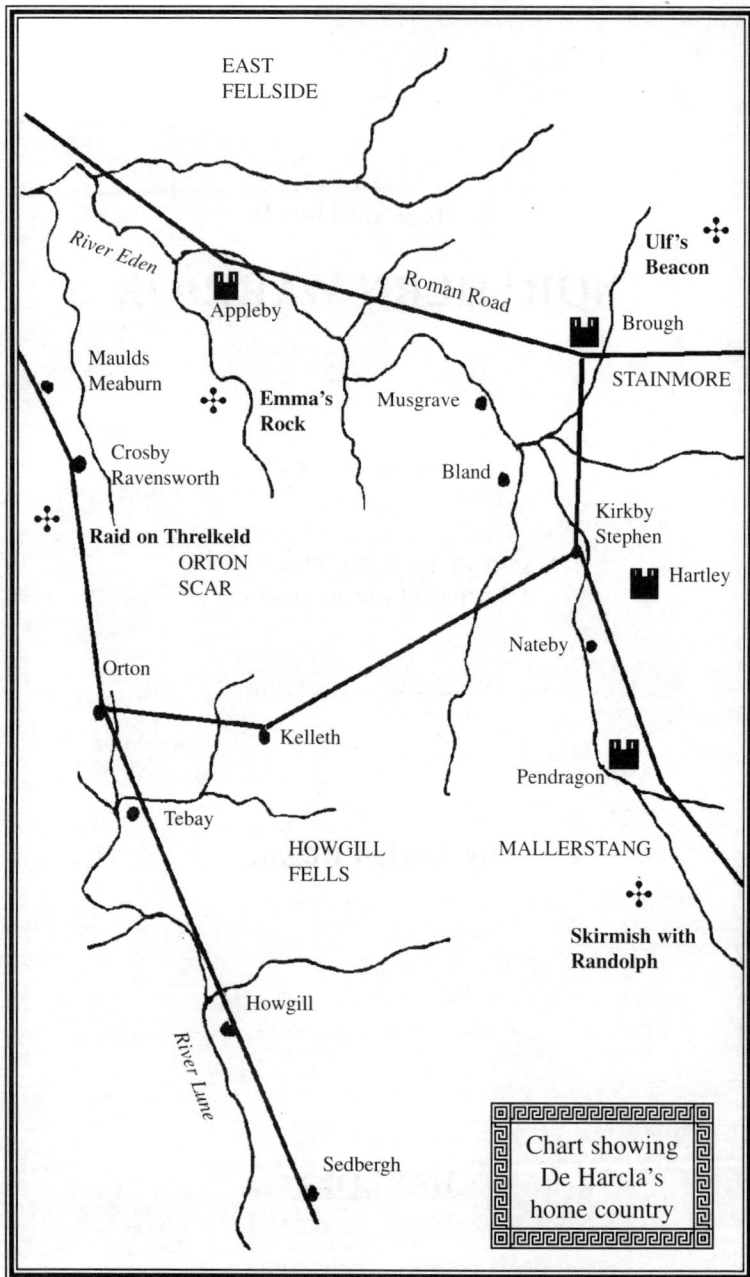

EAST
FELLSIDE

Ulf's
Beacon

River Eden

Roman Road

Appleby

Brough

Maulds
Meaburn

STAINMORE

Emma's
Rock

Musgrave

Crosby
Ravensworth

Bland

Kirkby
Stephen

Raid on Threlkeld
ORTON
SCAR

Hartley

Nateby

Orton

Kelleth

Pendragon

Tebay

HOWGILL
FELLS

MALLERSTANG

Skirmish with
Randolph

Howgill

River Lune

Sedbergh

Chart showing
De Harcla's
home country

Part of Ambrose's Chart

NORTHERN WARRIOR

First published 2001

by Hayloft Publishing,
Great Skerrygill, South Stainmore,
Kirkby Stephen, Cumbria, CA17 4EU.

Tel. 017683 42300 or Fax. 017683 41568
e-mail: dawn@hayloft.org.uk
website: www.hayloft.org.uk

ISBN 0 9523282 8 3

A catalogue record for this book is available
from the British Library

Design & production by Hayloft
Cover illustration by Jim Proudfoot, reproduced by kind permission of The
National Trust for Scotland.
Printed by Lintons Printers, Co. Durham

A farmhouse now stands on the site of the old castle at Hartley. Only the southern wall, several feet thick and fifteen feet high, remains standing. It forms one of the boundaries to the farm yard.

The wall continues below ground and drops into the hillside; at one end an inner stairway leads down to a vaulted chamber, filthy with the muck of centuries. It is dark and silent now but in past times was lively with the voices and clatter of men, for this chamber was once the guard-room. A circular stairway, the remains of which can still be seen in a dim corner, winds upward. In the old days this would have led through a trap-door to the stone ramparts of the castle.

It was outside this room, among the rubble, the detritus and the cow muck, that one winter some years ago, a visitor stooped to pick up a curious, perfectly rounded stone ball, about six inches in diameter. Standing on that spot, suddenly indifferent to the cold February wind, he examined the ball and guessed its original use; a solid reminder of the connection to a man who lived and died seven centuries before.

Beneath the ramparts the main gate once stood. It had been built in a sharp valley and the road to it falls away from the sloping banks down to the valley floor three hundred yards away. Here the track disappears from view among the thick beeches and rowans crowding the ford; today a neat wooden foot-bridge looks out on to fields of grazing sheep and the river running idly by. It would be from this spot that a man, emerging from the green road through the wood and resting his horse, might look up and glimpse the castle shining in the sun, and say quietly to himself, "Well, I'm glad to be home."

Kirkby Stephen
February 2001

List of main characters

Michael de Harcla, knight; tenant of Harcla and former Sheriff of Cumberland and Warden of Carlisle.
John, son; knight and Warden of Highhead Castle near Carlisle
Henry, son; rector of Dacre
Andreas, son; knight and Captain in the West Marches
James, son.
Isabel, daughter, married to Richard la Frounceise
Sarah, daughter, manages the running of the household at Hartley; engaged to Robert de Leyburne.
Emma la Frounceise, Andreas' cousin by marriage; friend to Sarah
Ketel Ormsson, Andreas' vallet and bodyguard
Conan of Askham) warriors and
Alexander of Kelleth) friends to Ketel
Richard le Bret (Uther Pendragon), the hermit of Pendragon; an Irish mercenary
Thomas of Howgill) two of Uther's
Patrick of Blande) young riders
Robert de Clifford, earl of Westmorland; head of a powerful border family, Harcla's mentor
Henry, his vallet
Clifford's knights:
Richard la Frounceise of Maulds Meaburn, philosopher and student of the ancient wars; married to Isabel de Harcla; guardian of Emma, his dead sister Alice's only child
John de Crumbwell, knight banneret of Pendragon Castle; married to Idonea, Clifford's aunt

Robert de Leyburne
Nicholas de Vipont
Richard de Musgrave
Walter de Strickland
John de Castre, knight banneret and Warden of Carlisle Castle
Antoigne de Lucy, lord of Cockermouth; Harcla's enemy
Henry Threlkeld, his lieutenant
Henry de Beaumont, Warden of Roxburgh Castle
Peter Claxton, dean to the Archbishop of Durham, Harcla's "spy"
Sylvester, his secretary
Ambrose, monk at Hexham, cartographer
Robert the Bruce, King Robert 1 of Scotland
Edward Bruce, knight; his brother
Thomas Randolph, earl of Moray; the King's nephew
John de Soulis, knight of Eskdale and Warden of Liddesdale; friend to Strickland
Mauchline, his lieutenant
Edward, King of England
Piers Gaveston, duke of Cornwall; the King's confidante and general in the field
Humphrey de Bohun, earl of Hereford; lord of England and Gaveston's enemy
Aymer de Valence, earl of Pembroke; friend to Hereford
Walter Reynolds, Chancellor; the King's playwright.

Notes

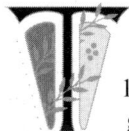

The *Northern Warrior* is an adventure story set in the year
1309/10; it describes a romance and, more largely, medieval
guerrilla warfare and a struggle for power in the borders of
England and Scotland. This period marks the beginning of the military
ascendancy of Robert the Bruce, crowned King Robert I of Scotland four
years before; the story, though, is narrated from an English perspective
and climaxes in the failed invasion of Scotland in September 1310.

The central character, Andreas de Harcla (Andrew of Hartley) is a
young warrior of an aspiring family who has a remarkable gift for lead-
ership and displays great martial prowess. It is these qualities which
allow him and his friends; in the long slide to defeat, to fight locally successful actions against the Scots. These are in spite of King Edward's
outmoded strategies and the divisions of loyalty wrought by his general
Piers Gaveston, the Duke of Cornwall.

Most of the characters existed in history, some, like Ketel, didn't –
although I now find it impossible to give credence to that fact.

Conan and Alexander take their presence from two fragments in the
Patent Rolls of Edward II's reign dated March 8 and June 19 1308. These
describe a legal injunction relating to an attack on a manor-house in
Crosby Ravensworth which was instigated by Harcla and in which they
participate. I have deduced from this, perhaps naively, that both men
were happy to be friends of Harcla and follow him in his adventures.

It is apparent, too, from these documents that Emma la Frounceise,
Harcla's cousin by marriage, was involved in the raid and she is thus
ascribed her warlike nature.

Sir Robert de Clifford was the most powerful man of a famous
Northern family. I hope there is in the narrative something of a proud
and martial spirit; although, by deferring to modern sensibilities, there
might be considered too much of benign democracy in his style of lead-
ership. He was certainly the prime force in holding the border marches
against King Robert I of Scotland, at least until 1312 by which time his
protégé, Andreas de Harcla, had risen from obscurity to fame and superseded him. Clifford was killed on 23 June 1314 in a preliminary skirmish at Bannockburn. He was forty years old at the time of his death.

NORTHERN WARRIOR

I have taken several liberties in the story regarding the placement of certain episodes - they are not always geographically or chronologically correct. The siting of Clifford's summer headquarters in 1310 at Wark-on-Tyne rather than Wark-on-Tweed is an example of this; it is done purely for the dramatic purpose of holding the main action within a day's ride of Hartley.

The skirmish near Pendragon, which is described in Chapter II, actually took place not in 1309 but in 1314, four and a half months after the battle of Bannockburn. I hope these and other instances do not diminish the real living picture I wanted to create.

Also, the influence and position of certain characters is sometimes at odds with that which is known to be true. Richard le Bret, an Irish mercenary who fought under Clifford at Loughmaben in 1299, is one in point. He appears in the story, at least initially, under the name Uther, a radical thinker in the art of warfare in whose ideas Harcla sees parallels of his own.

The aristocracy of the day were all of Norman descent and, naturally, spoke French. Contemporary documents were written in Norman French or Latin, or sometimes in a combination of both. This explains the French nature of some characters' titles and their style of speech.

Society was heavily influenced by the Church and everyday lives were structured around its holy days and feasts. To the medieval mind nothing was more certain than death and the final resurrection of the body. Earthly life was cheap and a brief forerunner to eternity.

The songs *Lenten is come* in Chapter five and *I have a young sister* in Chapter twelve are anonymous English lyrics of the 13th century. The blank verse pieces in Chapters seventeen and twenty-four are extracts from Shakespeare's play *Troilus and Cressida*.

This book, although based on fact, is a work of fiction and the characterisations are imagined.

Prologue

ndreas de Harcla stretched his legs to the fire and stared into the flames. From time to time a loose spark jumped and scorched the thick dark wool of his jerkin. He pinched at the smouldering marks absent-mindedly and studied the hot sootiness of his finger and thumb.

In this evening of early winter his vallet, Ketel, had already wrapped himself in his cloak and lain down in a dark corner of the room; he was now fast asleep, the sound of his snoring a deeper melody to the sizzling fire. A couple of candles stood on the table behind him and lit the room; the shadows they made on the walls rose and fell with the crackling of the flames.

Harcla settled back into his chair; he watched the flames, remembering the heat of a July day three summers before. He remembered the old king, the First Edward, looking out to mountains across the Solway Firth as though he were gazing on the Promised Land. Those distant hills of Galloway shone a hazy blue in the light of the summer morning and a soft breeze, coming in from the sea caused the pennants and bright banners of his army to rise and fill; the King's own great Standard stirred fleetingly.

The tide had ebbed from the mud flats of the Solway and Edward, looking across through flights of sea birds, could see the solitary Loughmaben Stone marking the northern end of the ford. His scouts were picking their way across the wet sands and indicating the path the army would follow with tall white wands; they snaked along the estuary like an enormous centipede. All was being made ready for the final onslaught.

But the sick King was failing. It was only his hatred for Robert the Bruce that had carried him this far; the journey from Carlisle to Burgh-by-Sands, just six miles, had taken him three days. It was the first time he had mounted a horse in twelve months and every step he took was an agony. Everyone had known he was dying; a scrofulous infection had taken hold of him but it was only now, in these last days, that Edward had become reconciled to his own mortality.

His confessor had been much with him since Carlisle. 'Just as well,' some men said.

The King stood and gazed towards Scotland. A fit of coughing took him and a stream of blood and mucous issued from his lips; he fell, clutching his mouth as though he could push back the rottenness. He called his captains to him; the young Harcla went with them and he heard the last words Edward spoke: 'Carry my bones at the head of your armies,' he said brutally. 'Every Scot must surrender, and kill me that Bruce!'

Harcla did not understand how, at the end of a life, the cup of wrath and bitterness could be still so full.

Two and a half years had passed since that day and the King's last commands lay unfulfilled, as though his words were echoing still with the cries of gulls by the sands of the Solway. In truth, far from achieving the surrender of the Scots, English power in the northern kingdom was failing.

And now, on a November night in 1309, in the castle at Hartley, a message had come from King Edward II at York appointing Harcla his new captain in the western borderlands. It was perhaps a measure of the haplessness of this new Edward that others had declined the honour, thinking any success to be impossible.

Sir Michael de Harcla, the tenant of the castle and its lands, pondered this news with the young men of his family.

John, the elder son who held lands of his own at Highhead near Carlisle, was wary. 'You shall not know who to trust, Andreas. Some, and not only Scots, will be eager to see you fail.'

'John is right,' said Sir Michael, 'our local English, Lucy and Castre, for two, are dangerous. They will harm you if they can. Lucy is still smarting over that affair at Crosby Ravensworth,' He chuckled happily, 'But, I must say that was well done.'

James, sixteen years of age and the youngest, could hardly control his excitement. 'But just think,' he cried, 'Andreas is become the new Captain!'

'You do not know the perils, James,' his father retorted. 'This is not a game.' He turned to Andreas. 'You will have need of Trojans,' he said solemnly, and, deep in thought, he began to twirl the rolled document in his hands.

'I would have much greater hope,' he continued, 'were the First Edward still alive. God! He would have finished the bastard! We nearly had him at Glentrool, you remember.

'And as for this new Edward!' He threw open his hands despairingly, as though they could grasp the air. 'Christ! He has his father's strength and looks, yes, but little else; he has no sense of duty, or love, for his northern kingdom.

'My lords Clifford, Lancaster and the others have been crying for military support these last two years. I know that Lancaster, thinking the effort futile, may withdraw his allegiance from the Crown altogether. Is it not incredible that the kingdom of England be in this perilous state? Christ in Heaven, my blood seethes to think of it! I believe I have more affinity with Robert the Bruce and Scotland than with this Edward and his England!'

Harcla exchanged glances with his elder brother; they both knew that a number of the border lords were re-thinking their loyalty to the English Crown; some men now thought that this Edward II was in actual danger of losing his kingdom. Of course, if Edward were defeated, and killed or exiled, his supporters would lose their lands and accumulated wealth – if not their own lives. Those lords in the borderlands must be clever enough, or lucky enough, to back the victor in this long war, be it Robert the Bruce of Scotland or King Edward of England.

Sir Michael got up from the fire and paced the room; he went on more loudly, 'Bruce is King of Scotland, by God! He claims an independent kingdom and asks we acknowledge this. And why should we not? He does not demand the throne of England, or at least not yet.

'Bruce waxes strong. He raids the borderlands whenever he has a mind, or at least when his cash runs low, the bastard. This never happened in my king's day. It was unthinkable, by the living blood of Christ it was! And now this......'

The old knight reached over to the long table and picked up the paper he had left there. 'Well, Andreas,' he said quietly, 'you are now Captain in the West Marches.' He was quiet for a few moments as he studied the document; and then he read aloud: 'and Sir Andreas is commanded to repair to his estate in the Marches in order to defend the same against the Scots.'

He threw the parchment down and his voice was bitter. 'What with, for Christ's sake?' he said bleakly. 'Where is a promise of more men, and of the means to pay them?'

Later, as he stared at the fire alone, Harcla considered his father's argument. 'My father is an old man,' he thought, 'and exaggerates difficulties - difficulties are not insurmountable.'

Harcla was young and confident. He looked to the future with eagerness and saw glory where his father in old age saw only death.

The candles began to splutter. The slumbering form of Ketel was just visible in the corner by his own straw mattress. Harcla rose, walked across the rush-strewn floor and lowered himself to bed.

'Is all well, my lord?' asked Ketel, disturbed in his dreams.

'All is well,' replied he, 'go back to sleep.'

Outside in the clear November night nothing stirred against the sky but the flight of an owl and, behind it, the young moon. Harcla dreamed and the high and wild fells of Westmorland rose starkly above him. The fell tops were this year already snow covered and the moon made a pale shining there.

AT HARTLEY CASTLE

Harcla opened his eyes. The movement of Ketel pulling away the wall-hanging had awoken him and pale beams of light threaded through the lattice of the shuttered window.

In this part of the castle the windows had not yet been glazed and he felt the cool draught of air on his face; he could hear the muted comforting sound of cows lowing in the dairy.

Ketel offered a morning greeting and re-kindled the fire. Harcla watched the flames for a moment before pushing away the heavy blanket that covered his bed. He rose, made noisy use of the chamber pot that stood in the corner, then washed and dried himself. His scarlet tunic, jerkin and hose lay on the press by the fire.

Ketel brought them to him and asked, 'Will you have fresh linen, my lord?'

'No,' he said. 'Just help me with these boots, will you.'

Ketel knelt to secure the fastenings at the back of his legs and then Harcla walked down the passage leading to the west doorway and out into the courtyard. He nodded to two or three people of the household as he made his way towards the main gate.

The castle was, more truly, a large manor house that during recent years had been heavily fortified. It stood on a plateau of rocky land about ninety yards square; the ground outside it falling sharply in all directions. The castle itself, timber built on two floors with a sandstone slab roof, was rectangular in shape and occupied about one quarter of this area. Surrounding it, on the edge of the plateau, stood a tall fence of sharpened stakes, each the thickness of a man's leg. A wooden parapet, lying some four feet below the top points of the stakes, ran round the entire circumference of the fence. Two raised towers stood at angles, one faced south-west and protected the track leading up to the castle and the other looked north-west down the valley to Appleby and the road to Carlisle.

The large double gate, to the left of the south-west tower as he walked toward it, had just been swung open for the day. Harcla jumped up on the ladder that climbed to the parapet and he stood on the widened rampart directly above the gate.

He saw Ketel riding down the road toward Nateby. 'Now where is he

1

off to?' he asked himself idly as he breathed in the cold morning air and looked across to the flank of Langrigg Fell as it turned northwards to the rising ground of Stainmore.

Two troopers, blowing their hands to warm them, came up to him as he stood there and they asked him questions of great things, like the state of the borders and Robert the Bruce's strength there. Afterwards they told him of other smaller things concerning minor jealousies against Godfrid, Sir Michael's reeve at Kirkby Stephen, and how accusations of favouritism in his sharing of guard duties were making discord. Harcla listened and promised he would be fair to all; the men nodded their thanks and went back to the gatehouse.

Between the outer fence and the castle was a large area of ground and Harcla gazed on the hodge-podge of small wooden buildings and animal pens within it; some of them lined the western wall and here was the far-riery, the stabling for the horses and the dairy.

Further along, almost behind the castle, stood the chapel; a covered passage led from it to the rear door of the house. Along this passage his father, two brothers John and James and younger sister Sarah, were walking; the chapel bell was ringing for mass and he went down to join them as they entered the church.

The chapel, a small high-roofed building, was filling up for the dawn mass; a dozen of the household and a few visitors crowded inside. Ketel hurried in behind his master.

The priest glided down the narrow central aisle; his common smock and hose could be glimpsed beneath the swaying folds of his priestly vestment. 'Introibo ad altare Dei,' he chanted as he walked.

Harcla and Ketel stood together in the rear of the nave. 'What have you been up to?' Harcla asked him in a whisper.

'Ah, my lord,' answered Ketel quietly, 'I thought I would ride to Nateby.'

'Nateby? Isn't that where, I forget her name, Wharton's daughter....'

'Yes, my lord.'

Harcla looked at Ketel's pious face and smiled.

The priest, Thomas de Leycester, the rector of Kirkby Stephen, told his congregation that this day was the feast of the presentation of our Blessed Lady. 'And soon,' he said, 'in two weeks time, the season of Advent will begin when we anticipate the miraculous and virgin birth of Christ.' The people pondered this, as they always did, in a perplexity of faith.

Harcla moved towards Sarah his sister and knelt beside her. The

2

flames of the candles upon the altar wavered and their light caught the golden threads woven within the vestments of the priest. The movements of his arm as he reached to turn the pages of his prayer book created ripples of light along his body.

The Latin murmuring of the priest Thomas began again and the crowd bowed their heads. 'Hoc est enim corpus meum,' he whispered. His words were like an incantation and he lifted the sacred host, showing it to the people; the altar bells chimed gently in the greater silence.

There was a movement at the door of the chapel and a cold rush of air swept down the nave; a candle flame puttered and was blown out. Harcla turned to see one of the guards in urgent conversation with Ketel.

His sister leant across and whispered to him. 'What is it, Andreas?' she asked.

Harcla saw that Ketel was motioning to him insistently. 'I do not know,' he answered her. 'I had best find out.'

He walked up to them standing in the doorway. 'Well?' he said, 'What news?'

Six miles to the north east of the castle of Hartley in the marches of England there is a pass in the bleak mountains known as Stainmore. It is a desolate place of bog and rock that is trackless except for the Roman road that leads from Carlisle and the plains of Eden to link with Dere Street, the great eastern route to Scotland.

On the heights above the pass the Romans had built a signalling station; it was one of several that formed a chain spanning the breadth of the Pennines alongside the road. In winter the road could be blocked with snow for weeks at a time and, by using a system of flags or smoke during the day and fire at night, simple messages, warning of attack or confirming orders, could be transmitted over long distances very quickly.

Henry de Harcla, an older brother and an enthusiastic student of Roman technology, had conducted an experiment several years before whereby he determined the speed at which a message could be sent from Bowes, above Greta Bridge in the east, and received at Brough, in the valley to the west of Stainmore; a distance of some twelve miles.

The exercise went ahead with some jollity one summer evening. Between Bowes and Brough Henry placed four parties at intervals on prominent terrain above the road, one on the site of the old Roman signalling station above Stainmore. He devised a code involving various groupings of short and long plumes of smoke to represent certain letters of the alphabet. It was a fairly cumbersome system but Henry believed

3

that common phrases, messages or orders could be given short distinctive codes that would quicken the process.

The message Henry instructed to be relayed from Bowes, requiring six letters, read: 'Ave Caesar'. Twelve miles away and ten minutes later Andreas, stationed at Brough, decoded the message as 'Eva Ceaser'.

In spite of the error Henry was pleased. 'After all, it was only the first attempt,' he said.

The others groaned, but Harcla smiled and, as he did with all things he thought profitable, stored it away in his mind. 'Ten minutes!' he thought, 'a fast horse would take an hour and a half with that climb!'

Robert de Clifford, the earl of Westmorland, had then ordered a beacon to be erected and manned on Stainmore. It was to connect with the beacon at Penrith, twenty-five miles away on the hill above the town; further north with the beacon at Carlisle Castle, and also, to the southwest, with one on Orton Scar.

At this time there was one man stationed there permanently, a retired foot soldier from the Welsh wars of the first Edward named Ulf, and one other, a youth from one of the manors, who travelled up nightly. That same night, as Sir Michael, in the warmth of his castle at Hartley, ranted against the new king, it was Adam, the son of a tenant from Brough, who had ridden up to Stainmore.

He never relished the prospect of a night on the fells, but he greeted the old man cheerily enough. 'Holloa, Ulf,' he had cried as he approached, 'Greetings, how goes it?'

'Quiet enough,' replied Ulf, and he turned to go back inside his hut.

Adam dismounted and unbuckled his pack. He tossed a blanket over the pony and followed Ulf inside. The hut was small and earth-floored. The smoke from a smouldering peat fire filled the air and by the gloomy light of a single candle he saw a straw bed, a chair and, about the hearth, some cooking gear.

Ulf handed the boy a bowl of some thick soup. 'I will wake you in six hours,' the old man said at last and, pulling a cloak over his shoulders, he went outside.

'Holy God,' said Adam to himself, chewing on his supper, 'he doesn't get more talkative.'

Ulf walked his round; even in the pitch darkness it was familiar to him. He knew every stone within two hundred yards of the beacon; he had trudged them often enough. It was a wild place. But this night at least there was no cold rain or driving snow; just a fresh breeze and a clear sky. He stood then and gazed down the valley to the north west;

the line of fells rising to his right, peak after peak stretching away in the huge bulk of the Pennines. The white tops of the mountains shone dully in the moonlight. Down below, the torches of the castle at Brough glinted warmly; but even they, one by one, gave way to the darkness and soon all light was extinguished.

During Adam's watch Ulf lay sleeping in the corner. The boy shoved a few more turves on the fire and wished the night away. Every half hour or so he went outside to gaze northwards; then he would return and sit with his knife, working a figure from wood which he intended as a gift to his mother. He dozed awhile.

Eventually he emerged into the half-light. Dawn broke behind him and the sky lightened; he was glad. He walked, shivering with the cold, across to his pony, fed him and then drew him to the near-by spring for water. He looked once more down the long valley. The glory of the new sun was behind him, and before him too, as though it were mirrored across space, for he gazed on the burning light of Penrith beacon.

'Aieeee!' he yelled, 'Aieeee! Ulf, Ulf!' He rushed to the hut and threw open the door.

Ulf started up, frightened, from his bed. 'For the love of Christ,' he shouted, wild-eyed. 'For the love of Christ.'

Adam burst through the doorway. 'Penrith beacon's alight. The beacon's alight.'

'Steady, lad, steady,' the old man said, pulling on his boots.

'It's the Scots, it's the Scots,' Adam shrieked.

'God's bones, be quiet,' Ulf muttered. He moved to the door and went out, striding up the slope; he rubbed the sleep from his eyes. 'Well,' he said quietly to himself, 'the beacon is lit alright. But so is Orton Scar.'

He turned to Adam, who had followed him from the hut. 'Which was lit first?' he asked.

The boy stared round-eyed at the flashing orange glow in the southwest. 'I don't know,' he replied. 'I did not notice that other.'

Ulf swore under his breath and thought quickly: 'If Penrith was lit first then we have plenty of time; but if it was Orton Scar....now that is more dangerous; and this fool of a boy....'

He said aloud: 'Listen, Adam, ride hard now to Hartley and ask for my lord Andreas. Tell him what you have seen.'

'You mean about the beacons?' Adam's wits were gone.

'Of course about the beacons, fool. Tell him we think Penrith was lit first but we are not certain. Do you understand?'

'Yes,' the boy answered. 'I do.'

'Good. Now go.'

Adam rode off and Ulf took some glowing embers from his hearth and set them among the kindling of the huge bonfire that would be his beacon. The flames jumped; soon the whole countryside would know the tidings.

After a little while Ulf, standing alone on his hilltop, could faintly detect the sound of tolling bells; it was brought to him by the morning breeze coming in from the west; many bells frantically rung. The messenger sent to Harcla, important though he might have felt, was a verbal confirmation only. My lord Andreas, Ulf knew, would soon be abroad, organising his men and sending out riders. The old man smiled grimly.

Harcla moved outside the chapel door and the guard said, his eyes wide, 'My lord, Stainmore beacon is lit.' He raised his arm and pointed northwards, behind Harcla's shoulder.

Harcla looked out over the castle's walls to see a thick plume of smoke rising and swirling over the shoulders of Langrigg Fell. 'The beacon is lit!' he muttered, 'Christ in Heaven! The beacon is lit!'

At this moment young Adam from Brough hurtled through the gates and leapt from his pony shouting: 'The Scots are coming! The Scots are coming!' He fell to the ground in his haste and, scrambling up, his eyes searched for my lord Andreas.

Ketel ran across to quieten him, and Adam told his story.

'Have any riders come in from Appleby or Orton?' Harcla asked the guard.

The guard shook his head. 'No, my lord,' he answered.

Harcla turned to Ketel and said, 'Will you bring two men to me in the great hall? I have messages to send.' Ketel ran off and determined to find his friends Conan and Alexander.

Harcla walked quickly along the covered passageway and into the castle. Mass had ended and his father, aided by John, approached him in the hall. 'So, Andreas,' he said sadly, 'I did not think this to happen.'

'The beacon is lit,' replied he, 'but of anything else we know nothing. We need Henry back, to devise a more effective warning system. We are ill-prepared.' He paused then and added: 'I did not mean any disrespect, father.'

Sir Michael looked at him in the dull light of the hall and waved his hand dejectedly. They could hear the bells of Kirkby Stephen and Nateby tolling, like a frantic lament. The villagers, at this advert of danger, would soon be making their way up to Hartley with their sheep and cattle.

6

'We shall have a full house within the hour,' John said.

Ketel appeared with Conan of Askham and Alexander of Kelleth.

'Listen, my friends,' Harcla said to them. 'We must determine the road they travel and the strength with which they travel it. Discover this and return to tell me.'

He sent Alexander to Maulds Meaburn to speak with Richard la Fraunceise whose men manned the beacon at Orton Scar. Conan went north to Lord Clifford at Appleby.

Harcla walked outside. The morning was turning foggy and a great mist swirled down from the mountains. The soldiers on the timber walls of Hartley were enwreathed and they peered uncertainly into the distance. The gates of the castle were still open and dozens of villagers with their families continued to enter the bailey, their pigs, sheep and geese manuring the ground. The noise from animals and men was tumultuous.

Harcla shook his head and reminded Ketel to close the gates when all were inside and to keep alert the guards on the outer walls. He climbed up to one of the raised towers; it was quieter there.

After three hours the two riders returned within a few minutes of each other. Harcla went down to the Hall.

'My lord,' said Conan, the first to arrive, 'Sir Robert de Clifford at Appleby presents his compliments and begs to inform you that there are no enemy bands approaching from the north or the east. He assumes, therefore, the potential danger to come from the south. With regard to that, he sends Sir Richard de Musgrave with six men-at-arms to aid you.' Conan paused for breath and added smiling, 'They should arrive at Hartley within the half hour.'

Harcla listened and mentally totalled his force. 'Ten horse from Hartley say, three with John, four, makes fourteen; Musgrave and six, twenty-one; myself and Ketel, twenty-three. Also twenty foot to defend the castle.

'Well, we would be strong enough at Hartley itself,' he thought. 'If we do nothing they will, like as not, push straight on through Kirkby Stephen; they must want to reach the border as quickly as they can.'

He was considering this when Sir Richard la Fraunceise walked into the Hall with Harcla's second rider, Alexander. Fraunceise saw Sir Michael sitting apart and greeted him cordially; he began to ask after his health.

Harcla coughed impatiently. 'Richard,' he said, interrupting his father's reply, 'tell me why Orton Scar is lit?'

'Yes, good morning to you, Andreas, also,' la Fraunceise said good humouredly; and he paused.

'Good morning, Richard,' said Harcla at last.

Fraunceise laughed. 'Well, my friend,' he said, 'we thought it should be lit, you know. There is news of a Scots company marching up Wensleydale.'

'Wensleydale! Have they come that far south before?'

Fraunceise looked across at Sir Michael, who said: 'Not for ten years, since the days of Wallace.'

Harcla sat back in his chair. 'We learned of a Scots force moving south on Dere Street seven days ago,' he said. 'They raided some steadings by Richmond.'

'It must be the same band,' said John de Harcla. 'They have turned up Wensleydale to return home by the western road.'

'It's possible,' said Harcla thinking hard.

Suddenly it seemed everyone was speaking.

'What is their strength, I wonder?'

'The report from Richmond put it at two hundred.'

'That could mean anything from fifty to five hundred!'

'They may have separated. One party returning the way they came, the other going north-west.'

'If we remain in the castle they will pass us by.'

'Yes, they cannot afford to waste time on a siege.'

'Enough, enough,' shouted Harcla into the babble. 'God's blood! Let us think clearly! How many men have you brought, Richard?'

'Four.'

'Very well,' he said, hiding his dismay. 'When Musgrave arrives we will total twenty-seven horse, a good number. Richard, tell me precisely the information you received.'

La Fraunceise breathed in deeply and said: 'This morning, before dawn, a rider from Middleham arrived at Howgill. He had overtaken the Scots during the night at Bainbridge. They were camped by the river near the old Roman fort.'

'Good so far. Their numbers?'

'He reckoned one hundred and fifty, all horse, and a train of wagons, perhaps a dozen.'

'Excellent. They must move slowly. Bainbridge last night, say twenty-two miles. They must intend to travel down Mallerstang; if they broke camp at first light they would ride through Kirkby Stephen at....when? Early afternoon? Say, three hours from now. Their plan must be to rest tonight on the lower fell side between Appleby and Penrith.'

The others nodded their heads in agreement.

'Well, I think we should intercept their progress in Mallerstang,' Harcla continued. 'You all know where the valley narrows at Shoregill above Pendragon, where the Bainbridge road drops down to the river from the shoulder of the fell. That is our place, if we have time. We are twenty-seven - we should ride light, be mobile. Perhaps we can be the cause of some damage before they reach Scotland. Christ, it is not before time!'

He paused to look around him. Their faces were solemn now. 'We should ride in four units, each commanded by a knight - you Richard, John, myself and Musgrave.' Harcla stopped as he said this, trying to pick out Musgrave's face among those crowded around him at the table.

'If any of us encounters a serious attack we can as individuals, that is in our units, retreat here to Hartley. Agreed? Good. Richard, I don't suppose you learnt of their leader?'

'I do not know, Andreas.'

'No matter. How many of our riders are equipped with bows?'

'Bows?' They all queried this, as though mis-hearing the juxtaposition of the words. 'None,' they said.

John de Harcla looked at his father.

'Well, six of my men from Hartley will be. Is that right, Ketel? Ketel.'

'Yes, my lord.'

'Good.'

Harcla turned then to his younger brother and asked, 'James, will you ride with us?'

James had thought to be left behind; he said, his eyes bright: 'Yes, Andreas.'

Richard la Fraunceise laughed in good humour, trying to dispel the gloom of others. 'Christ's blood, Harcla,' he said loudly, 'we nearly had my niece Emma with us also. It was all I could do to prevent her coming. She is locked in her room. My lady Isabel, your sister, cannot quieten her.'

'She is a war-like creature,' Harcla said smiling, 'and her heart is full.' And he laughed then also. A strained hilarity was upon them as they went away to make preparations for the ambush.

~ 2 ~

A SKIRMISH IN MALLERSTANG

An hour later, at midday, Harcla's small force was mounted and ready to depart. The knights of the company were made distinct by the bright steel of their helmets and the coloured plumes that issued from them, like the tendrils of flowers. Each rider displayed the knight's crest, mostly on a white surcoat but some on a red or blue. Harcla's men bore his own coat of a red cross with a martlet drawn in the upper right quarter; martlets were swallows, or swifts, shown without legs to imply landlessness, for Harcla was the fourth son and destined for no inheritance.

These devices, imprinted on each man's chest, were also emblazoned on their round shields, or targets. Harcla's men slung their shields around their bodies in the border manner, to rest on the saddle at their backs.

The horses, excited by the promise of running and chasing, pawed at the ground and the pike-men stationed on the walls clashed their shields and spears together. This strident noise rolled around the bailey and the villagers took up a shout that had begun with Ketel, who, with fixed eyes was circling his horse impatiently: 'Harcla! Harcla! Harcla!'

The cheering and yelling grew louder, reverberating against the dark timber of the walls. The gates of the castle were pulled open to a last deafening shout and the company rode out into the mist. They forded the beck at the bottom of the hill, just above the place where it runs into the Eden, and climbed the green road towards Nateby. The blood was pumping in men and horses alike as the noises from Hartley sounded in their ears. Harcla spurred them hard to the castle of Pendragon and they arrived there fifteen minutes later, panting. He walked round his men saying, 'Do not worry, we will take the last couple of miles more easily.'

He looked up the valley, into the mist, and called Ketel and James to him. 'Ride forward quietly,' he told them. 'Keep the river to your left. When you come to the enemy note their position and how fast they are moving - then return.' He stopped for a moment, thinking the way ahead. 'The company here shall walk forward to Shoregill,' he went on. 'If you do not come back to us by that time we shall lie there as planned.'

Ketel and James nodded their heads and rode off.

There was a guard at the gate of Pendragon, looking down upon them and about to ask their business when Harcla shouted up to him: 'Send for Sir John de Crumbwell!'

The man hesitated, astonished at this sudden and wild appearance.

'Quickly, man!' Harcla said again.

Crumbwell, the warden of this remote castle had become aware of the commotion about him, and appeared on the rampart above the gate. He peered down. 'Is that you, Andreas?' he asked.

'Yes, my lord.'

'What in the name of Christ is going on?'

'We go to waylay a Scots army,' Harcla told him. 'We believe they march down Mallerstang this very day.'

'Good God!'

'I shall send you word by evening. But for now, open your gates and let in your people. Be vigilant!'

'Consider it done, my boy,' Crumbwell replied stoutly, 'I would be with you but for this damned leg.'

'Adieu!' said Harcla, and he smiled to himself thinking, 'Pandarus is of little use to me.'

They moved out and the mist rolled down from the mountains. They kept to the higher ground above the river and Harcla rode up and down the line, telling his men of the need for silence. He would raise a finger to his lips saying, 'Quiet, my friends, quiet. For therein lies our hope. They do not think to find us here.'

The company picked its way southward for a mile or thereabouts, the sound of the river always below them and to their left. Richard de Musgrave cantered to the front of the band of men and said: 'Harcla, I have my doubts of this enterprise. My lord Clifford summoned me to defend Hartley itself, not to roam the countryside, which I cannot see by the way, in search of invisible Scots.'

The new captain in the Western March turned to Musgrave and said: 'Sir Richard, my duty is to harass, disrupt and destroy the Scots wherever I may find them; I thought you knew that. This is one such place. Please return to your group. Should we need to, we can defend Hartley later.'

Harcla, gazing through the mist, rode on; Musgrave allowed his horse to fall back, annoyed at Harcla's abrupt manner, and he re-joined his men.

Two riders appeared out of the fog; they were Ketel and James.

The company halted as Ketel spoke to Harcla. 'My lord,' he said, 'the Scots are resting in a flat pasture about one mile below Hellgill, only twenty minutes ride. Their captain, who I think is Randolph, has just now sent two riders northwards out along the river. They must intend to follow its course through the valley - what else can they do in this fog?'

'How many are they, Ketel?'

'It was difficult to tell, my lord,' he replied; then he turned to James and asked: 'How many would you say?'

'My lord la Fraunceise's information is not far out,' said James, 'I would guess less than two hundred. But with them a good number of carts, heavily laden, and also cattle.'

Ketel nodded in agreement as Harcla glanced at him. Ketel added, 'They have lit fires and they are noisy.'

'So much the better!' cried Harcla. 'They think they have the valley to themselves. Ketel, take James and two bowmen, watch for these scouts of Randolph. If they come near us capture them; kill them if you have to. Otherwise leave them be. In any event send me news within the half-hour.'

Harcla looked about him. The land fell towards the river; below the track, on a raised bank of boulders, a line of hawthorns ran. He rode down with his brother John. The rushing noise of the river was clearer and louder here. Dismounting, they peered between branches to see a gentle grassy bank falling to the water twenty yards away. The mist swirled.

'Well, my brother,' whispered Harcla, his eyes bright, 'what do you think?'

'For an ambush?' John replied cautiously. 'I've seen worse.'

'Come, John,' said Harcla, laughing at his brother. 'It's near perfect!'

Ketel's small party rode forward among rocks and fallen boulders. After a quarter of an hour Ketel, walking ahead, stopped suddenly and raised his arm. One of the bowmen, Conan from Askham, ran up and knelt beside him, notching an arrow. They could see no more than twenty yards distant; emerging from the mist and dead ahead were two riders. They appeared to be speaking quietly together.

'Loose!' Ketel said quietly.

By chance the riders looked up as he spoke and their absolute surprise turned to great fear as Conan's arrow whistled through the air and buried itself in the chest of the first man. The force pushed him backwards off the saddle and, lurching for a moment, he fell to the ground with a shout. The second rider, his face white with terror, screwed his horse about wildly to flee. The horse, scrabbling noisily for a foothold in the gravelly ground, almost threw its rider.

Ketel unsheathed his sword and ran forward a few steps. 'For Christ's sake!' he shouted back to Conan. 'Shoot! Quickly.'

The second arrow was loosed as the mist enveloped the Scot; there was a cry of pain, a receding beat of hooves and then silence.

'He got away,' said Ketel simply. 'My lord Andreas will have my guts pulled out for this.' He walked across to an old rowan tree where the dead Scot's pony was standing and, speaking quietly, he grasped its bridle.

James and the second bowman came up and they approached the fallen rider. They pulled the body over; under his cloak he wore a simple jerkin that had been pierced neatly by the arrow.

'A nice shot, Conan,' said Ketel, looking down.

'I am sorry I did not make two,' Conan replied. 'My kill, I think,' and he rummaged through the pockets and purse.

The wounded rider approached the front of Randolph's little army. He rode awkwardly, his head drooping to the horse's neck. A trooper helped him to dismount and he saw a length of arrow protruding from his back. The crippled man pointed northward into the mist. 'Ambush,' he mumbled.

'How many?' asked Randolph, who had ridden forward quickly.

'How many?' repeated the scout, as though confused. 'My lord, they were outriders. I saw two.'

Randolph thought rapidly. He was surprised that he should encounter English forces here in this quiet valley; that was the very reason he had chosen it. He knew of Harcla, but his source at Durham had said he was in York with Clifford and the king.

He looked up to the dying man, slumped heavily between the two troopers supporting him; he uttered a strangled cough and blood issued from his mouth.

'Did you see their colours?' Randolph asked urgently.

The scout's eyes rolled in his head as he attempted to speak. He licked his lips. 'Yes, my lord,' he said, 'a red cross and....'

'Yes, yes, what else?' urged Randolph.

'A black martlet.'

Randolph sat back and swore. 'It must be Harcla,' he said.

Thomas Randolph, the earl of Moray and a nephew to Bruce himself, surveyed his forces and his position. He thought they should be strong enough to repulse a raid, but he did not want to be harried all the way to the border.

13

His little army lay two miles south of Pendragon Castle and his possible actions were limited in the narrow valley. He could not pass by the higher ground to the west because of the wagons and cattle. 'There is no road there,' he said to himself. 'And this damned fog! Christ's blood, there is nothing else for it!'

He ordered his army to move out and follow the river. The cattle and wagons he placed in the centre, with riders out front and to the left and right. Randolph put himself to the rear of the leading group and rode forward doggedly.

Ketel and James returned and delivered their news to Harcla and the others.

'Well, it is done,' he remarked grimly. 'Randolph will come anyhow. Is all ready John, and Richard?'

'Yes, Andreas,' they replied. 'But will he come? Are you sure?'

'Sure? What else can he do? He will be more careful that is all. We must wait, as still as the grave. Tell the men that, or I will throw the noisy whoresons in one. Wait for my word.'

John de Harcla and Fraunceise smiled a little and walked off to give the final orders.

Harcla turned to Ketel, 'Now, my friend - our bowmen. You know what I want. Fast and thick; I want the air to whistle, by Christ. Aim high, to fall like hail; like steel-tipped hail, Ketel. But fast - twelve a minute. One quiver for each man, two minute's work and then we mount and charge. Do you understand?'

'Yes, my lord.'

'Good.'

The world was perfectly still; no bird sang and no creature stirred. It was as if time had ceased to pass and the sun, unable to pierce the heavy veil of mist, hung immobile and invisible. Into this weird silence crept a rhythmic plodding; imperceptible at first, it grew by degree until there was an absolute roaring in Harcla's brain and he imagined his ears would burst. Abruptly a group of men on horseback swirled into view below him.

He waited, counting the seconds, until the wagons passed; then another ten seconds. Ketel looked across, his eyes grave. Harcla nodded his head deliberately and the inner roaring ceased.

And now another sound began, like a rushing wind through a quickly opened doorway; like a whistling exhalation of breath, many times.

This sound grew, and then mingling with it were the shrieks of men. Terror-stricken horses reared, throwing their riders into the paths of carts that were pulled crazily in all directions. The cattle broke their tethers and plunged on into the river.

Randolph was shouting orders; those nearest to him heard and formed small crouched lines, their round shields held over their heads against the deadly hail. Outside these there was, for the moment, chaos.

As suddenly as it had begun, the barrage of arrows ceased. Harcla and his knights and men were ready. Their horses stamped the ground. He let them go and they broke like a wave over the Scots.

'With me, with me!' he yelled and his blood surged.

He aimed for Randolph, striking out as his horse rushed him past. Randolph cried aloud and clutched his shoulder. Blood dripped from Harcla's sword as he brought up his stallion and wheeled quickly.

A Scots horseman appeared from his right and struck wildly; Harcla parried with his shield arm and slashed downwards. The Scot sank from his horse with a wild cry and his gut spilled open.

Harcla looked round for Randolph.

Ketel, James and the others had stormed down the slope after his charge and were fighting hand to hand. Fraunceise and his party had charged the opposite flank, but there was no sign of Musgrave.

'Fraunceise!' called Harcla, 'Fraunceise!' He moved closer into the melee; his horse lashed out with its hooves at men on foot, and trampled them on the ground.

'Richard,' Harcla shouted across to his friend, above the shrieks and yelling, 'we must depart. Randolph will soon restore order. They are too many! Ride for Pendragon.'

Fraunceise was happy to nod his head in agreement.

John de Harcla was hard pressed further forward. Harcla spurred his horse and clattered into two or three of the enemy. He swung his sword at a tall knight who threw his shield forcefully to break the blow; Harcla's sword shattered at the grip.

The tall knight laughed, 'Surrender, Andreas de Harcla. I will treat you well.'

'You shall not have the chance,' answered he. 'But I thank you all the same.' Harcla brought his shield arm up with great power and, before the tall knight could turn, Harcla barged him from his horse. He grabbed the bridle and laughing, brought his prize away. The Scots knight was shouting at him from the ground.

'Come, John,' Harcla cried, 'It is time for us to go.'

15

They saw Randolph gathering a group of riders about him. Harcla, John and Fraunceise climbed towards the higher ground; the mist was beginning to clear and they saw, thirty yards away on a little knoll, Ketel with his own men; but there were only three.

'Andreas!' John shouted in his ear, pointing.

James de Harcla, still fighting, was in danger of being engulfed. 'The young fool. He has over-stayed. Good Christ! They have unhorsed him. He is trying to disengage. Andreas, we must go to him!'

Harcla put a hand on his brother's arm and pointed to Ketel's small band. 'Look!' he said.

They saw Ketel and his three companions ride down, arms raised and yelling. They broke into the fight and Ketel shouted to James. 'Jump!' he called out. James leapt up and, throwing his arms around Ketel's waist, hung on. 'Thank you,' he panted out.

'Don't thank me yet!' Ketel answered. He dug his horse out from the muddied ground and spurred hard for Pendragon.

SIX MONTHS LATER

Robert de Clifford, the earl of Westmorland, regarded the strong gates of York from the steps of the Palace. He had been there three days but, during his stay, the pleasures of the city had been lost on him.

'Dear God,' he muttered to himself, 'three days of hanging about in waiting-chambers, with the king either locked in the hall with his great earls Hereford and Pembroke, or, for the most part, out practising farriery and other rustic games with Gaveston and his queer friends. Christ, what a way to run a kingdom!'

Clifford screwed up his face in a mixture of frustration and rage.

'And then, at last,' his thoughts ran on, 'this morning, an hour's audience with Edward the King, but with that damned Gaveston smirking in the background; and Pembroke and Hereford playing at being strategic in this war that is no war.

'There is no love lost,' he considered, 'between Gaveston and Pembroke, that is clear enough. What was the nickname Gaveston ridiculed him with? Yes, that was it, Joseph the Jew! Good Christ! Edward's most loyal earl a laughing stock because of his large hooked nose! No wonder Pembroke hates him.'

It was Gaveston who had pushed Pembroke out from the bounds of prudence he usually inhabited; for Lancaster and the other earls had tried in vain to persuade Pembroke to break his allegiance these last eighteen months. In truth, Thomas, the earl of Lancaster and the king's cousin, had begun to believe the whole kingdom was in danger of disintegration.

Lancaster had spent ten years of his life fighting shoulder to shoulder with the first Edward in the Welsh wars; and then, with the Scots all but defeated and Robert the Bruce nearly captured in 1307, Lancaster could not now be reconciled to the first king's son and witness the brainless destruction of all that he, and others, had sweated and bled for.

Bruce was gathering power in Scotland. The year before he had held his inaugural parliament at St Andrew's and the Scottish Church had recently recognised him as the true heir to the Crown. The English borderlands were coming under increasing threat from his three lieutenants Edward de Bruce, his brother, Thomas Randolph, his nephew, and Sir James Douglas.

Lancaster, as a last resort, had persuaded the Lord Chancellor - Archbishop Langton of Canterbury - together with six of his bishops, and eight earls to demand the appointment of an executive of Lords Ordinaires to "order and establish the estate of the realm according to right and reason".

The king, when he heard this in the Painted Palace at Westminster on the 17 March 1310, went white; at first with anger and then with fear, for the Ordinaires added that they would no longer hold him as king unless he agreed to these principles. Even Gaveston's mockeries were silenced.

The king wished to consider his position, and so took Gaveston and his whole court to York, ostensibly to prepare for the re-conquest of Scotland. Once there the king ceremoniously, and in his absence, stripped the Archbishop of the chancellorship and appointed in his place Walter Reynolds the bishop of Worcester, his former chaplain and favourite playwright. Lancaster could not believe it.

And so, at York two months later, in the second week of May, Hereford and Pembroke were acting as mediators on behalf of the incensed Ordinaires and discussing the Scottish question with Edward II. Lancaster would not even go to the King. 'A waste of time', he said, 'the man is a child'.

It was Pembroke who had summoned Clifford to York. The king, he knew, held Clifford, his earl of Westmorland in high regard, and Pembroke hoped, with the added weight of Clifford's argument, to disabuse Edward of his new plan for the invasion of Scotland.

On the third morning of his stay in York, Clifford heard mass at the Church of Saint Peter in the city and at about ten o'clock made his way to the Palace. The noisy scene in the ante-chamber to the great hall was one he was becoming used to, for the hubbub always accompanied the occasions of the king in residence. Litigants and plaintiffs had journeyed in from the surrounding towns and villages in the hope of an audience with him. Fifteen or twenty men, merchants, knights and local lords, were clustered round two tables where the king's clerks were deciding the order of the day. Clifford recognised some faces from the day before.

After an hour the door of the hall opened, an usher emerged and shouted, 'Sir Robert de Clifford, earl of Westmorland.'

'At last,' Clifford muttered to himself and he stepped forward.

The usher bowed and said: 'This way, my lord, if you please.'

Clifford moved past him and entered the hall. Sunlight streamed in through the tall south-facing windows and he walked amid the bright beams towards the king. 'Your Majesty, my Lords,' said Clifford bowing.

The king was sitting at the end of a long table. There were four men around him, and off to one side at a tall desk a secretary was at work, shoulders hunched. Nearest to Clifford as he approached, on the king's right was Walter Reynolds, the newly created chancellor; next to him, and closest to the king, was Piers Gaveston, Edward's confidante. Opposite these two, on the king's left, were Sir Aymer de Valence, the earl of Pembroke, and Sir Humphrey de Bohun, the earl of Hereford.

Clifford knew the earls well, Gaveston he had seen once or twice and the Reynolds, the Bishop of Worcester he knew not at all. He sensed that the atmosphere around the debating table was not one of friendship. There was a tangible antagonism in the air.

'Come in, my lord, come in,' cried the king enthusiastically, as though trying to break the spell, 'Ahh! It is good to see a smiling face, is it not, Piers?'

Gaveston looked up at Clifford and said sourly, 'Beware the smiling face, sire. It is like the false challenge of Troy.'

'Gaveston, you are too melodramatic. Take no notice of him, Clifford. He means well. Come, join us.'

Pembroke had risen to allow Clifford room to sit. 'Leave Gaveston to me, Robert,' he whispered.

Hereford was silent; he had not raised his eyes from a document in front of him.

Walter Reynolds, ignoring Clifford, was saying something in an undertone to the king, who was bravely trying to maintain his air of amiability.

Clifford settled himself and looked up; Gaveston was staring hard at him. 'God's holy blood,' he thought, 'a nest of vipers.'

'My lord Clifford,' Reynolds began, 'You arrive at a difficult point in our discussions.' His soft cultured voice had a slight nasality which gave it a reptilian charm. 'Pembroke here was anxious that your views be sought, especially as, in your capacity of Lord of the Marches, you have, as it were, first-hand experience of the perils we face.

'I'm sure you are aware that His Majesty the King has been placed in an impossible position.....'

'We all know the background, Reynolds,' Gaveston interrupted. 'Pick your way to the bones of it, if you can. We haven't got all day.'

'My lord Clifford,' continued Reynolds imperturbably, 'the king

19

wants to secure Scotland against the maraudings of the traitor Bruce. All sensible and honourable men must surely agree.' He paused, waiting for Clifford to affirm this.

'Yes, my lord Bishop,' said Clifford resolutely. 'But it is not the ends but the means that must have debate and clear thought.'

'What! Clifford,' exclaimed Gaveston, 'are you suggesting that His Majesty's plans are ill-conceived?'

'My lord, my lord,' said Pembroke soothingly. 'Clifford intends no such effrontery. His Majesty knows well the love his liege bears him.'

The King nodded his head and then raised his hand as Pembroke was about to continue. 'Robert, my friend,' said Edward, looking closely at Clifford, 'I need your support. As the king I could command it, but I ask. Bruce's power must be broken. I intend to gather an army of ten thousand and march into Scotland this September. We shall crush him. Are you with me?'

The King had spoken with great honesty, almost with desire, and Clifford was moved. 'Sire, you know I am yours to command,' replied Clifford. He felt Pembroke's eyes on him; even Hereford was listening. 'But if you bring an army of ten thousand Robert the Bruce will not fight you.'

'Will not fight?' repeated Gaveston, 'Is he a coward?'

'No, he is not a coward. He knows he would lose, that is all.' Clifford turned to Pembroke for support.

'Your Majesty,' said Pembroke, 'your liege lords.....'

'Bah! Lancaster and the rest of you....' sneered Gaveston.

'Your liege lords,' continued Pembroke, 'the Ordinaires, are not certain that this offensive, at this point, will bring what we all desire. That is, absolute success. Such a mobilisation into enemy territory at a time when our intelligence of Bruce's strength and movements is poor, when the disposition of the border lords is unclear, must be fraught with dangers. Our advice is to wait.' Pembroke fell silent and, in thought, ran a finger along his nose.

'Wait? You disappoint me, Pembroke,' said Gaveston, 'you sit there rubbing your nose like some biblical Jew and expect us to defend the kingdom while you wait for more propitious circumstances! Well, Joseph, go back to your friends and procrastinate. We will act!'

Pembroke sprang to his feet. 'You insult me, my lord. By God, if we were not in the presence of the king I would kill you instantly.' Pembroke, his voice choking, was beside himself with rage.

Hereford, for the first time, butted in. He said, in his slow gravelly voice: 'Sire, it is not enough that your counsellors offer doubtful advice but that they insult and ridicule your loyal subjects of many years, men who have served your father, is beyond endurance.' Hereford, the king's brother-in-law, had said what Pembroke dared not say. Clifford was surprised, he had not thought Hereford to have it in him.

Reynolds evidently did not support this. 'What *is* beyond endurance,' he interjected, 'is that the lords of England, in withdrawing their allegiance from the Crown, are placing at risk the very institution they claim to uphold.'

'If we had confidence in the King's advisors the situation would not arise,' retorted Hereford.

'You lack confidence, my lord?' asked Gaveston, 'in the same way you lack guts?'

'Sire, this is insupportable.'

The king made a gesture of impatience. 'Mort de Dieu! Stop this bickering, all of you. Let us return to the military point. Tell me, Clifford,' he said, turning to his northern earl, 'why you believe Bruce will not fight.'

Clifford gazed over to the secretary, scribbling at his desk, and gathered his thoughts as all eyes turned to him. 'Sire,' he said quietly, ' Bruce does not fight according to the rules. He cannot. The resources he has to draw on are limited. I would be surprised if he could raise a force in excess of two or three thousand, and that could not be maintained for longer than a few weeks. He fights, therefore, with small bands. They raid, they harry, they ambush. If he stood to fight a pitched battle against such a force as you could muster he would be destroyed. He knows this. If you march into Scotland with ten thousand men I lay my oath you will not even see him!'

'My lord,' returned the King, 'you therefore recommend to me to do nothing? To allow him free and wanton access over my kingdom? It is lunacy.'

'Sire, with respect, I did not say do nothing, but we must fight him on his own terms.'

'What! Skulking about under cover of darkness in raids on farms? No, my lord, I cannot admit to this,' the King's eyes shone with anger. Clifford dropped his gaze, realising that Edward's pride was unassailable.

'You perhaps forget, Clifford,' said Gaveston, 'that we are knights and beholden to our vows. Some of us still hold to the notions of chivalry. It would appear you have misplaced these higher feelings, possibly by long association with barbarians.'

'Sire, I must protest,' said Pembroke angrily, 'Sir Robert de Clifford is the most loyal and honourable knight in the northern marches. His valour and virtue are undeniable. This man,' he said pointing to Gaveston, 'is an insidious influence. He sows nothing but discord.'

Gaveston sat back, sensing his victory, and he smiled.

'We are getting nowhere and I am becoming tired,' said Edward the King. 'My lord Clifford, it is in my mind to invade Scotland. I will send word.'

On this abrupt conclusion Robert de Clifford, realising he had been dismissed, bowed and left the chamber. Pembroke made a sign to Clifford to await him.

He regained the ante-chamber where the plaintiffs of the county still mingled. At his appearance, and assuming the King was ready to see others, they hastily approached the clerks' tables to press their claims anew. Clifford paced the room, his temper cooling. He hoped that Pembroke would not keep him waiting long.

Pembroke did not disappoint him, for within a few minutes he emerged from the Hall and joined him in conversation.

'Robert, I congratulate you,' he said warmly, resting his hand on Clifford's shoulder. 'Your control of emotion is admirable.'

'I may have controlled myself, my lord, but I lost the argument.'

'A forlorn hope. I am sorry I put you to the trouble of journeying here. But I thought it was worth trying.' Pembroke smiled wryly. 'Well, the king is fixed on a September invasion; the Ordinaires will not support it, except perhaps Gloucester. Will you?'

'If the King calls me I must answer,' replied Clifford simply.

'Robert, you are a Trojan!' Pembroke declared. 'Are there many like you in the north?'

Clifford was silent. He could not answer diplomatically for he had begun to think there were too many for this careless King.

Pembroke perhaps understood his mind and he said, 'Thank you once again. I hope Reynolds and Gaveston do not give you too much trouble. I bid you adieu.'

'My lord.'

The two men parted and Clifford, walking away, looked around for his lieutenant. He found him by the outer doorway in conversation with a group of soldiers.

'Holloa, Andreas,' he cried, 'we are going home. Middleham tonight. We dine with friends.'

THE ROAD TO MIDDLEHAM

They rode out through the gates of York in sunlight and took the road for Boroughbridge. Clifford was silent for a while, his mind recapturing the arguments and enmities which he had found surfacing, like malignant sores, at the court of the King. He glanced across at the young man beside him; he had known Andreas de Harcla for seven years, since his first campaign as a boy under Edward I in 1303. He had grown since then and was now a powerful man of twenty-five years. But there was almost, Clifford thought, a lightness about him that contrasted strangely with his physique. This dichotomy was apparent too in his face, which could have had something in it of the nature of Hector, the proud son of Priam. That is not to say he was displeasing to look upon for his chin was firm, his mouth well-shaped and his eyes, beneath thick auburn hair, were dark grey and sometimes unfathomable. While some found this alluring, equally, to others, it was disconcerting: on occasions, in conversation with him, an questioner might not hold his gaze and would find himself staring at the small scar below his right cheekbone. It was shaped as a star in miniature and when he smiled the short rays of the star defined themselves like the stamens of a flower. Put simply, his face, as an image and likeness of God, was a reflection of his ultimate ungovernableness.

Clifford turned to his young companion and asked amiably, 'Andreas, you have never told me how you acquired that distinctive scar.'

Harcla looked askance.

'Come, dear friend, entertain me with the story.'

'There is little entertainment in it, I assure you,' Harcla replied. He uttered these words with such a serious countenance that Clifford could not help laughing.

'Andreas, you intrigue me.'

'No, my lord, it is an embarrassment,' Harcla began to smile.

'Ah! But there should be no embarrassments between friends. You and I are perfectly easy with one another, are we not?'

'Yes, my lord, we are.'

'Well then, be frank. Tell me the story. There can be no dishonour in it?'

'No, there is no dishonour. I imagine, though, that there are secrets you, on your part, would wish to keep from me.'

'Secrets? What secrets?'

'That is the very question, my lord,' said Harcla shrewdly.

'Are you trying to baffle me, Andreas?'

'No. I'm simply making a point for discussion. The face you or I, or any man, shows to the world is an image of his character and his life heretofore. Do you not agree?'

Clifford paused at this and, in deep thought, was silent for a few moments. At last he said: 'If you mean a man's nature can be determined by looking at him, I'm not sure I do.'

'There are some given to making loose confidences and several allegiances....'

'Andreas, you injure me. I am not given to discussing private conversations at large.'

'Robert, I did not mean to offend. Some find it easy to make confidences, that is all.'

'And others do not?'

'Precisely so, my lord,' said Harcla.

'In which latter group you place yourself?'

Harcla moved his body sideways on the saddle and, smiling, made a slight bow.

'And am I to deduce that fact by virtue of the scar upon your cheek?'

'No, my lord, for I was not born with it,' said Harcla and he laughed.

'Then what is your point?' Clifford asked, slightly put out.

'I was being evasive. Forgive me.'

'But, in any event, you say you do not readily reveal intimacies; that is a laudable trait, I suppose. But a man can be overly circumspect.'

'You imply you are not? I would say you are meticulous in preserving your own counsel - until you reckon the moment ripe.'

'That is common sense, surely.'

'Perhaps,' said Harcla simply, 'but not all men practice it.'

'And that is why some lead and others follow, my friend,' said Clifford, returning to basics. 'You for instance, Andreas, in your demeanour, display to me certain forms of character that mark you out as a commander. I do not, however, claim to discern these in your face.'

'Ah, my lord, but I read them in yours.'

Clifford stared at his companion in astonishment.

They were approaching Boroughbridge; the horses for the last mile had been at a walking pace. The two knights began to look around them.

'How goes it, you two there?' Clifford called, and he swivelled round to see the servants who were riding a respectful distance some thirty yards behind them.

'Well enough, we thank you, my lord,' they answered.

'Good. We shall rest here an hour to refresh ourselves and the horses.'

The two vallets, Ketel of Hartley and Henry of Appleby, smiled and nodded at each other. They had been discussing this very point themselves.

The small party had ridden steadily for a couple of hours and were now about twenty miles from York. They were travelling Dere Street, the great Roman military road that led through the Eastern Marches into Scotland. After Boroughbridge they would leave Dere Street and ride to the north-west through Ripon and Masham to Middleham. Robert de Nevil, a long-standing friend of Clifford, held the castle. It was twenty-five miles from Boroughbridge.

They rode into the township. The small steadings on either side of the road led in a straight line to the river. The women of the town shouted to gather their children and they watched the group of riders as they passed. A dirty looking boy of eight or nine years, dressed in a common smock stood in front of them, forgotten by his mother; he was gaping at the horses.

'Out of the way, boy,' yelled Ketel. 'You will kill yourself.'

They could see the narrow bridge over the Ure as they approached. The river, twenty yards wide here, was deep in the slow-moving stretches of water. On the far side were meadows rising to a walled manor house. The gates were held open and through the passageway they saw a number of dogs jumping madly around a villager who carried a bulky sack across his shoulders. He was endeavouring to manage the sack, which must have contained some mutton or beef, and at the same time lash out at the dogs with his legs. It was a comical scene which gave huge enjoyment to some idlers of the village as they lounged about the timber walls.

Over to the left, as the road swung round, stood the priory. Several monks were busy working in the garden, and in the neighbouring field a few cattle were grazing. One of the monks stood to watch the strangers as they paused by the bridge.

Harcla seemed mesmerised by the scene. He stood his horse solitarily a few yards from the others. He gazed silently about him.

'Come on, Andreas,' said Clifford. 'My belly is growling.'

'You could hold an army at bay here,' Harcla said, almost to himself.

'What?'

'The bridge. I was thinking.'

'Come on. There will be no war here.' Clifford wheeled around but Harcla stayed, deep in thought with his horse calm beneath him.

Ketel and Henry had dismounted and were walking towards the monk. He had not moved but was standing, clutching a long-handled hoe. The other friars had walked behind him and looked doubtfully at the well-armed visitors.

Clifford called out: 'Good day to you, Brother, and Christ be with you. My name is Sir Robert de Clifford.'

'God's blessing, my lord,' replied the monk, relieved. 'I thought I recognised you. My name is Brother Jerome, at your service. You have passed here before, I think?'

'I have indeed,' Clifford answered, 'several times.' He indicated his companion, 'This is my lieutenant, Sir Andreas de Harcla.'

Brother Jerome bowed.

'We would be grateful,' Clifford continued heartily, 'for a morsel of food, and something also for the horses. Naturally, I shall be delighted to make an offering to the church.' With this gesture he was not acting purely from Christian motives; he also wished they should receive a good dinner.

'You are generous, Sir Robert,' replied the monk. 'We thank you. Your vallets can rest the horses over there.' Brother Jerome pointed to a low-roofed stable. 'Brother Martin will act as their guide from there to the kitchens.'

A young man detached himself from the group of monks and stepped forward smiling.

Brother Jerome continued, 'If you, my lords, will follow me.'

'Willingly!' cried Harcla and Clifford together.

Clifford and Harcla rested at Boroughbridge Priory a little longer than they anticipated for Brother Jerome, having escorted his guests to the refectory, informed the abbot Father Malton of their presence and this worthy proved to be insatiable for news of any great events that were shaping the kingdom. Clifford, though, only paid him the attention demanded by virtue of the dinner provided for them, and in between mouthfuls his answers were somewhat short, although courteous.

The Abbot seemed untroubled by this and opened up his own account with a statement that shocked the earl from the enjoyment of his meal. 'By the by, my lord,' he said, 'I heard that Robert the Bruce rode into Durham three days ago.'

26

Clifford almost choked on his food. 'What!' he exclaimed in disbelief. 'What did you say?'

Harcla pushed away his plate.

'A travelling friar stayed here last night,' said the Abbot, disarmingly. 'He had seen him there.'

'What! What was he doing?'

'Oh, there was no question of fighting,' the Abbot said almost carelessly. 'He only had about a dozen men with him. He wanted to talk with the bishop.'

'He wanted to talk with the bishop!' Clifford exclaimed. 'So he just rode in for a quiet tête à` tête. What about? Do you know?'

'No, my lord, I am sorry.'

'I can't believe this,' said Clifford, his eyes popping. 'I tell you, my dear Abbot, I left the King three hours ago and I swear he knows nothing of this.'

'Perhaps he does,' said Harcla, 'and it doesn't signify anything.'

Clifford was incredulous. 'Doesn't mean anything?' he cried. 'When the kingdom is being bargained for like a ...a...God's holy blood, Bruce has nerve, I'll give him that. He fought with us five years ago, Andreas, did you know that?'

Harcla nodded; he knew the story well enough. Abbot Malton listened.

'Yes, of course you know that. His father always remained true to Edward I but Robert supported Wallace, and then changed sides more times than I have loved my wife.'

Clifford paused, thinking. 'We are the same age,' he said after a while. 'I know him well; he is very, very clever.'

'The point is, my lord,' said Harcla, 'what do you intend, if anything, with this information? The king must have had intelligence.'

'Must he? Who could say for certain in these times,' he glanced at Harcla as he spoke, as though unwilling to say more in front of the Abbot.

Clifford turned and said, 'Listen, Father. You must send a messenger to the King with this news; apologise first, in case he is already aware of it, but say you thought it important enough to inform him. Say you have spoken with me.'

Abbot Malton looked unhappy at this. 'My lord Clifford,' he said, 'we servants of the Holy Church do not wish to meddle in these temporal matters. It would be better if Sir William sent a message.'

'Who is Sir William?'

'The local lord, William de Aldburgh.'

'Well, in the first place,' Clifford said, 'I am not talking to him, and in the second, you have it at first hand. If you must justify your stance with the Bishop direct him to me. Come, time is precious. Write your letter; and we, Harcla, must depart.'

Harcla was about to ask a further question when Clifford motioned him to be silent, 'No, Andreas, there is no time for debate. Thank you, my lord Abbot, for your generous hospitality. Do not forget that letter.'

Within a few minutes Clifford and Harcla, together with their vallets, were riding towards Middleham. As soon as they were clear of Boroughbridge Harcla said, 'Well, Robert, that letter will never go.'

'Yes,' Clifford agreed, 'and if you are right then I have learnt something of import. Something that has been unclear to me for a while.'

Harcla waited for him to continue.

'Abbot Malton was uncomfortable when it came to the point, was he not? Is Bruce, then, seeking the support of the northern bishops? Or if not actual support then a passivity through inaction. The Scottish Church formally recognised him as the rightful heir to the crown in March. There are moves afoot, Andreas. The non-arrival of our letter will fit one piece of the jigsaw at any rate. It may help us at a later date.'

Clifford laughed. 'That fat Abbot has got something to worry about anyhow. He shouldn't have let it slip.'

At the time they rode up the hill to Middleham Castle the sun was beginning to sink behind the fells to the west. In the meadows before the castle the tall beech and rowan trees cast long shadows on the grass. The air was fragrant with spring blossom and the castle stood clean and strong in front of them. Impulsively they swung down from their horses and with light hearts gazed around them, walking the pleasant stiffness from their joints.

THE CROSBY RAVENSWORTH AFFAIR

In the cold hours before the dawn of a July morning, two months after the journey to York, Harcla led a small band down the hill from the castle at Hartley; the others of his group were Ketel, James, Conan and Alexander. They rode inelegantly in the falling of the ground as the sleep went from them and they made miserable noises about the unholy start so early in the day.

The sun had not yet risen above the fells behind them and, in the pale light, small traceries of mist rose like wraiths in the air around the river. They splashed across the Eden at the ford below the church and climbed up the steep track towards it. The great stone building with its central tower rose up before them and the new stained glazing in its southern wall shone from lighted torches within. The riders could hear the low murmur of voices chanting psalms before the dawn mass.

Harcla and his men blessed themselves as they walked their horses past the church. Once they were clear of the township they quickened their pace and, riding now in silence, they followed the road to Appleby. After an hour, with the sun fully risen, they rattled through the gateway of the castle there and Ketel leapt down and took the bridle of Harcla's horse. The bailey was busy with noises and the air within it seemed to hang with animal smells.

Two men dressed in Clifford's livery appeared from the steps of the keep; one of them was Henry, the Earl's vallet. Harcla swung to the ground and, walking across said, 'Good morning, Henry. I am here to see Sir Robert.'

'Yes, my lord, he is awaiting you. This way if you please.'

Harcla glanced over his shoulder to James, who was tending his horse. 'Come, thou nursemaid,' he said to him, 'our breakfast awaits. Conan, will you see to James' horse.'

A wooden staircase had been built on the outside wall of the keep. It was protected by an elaborate forebuilding and gave direct entry to the Great Hall at first floor level. Harcla and James followed Henry up the steps and through an open doorway into the Hall.

A huge fire was blazing in one wall and in the centre of the chamber a long table stood with a bench on either side. At the end of the Hall was a raised dais holding two large chairs, and behind these a curtained

29

recess. Henry led them the length of the Hall to the recess and opened a door within it.

Clifford was seated at a desk in conversation with a tall man standing before him. The earl rose and stepped forward to greet the two newcomers.

'Good morning, Andreas, and James; my friends, you are welcome. This is Sir Antoigne de Lucy,' he said, motioning to the tall man 'Sir Antoigne has recently arrived from Allerdale. He serves with us.'

Harcla started at the name and looked across to the young knight during these introductions. He was of a similar age, but taller and slimmer, almost thin. He wore his black hair long, framing a pale face and a deep forehead. His eyes were dark, or at least it seemed so, for they protruded slightly and contrasted with the whiteness of his skin.

'Cold in heart,' Harcla muttered to himself, but then he said aloud, 'Your father and mine, Lucy, were comrades in arms in the service of our late King; it is appropriate that now you and I may together serve his son.'

'Well spoken, Andreas,' cried Clifford, 'a neat word for every occasion. I am pleased that you place family differences secondary to the safety of the kingdom.'

Harcla's eyes creased a little as they caught the earl's gaze.

'Have you breakfasted?' enquired Clifford. 'No? Come then, I don't expect the others until mid-morning. We can hardly wait that long.' He motioned to Henry for food and drink. 'These are perilous times, my lords. Come, to business; we can talk as we eat.'

The family differences alluded to by Clifford were well known to him. He had had to play a conciliatory role on more than one occasion. Their origins lay ten or eleven years before when Edward I was still King.

Sir Michael de Harcla, Andreas' father had been at various times the Sheriff of Cumberland and the Keeper of Carlisle Castle. He was an able man, although prone to occasional bouts of intemperance. He conducted his military obligations competently and, through them, had earned respect and friendship.

Sir Berthold de Lucy, Antoigne's father, was a wealthy man from the west of Cumberland; he held several manors in Allerdale together with the castle of Cockermouth. But he was avaricious and he coveted the positions of power held by Sir Michael; he abhorred this ascendancy over him and his own family.

Over the years the two men became bitter rivals in securing the patronage of the King. This bitterness had first spilled over into actual violence five years before, in 1305. Sir Berthold was resentful of Sir Michael's position of increasing influence with Edward I and the air of superiority displayed by Harcla's tenants and reeves infuriated him; it seemed to him that the whole county scoffed at his family.

Then, in that year, the King conferred upon Sir Michael a part of the valuable manor of Culgaith, a pleasant village near the town of Penrith. Sir Berthold was incensed; he thought it should have been granted to him.

The story goes that Master John Wharton, Sir Michael's new reeve at Culgaith, together with two men of the village, were returning home late one afternoon two months after this manorial gift of the King. Wharton had been conducting some business relating to the manor with Guillame Vespucci, the Italian merchant and banker at Carlisle.

It happened that Sir Berthold was also in Carlisle that day; he had business of his own with John de Castre, the keeper of the city. Sir Berthold saw Wharton enter Vespucci's house in Castle Gate. His simple but malignant mind saw the opportunity; he drew his lieutenant, Henry Threlkeld, to one side and ordered him to take half a dozen men, well-disguised, and make an assault upon them before they reached the manor at Culgaith.

'And Threlkeld,' he added, 'it must seem nothing more than a robbery on the highway.'

Threlkeld, not one to allow scruples stand in the way of a little easy profit, received the order with some relish and went about its execution.

Wharton concluded his business with Signor Vespucci and, together with his two men, set off homeward. The party was approaching High Hesket, a village about seven miles from Carlisle, when they were attacked at a lonely spot by Threlkeld's armed band. Sir Michael's reeve was robbed of the gold and other valuables he had kept in three leather saddle-bags, beaten and left for dead. One of Wharton's two companions, whose sole reason for travelling was to provide some protection, had ridden off at high speed the moment the attackers revealed themselves. This man returned half an hour later with the warden of Hesket and three apprehensive villagers.

Wharton and his single remaining guardsman were both lying on the road covered in blood; their horses were gone. Wharton suffered a broken head, but at least was alive; the other was dead by a sword thrust through the body. The leather satchels, now devoid of their precious contents, had been thrown away and lay in the mud by the side of the road.

Leaning over the wounded Wharton, they tried to make him drink a little water. But he wanted to sit up and speak. 'I know them now,' he mumbled, slurring his words. 'I know them, the bastards.'

'Fetch the priest,' shouted the warden of Hesket to one of his villagers. 'This man is dying. Go on, quickly!' He turned back to Wharton, who was unable to catch his breath. 'Be easy now,' he said. 'Be easy.'

'The leader is called Henry,' said Wharton, rushing his speech in gasps. 'I heard them. He leaned over me, his cloak fell to one side - I saw the crest, three silver fish. He ripped the cross from my neck.'

'Who does he mean?' the warden asked the man from Culgaith. 'A crest? No knight or lord would do this, or allow it.' He shook his head and looked down on the dying man with some sorrow.

Wharton gripped his sleeve and said, 'Tell Sir Michael.'

When Sir Michael was told of the ambush the following day he sent for the survivor to come to him at Hartley. He listened to the story, his face grim as he learnt that John Wharton had died of his wounds during the night.

One week later Michael de Harcla confronted Berthold de Lucy in the Great Hall at Carlisle Castle. He approached Sir Berthold and said bluntly: 'A murderous attack was made upon John Wharton, my reeve at Culgaith, on the road to Penrith. He was robbed of sixty marks of gold, my gold. One of his men was killed.'

'I am sorry to hear it, Sir Michael,' Sir Berthold replied calmly. 'The King's highway is still prey to outlaws and thieves.'

'Which band of outlaws, then, do you think responsible?' Sir Michael asked him keenly.

'Oh, I understand there is a particularly vicious gang out towards Geltsdale.'

'One that carries its own coat of arms?'

Sir Berthold became pale as he heard these words and glanced away as he tried to compose himself. 'A coat of arms? What can you mean, my lord?'

'I mean that the murderers were disguised as common robbers. My reeve saw a crest as he was beaten to the ground.'

'I cannot believe it,' said Sir Berthold. 'Who would stoop to such a thing?'

'My sentiments, Sir Berthold; the miserable trash of humankind.'

Sir Michael's hostility was plain and his voice harsh.

'But, Harcla, were you able to identify the crest? We must question your reeve more closely.' Lucy's palms began to sweat.

'He is dead, Sir Berthold. Two men were murdered in the ambush.'

Sir Berthold relaxed a little; but then he thought to himself that Harcla might trick him and he was troubled. 'Whose was the crest?' he asked uneasily.

'Whosoever it was will pay,' Sir Michael said and, in uttering these words with great deliberation, he broke a prolonged and strained silence. He turned his back and walked away.

Sir Berthold stared after him, cursing.

Sir Michael de Harcla would have preferred to have gone to the high court of the King but, ultimately, he could not prove the events he believed to have taken place. He determined to wait for an opportune moment when circumstances would dictate his course.

As time went on the dread apprehensions of Sir Berthold receded and Henry Threlkeld, sure of his escape from justice, and a braggart by nature, would drunkenly repeat to his cronies while laughing, 'Well, we taught that clever bastard from Hartley a lesson he won't forget - and sixty marks for doing it!'

In this way the truth of the matter became an open secret throughout the district and a talking point whenever men came together. This state of affairs continued for some two years, and the story was resurrected afresh after each drunken outburst of Threlkeld.

Andreas de Harcla, then about twenty-two years of age, heard all the rumours and snatches of gossip. It came to the crux when he was told by a journeyman from Penrith that Threlkeld had threatened to repeat the deed. The young Harcla, believing his father now too old to act, decided to take the matter into his own hands.

Threlkeld had been given the manor of Crosby Ravensworth by Berthold de Lucy; through simple bad management and corrupt practices the manor was gradually slipping into debt. A substantial sum was owing from the period when Sir Michael had been Sheriff of Cumberland. Threlkeld was attempting to buy off his creditors with occasional payments that took the form of timber or grain from the lands of the manor, or gold from the withheld wages of serfs.

Harcla believed he had discovered an authentic pretext in this and he resolved to surprise Threlkeld at Crosby Ravensworth with a demand for recognisance of the debt that he, Harcla, had assumed. If he could not destroy the beast itself he would at least hack off one of its limbs.

33

He brought together a band of seven men, some from Hartley and some who had, in one way or another, good reason to despise Threlkeld, and one young woman, Emma la Fraunceise of Maulds Meaburn, the niece by marriage of his elder sister Isabel. Emma's uncle, Sir Richard la Fraunceise, had for some time suspected Threlkeld's men of stealing his cattle.

Harcla attempted to dissuade his cousin from accompanying them, pointing out the dangers inherent in the enterprise. But Emma, as he well knew, was spirited and she would not be deflected from her course. 'I want to be part of the campaign,' she stated emphatically.

'It is hardly a campaign, Emma,' Harcla corrected her. 'More of a raid, there will be no knightly rules of combat, you know, it will be dog eat dog; or bitch.' And Harcla laughed.

'Andreas, why do you mock me so?'

'I do not mock you,' replied Harcla, disarmed. 'But you need to realise the perils we may face. It is no place for a young girl, especially a beautiful one such as you.'

Emma chose to ignore the compliment, probably temporarily; she instead retorted: 'You are no older than me. Besides, as you know to your cost, I can fight as well as any man. You said so yourself last summer.'

'Look, Emma, come then,' Harcla said, relenting. 'But you must always stay close to me.'

Emma la Fraunceise wished for nothing more on this earth.

It happened, therefore, that in the middle of May, on the vigil of the Ascension of Our Lord in the year 1308, Harcla and his band met by prior arrangement outside the church of the village of Maulds Meaburn. When Harcla rode up at six o'clock in the evening with the undetachable Ketel by his side, he learnt that Emma was inside the church at her prayers.

'She is a good girl, Ketel, is she not? She will have heaven on our side.' Ketel nodded his head and smiled a little, but he was uncertain of her value.

Harcla though, did not expect too much difficulty in the enterprise. He thought Threlkeld was likely to have half a dozen troopers of Sir Berthold's with him; but he very much doubted that the villagers of Crosby Ravensworth would aid their master.

Of his own force he could count on three, Alexander of Kelleth, Conan of Askham and, of course, Ketel. As for Emma, it was her unpredictability that was cause for some unease; she just had to stay by him.

Once he had subdued Henry Threlkeld all would be over; the rest of them would not be much inclined to fight and then the independents of his party could help themselves.

Harcla looked around him in wry amusement as these others arrived at the church. 'Good God!' he exclaimed, laughing. 'What's this? A travelling fete?' Three horse-drawn carts came to a halt in front of him.

'We do not intend to leave empty-handed, my lord,' they said.

'So I see,' admitted Harcla. 'Well, we await Emma, our saintly mistress.'

Emma la Fraunceise appeared at that moment from the darkening portico of the church. Her long fair hair fell in waves upon the shoulders of the robe she wore. It was woven of perse, a fine grey blue wool, and lined with squirrel fur in a delicate design of light and dark.

'This,' she said proudly, looking at Harcla and pointing to the pattern of fur, 'is called vair. Is it not beautiful?' Emma la Fraunceise stood there before him as though she were Andromache in great beauty.

'My lady, it may well be; but now is not the time,' he answered. 'I thought, anyway, you had been contemplating God and not the uses to which we put his creatures.' Beneath the extravagance of her cloak she wore, more sensibly, a thick quilted tunic, called a gambeson. 'She must have borrowed that from her uncle's wardrobe,' he thought.

'I prayed our Ascended Lord,' she said theatrically, 'that he watch over you, Andreas, and all of us this night.' In truth, if one could criticise Emma's nature, one would have to admit she adored drama for its own sake.

The village of Crosby Ravensworth lay no more than a mile and a half from Maulds Meaburn and as they forded the beck below the township the sun was still visible above the fells to the west. Threlkeld's house stood just four hundred yards from the ford on rising ground. It was protected by a simple fence of sharpened stakes and the road to it led upwards to a central gateway.

The gate was open and as they rode in the house-dogs snarled and jumped around them. Harcla, Ketel, Conan and Alexander remained mounted and waited in the open courtyard quietening their horses with gentle words. A few yards behind Harcla was Emma. The others with their carts had pulled up outside the fence; they jumped to the ground and ran quickly, armed with forks, to join her.

The noise from the dogs was intolerable and Harcla could not hear what movements there might be inside the house. One of the dogs bit the off front leg of his horse. He shouted above the racket, as the animal reared, 'Ketel, kill that damned dog.'

Ketel withdrew a slim-bladed dagger, called a stylet, from his belt and threw it with expert precision. The brute collapsed and its mates, with low growls, sniffed at the corpse. In this new silence Harcla observed a movement of figures behind the narrow windows flanking the main door of the house. 'What if they have bows?' he asked himself.

Suddenly the heavy door was pulled open and a man emerged, a sword swinging freely from his waist. 'Who in hell are you?' he yelled. 'You've killed my dog, you bastards.'

Harcla knew he must act, for his small force might soon be skewered by arrows. It was the prospect of humiliation that prompted him and not only a sudden and sordid death.

'Good evening, Henry,' he called to the man in the doorway, and he swung down from his horse. 'You do not need to alarm your men there,' he said pointing to the crouching figures behind the windows. 'I only wish to accomplish one thing.'

'What is that, Harcla?' retorted Threlkeld in recognition, and he unsheathed his sword.

Harcla walked steadily towards the doorway as Ketel and the others dismounted, pulling down the horses and sheltering behind them. 'The payment of a debt,' Harcla called back. 'Two men's lives and sixty marks of gold.'

Threlkeld laughed and raised his sword; then, looking to the side, he brought it down with deliberation. A discharge of five or six arrows was loosed from the windows with one finding a mark and killing Ketel's horse. Harcla ran forward and threw himself upon Threlkeld. He disarmed him with a sweep across the body and knocked him unconscious by a second blow with the flat of his sword.

Threlkeld fell and a stream of blood covered his face. Harcla walked over the prostrate body and into the house. Ketel sprang toward him as he moved inside.

'Do you wish to fight me?' Harcla asked Sir Berthold's men as they backed away into the chamber. 'Do you wish it?' he repeated, more loudly.

'My lord,' they said frightened at his countenance.

'Then get out! Now! And take these women with you; and the children.'

They dropped their weapons and ran from the house, kicked and buffeted as they went.

Emma came up and said, 'Andreas, what about the children?'

'They can stay in the village,' he answered brusquely. 'Someone will take them in. Emma, will you supervise the clearing of the house? Goods to the value of sixty marks - no more. Come on quickly.' Then turning to his men he said, 'Ketel, Alexander, tie our friend Henry to that door post. Conan, stand guard at the gate.'

The others drew the carts into the yard.

Harcla, looking at Threlkeld's bloody head with some satisfaction, said, 'Ketel, wake him up. I wish to speak with him.'

Ketel brought a pitcher of water from the kitchens and threw the contents in the face of the prisoner. Threlkeld recovered consciousness, coughing and spluttering.

'I wish you to know, Henry Threlkeld,' Harcla said harshly, and pricking with his sword the hollow of Threlkeld's neck, 'that I spare your life; and that consequently, worthless though it is, it is henceforward mine to dispose of. I have ejected your servants and your women, and my men are clearing the house of its valuables. Also, if you possess three horses of any value I shall take them.'

Threlkeld stared at Harcla, astonished at his coolness.

'This is in settlement of several debts which I have assumed,' Harcla went on. 'The papers are here. You can tell your master Sir Berthold whatever you like, but I tell you this: Do not cross my path again, for on that occasion Threlkeld, and mark me well, I shall dispatch you to your other master in Hell.' He paused before continuing, 'Before I go there is one other reckoning to make.'

Harcla reached down towards Threlkeld who, fearing a beating, struggled in his bonds crying, 'Leave me, Harcla, leave me.'

Harcla pulled Threlkeld's tunic from his chest to expose a golden cross resting there. 'This belonged to my father,' he declared. 'It was a gift from him to John Wharton, his reeve at Culgaith. And now, you miserable wretch, I retrieve it.' Harcla uttered these words with great contempt and, as he did so, he ripped the cross from Threlkeld's neck.

'Remember what I have said,' he concluded and turned away.

'You bastard,' Threlkeld gasped out.

Harcla stopped and looked back over his shoulder. Their eyes met then and Threlkeld shut his mouth and dropped his gaze to the ground.

All this time there had been much coming and going of Harcla's party as they emptied the house. He walked outside and saw that the three carts were very nearly filled with chairs, cupboards, wall hangings, linens, silks and all manner of goods. Tethered to the carts were three horses, fully equipped. Already two of the band had departed driving six of Threlkeld's young stock before them; the rest mounted up and, with the carts, moved at walking pace out through the deserted street of the village.

Ketel looked back to the manor house. 'I wonder who will wish to free Threlkeld,' he said laughing.

'They should leave the villain to rot,' Conan said.

'One day he will,' said Harcla. 'But we should think of pleasanter things now.' He glanced at Emma la Frounceise. The freshness of the evening air, together with the recent excitement, had imparted a radiance to Emma's cheeks and her eyes were bright as she jogged side by side with Harcla.

Theirs was indeed a pleasant situation. The lane they rode along was, above the creak of cartwheels, resonant with the singing of blackbirds; and from further off they heard the wilder cry of the curlew. Looking upwards they saw the tops of trees still catching the last glints of sun, turning the new leaves an almost mystical golden white, like the glowing raiment of the Ascended Lord. The evening sky was a rich dark blue and displayed, in one or two faint stars, the boundlessness of Heaven.

Emma began to sing, her light and strong voice mingling with the bird-song all around:

> *Lenten is come with love to towne,*
> *With blosmen and with briddes roune,*
> *That al this blisse bringeth.*
> *Dayeseyes in this dales,*
> *Notes swete of nightegales,*
> *Uch fowl song singeth.*
> *The threstelcok him threteth oo,*
> *Away is huere winter wo,*
> *When woderove springeth.*
> *This fowles singeth ferly fele,*
> *Ant wliteth on huere winne wele,*
> *That al the wode ringeth.*

'That is one of my favourite songs of spring,' she said, 'although I sing it better in Gaelic.'

'Then do, Emma.'

'Well, there is quite a lot of it, you know, and I am tired now.'

'You must sing it for me on another time,' Harcla said.

'Yes, I would enjoy that,' and she laughed. They were quiet for a few moments.

'We did well, did we not, Andreas?' asked Emma, smiling broadly in complete happiness.

She looked at him for some short time and her eyes held his by a hidden force of which he had been unaware. In these seconds we spend eternity. After an age he realised he was gazing not at her but rather on the paradise within her; and he further realised this was only possible because she allowed it, or more than that, she willed it.

He tried to wrench his eyes away from hers; he succeeded but only so far that they rested on the thick waves of her hair, escaping freely from the hood of her cloak. Emma continued to smile and, as she re-captured his gaze, said again, indescribably softly, 'Andreas, we did well. Are you pleased with me?'

Harcla was overcome, 'Emma,' he whispered. 'My lady, I am yours for you to command.'

'Then stay with us tonight,' she said, and paused before adding, 'my aunt and uncle will be pleased to hear of our adventure.'

The talk around the table of that small room in the castle of Appleby had ceased for some little time. Harcla, musing on this episode, was smiling to himself and gazing with unfocused eyes beyond the windows to the swaying branches of rowans. He saw the interlacing greenery and in the swaying gaps a supernatural blueness of sky.

The earl of Westmorland watched him for a moment and said, 'Are you with us, Harcla?'

Harcla started and said, 'I beg your pardon, my lord?'

'Did you manage to catch any of it?' Clifford asked dryly. 'Perhaps I should recapitulate: The King has called me, Harcla, to raise a force to hold the border in readiness for a September invasion of Scotland.'

'When, precisely, is the invasion to be?' Harcla inquired attentively.

'On the eighth day of the month; that is, the feast of the Nativity of the Blessed Virgin. The army is to gather to the King at Wark in Northumberland, which is where I shall be based throughout the summer. During that time we shall have a total force of one hundred and fifty riders to glean what intelligence we can of the Scots and also, of course, to prevent any enemy incursions into England.

For your information, my lords, some one hundred men of this force will be quartered in the far north east, at Berwick, until Michaelmas next under Sir John de Segrave, the new Warden of Scotland.

'I shall go into the details when the others arrive. Suffice it to say that you, Andreas will, with me, be based at Wark. You serve under Sir John de Crumbwell, knight banneret of Pendragon, along with four other knights; you know them all, of course: Richard de Musgrave, Walter de Strickland, Nicholas de Vipont and your future brother-in-law Robert de Leyburne.'

Clifford stopped for a moment and, in thought, ran a hand through his hair. 'I should say, Harcla, that Crumbwell is not in the best of health, nor does he possess the sharpest acumen. I mention this to you privately so that you may know, although he holds seniority by rank, I charge you to assume command should the need arise.'

Harcla nodded his head in assent.

'You, Antoigne,' Clifford went on, 'serve under John de Castre, knight banneret and Keeper of Carlisle. You know him well, I think?'

'My late father knew him better. But, yes, I know him.'

Harcla looked across, interested in this news. 'I did not know your father had died, Lucy,' he said. 'My condolences.'

'Thank you,' Lucy said and he looked at Harcla, doubtful of his sincerity. 'It was very recent, two weeks ago in fact. A hunting accident.'

'Probably too full of Bordeaux wine too early in the day,' Harcla thought.

'He talked of you often,' added Lucy, and his dark eyes slid away.

'Castre is an able man, Lucy,' continued the earl quickly, 'you serve with Patrick de Curwen, John de Penrith, William de Mulcaster and Hugh de Moriceby.'

Lucy, in his turn, agreed by a short nod of the head.

'Each knight in this intelligence-gathering force,' continued Clifford, pressing the palms of his hands firmly upon the table to make his point, 'will command six men-at-arms. Choose wisely, gentlemen; we are summoned for two months, until September, and after that the invasion itself. I don't need to tell you that, at times, this adventure will be uncomfortable.'

The earl paused and looked at the two men before him. He thought them to be his ablest young lieutenants in the north and he hoped, by treating them in this like manner, that their feud would die.

THE HERMIT OF PENDRAGON

castle of Pendragon stands some four miles to the south of Hartley in the upper reaches of the valley. The ground narrows markedly here: at its widest point the dale is no more than half a mile across and is bounded by the high fells of the Pennines.

The stretch of land thus encompassed was named Mallerstang Forest and renowned for the great quantities of timber it produced, and for its stocks of deer and game-birds, especially mallards. The lords Clifford, part of whose estates it now was, often took visiting parties there for the excellent hunting.

It was considered therefore a valuable manor to possess, but one with a curious history. One hundred and fifty years before it had belonged to Hugh de Morville, one of the four assassins of Archbishop Thomas Becket. After the assassination at Canterbury Hugh de Morville was said to have fled to Pendragon where, wracked by guilt, he paced the walls of the castle night and day, unable to find tranquillity. After a time he began to believe he was haunted by the spectre of the murdered archbishop, his mind sinking under the weight of the sin. Indeed, in the jutting edge of the gaunt fell above the valley a traveller can see, from a point a quarter of a mile up stream from the castle, that the profile of a bearded face wearing a tall mitre is outlined in the rock.

Eventually Morville, unable to bear his remorse, sought solace over the seas in France. Whether he ever found the peace he craved is not recorded but his estates were forfeited by the Crown and, after some years, these lands passed by marriage to the Clifford's, which family, in the time of our history, still owned them by grace of the King. The knight banneret John de Crumbwell had married Robert de Clifford's aunt Idonea some twenty-five years before and it was thus that he held the manor for his life.

Some say Mallerstang, hidden away by its misty remoteness, is still a dolorous place. The castle itself was built on an ancient site. Old stories held it to be the birth place of Uther Pendragon, the father of King Arthur. Edward I had, from early youth, been strongly influenced by the legends that surrounded King Arthur and his chivalrous knights. He learnt of the link Pendragon had with Arthurian tradition through Clifford's grandfather early in his reign and on occasion, before the bitterness of life had overtaken him, he liked to rest there during his journeys to Scotland. He would walk with quiet excitement the ground that provided so close a connection to his lost hero; ground that Arthur himself may have walked.

The mountains rose steeply above the castle on the western side of the river and somewhere among the lower cliffs of the mountains, beneath the haggard image of Saint Thomas, there lived in a cave a hermit who became known locally as Uther. He had been there a long number of years and was generally thought to be mad. Nobody knew anything of his origins; some said he was from Wales for he spoke limited English, and French with an unusual accent. He was never known to hear mass but he walked into the villages of Nateby and Kirkby Stephen from time to time to trade for food the bracelets and charms he fashioned. The priests of the Church frowned on discourse with him and generally he was left alone; which is, perhaps, what he wanted.

This man, in his eyrie, watched as two riders made their way one July morning, along the road by the river towards Pendragon.

It was four days after the meeting with Clifford and Lucy at Appleby and Harcla had received a summons from John de Crumbwell to attend him at the castle in Mallerstang. Harcla was accompanied by Ketel.

Uther could see that the two men were chatting together and riding easily, the sunlight glinting on the hilts of their swords and the clasps of their cloaks.

They approached the castle through a long row of small huts; the blackened wet thatching of the roofs, as they dried in the sun, stank of mouldered straw. The riders crossed a narrow bridge that spanned the deep dry moat. As they dismounted and glanced back they saw a strange figure running towards them from the bridge; he was pushing his way through the small crowds of women and children who had gathered in the roadway. He wore a long brown robe tied at the waist and he had sandals on his feet, almost in the manner of a mendicant order. His hair was long and his beard unkempt; both had streaks of grey in them. He looked about forty years old but he was running like a younger man.

'What in God's name is this?' Harcla exclaimed as the wild man crossed the bridge. He drew his sword.

Uther stopped in front of them with palms upraised, gathering his breath in deep gulps. 'Art thou Harcla?' he gasped out.

Harcla said: 'That is my name, but you have the advantage over me.'

THE HERMIT OF PENDRAGON

'Thou can call me Uther, if thou likest. But it matters not.' He spent some seconds regaining his breath and he studied Harcla's face minutely; and then, appraising the lines of his body, he scanned him from head to toe. It was almost as though he were an artist about to make the single most telling stroke of the brush, which would define the portrait forever.

Harcla became impatient. 'Is there anything you want with me?'

Uther did not answer immediately but began to scrutinise Harcla's sword in the same way he had his face.

'For God's sake, man. This is enough,' and Harcla lowered his sword and turned to enter the castle.

'Can I see it, please?' asked Uther then, and he reached out his arm for Harcla's sword.

Harcla, surprised, and after a small hesitation, handed it to him. The hermit grasped the heavy broadsword firmly and, flexing his arm, made several forward feints; then, to Harcla's amazement, threw it in the air above their heads. It spun in imperfect arcs; Harcla and Ketel backed away from the lethal twisting flight.

Uther caught the sword expertly as it fell, still spinning, towards the ground. 'I can make thee a sword,' he said smiling, 'better than this. A thousand times better.'

Harcla, in some confusion, looked at Ketel and then back to Uther. 'Why would you wish to make me a sword?' he asked.

Uther raised his eyes to heaven, as though the answer was obvious. 'Thou shalt have need of it,' he said, 'I saw thee fight at Shoregill.'

Harcla looked strangely at him as his sword was returned. 'You mean last November?' he asked.

Uther nodded, 'I watched from a place in the mountains,' he said, and he smiled secretly. 'A better sword is deserved, perforce. I will have to use thy forge at Hartley. The one here is useless.'

'How do you know that, you lunatic?' exclaimed John de Crumbwell, emerging from the gateway of the castle. 'Go on, be off! Sir Andreas does not require anything from you.'

'I shall call on thee at Hartley,' said Uther and he walked away. Harcla watched him go.

Ketel said: 'With your permission, my lord, shall I make enquiries of him?' Harcla nodded.

'Dismiss him from your mind, Harcla,' said Sir John, 'he is mad. I, for one, know nothing much of him. He turned up here about ten years ago. He sells trinkets in the villages, I think. But come into the Hall; I

43

wish to speak with you about this Scottish business.'

Crumbwell led them through a chilly passage with a circular stone stairway leading upwards on each side. They climbed the one on the right to the first floor, Crumbwell wheezing somewhat with the effort; the flagged corridor in front of them was enclosed with narrow slitted windows looking north. Crumbwell pushed open a door on his left and ushered Harcla and Ketel in to the Hall.

'I can talk in front of your man, can I?' he said, sitting himself down.

'Yes, my lord, he is as safe as gold.'

'Well, Ketel is it? Outlandish names you christen your children with here. I can never get used to them. Pour me and my lord some wine. It's over there,' and he pointed Ketel to a covered trestle in the corner.

'Christ knows what I am still doing in this draughty hole,' Crumbwell continued. 'Cold for half the year and wet the rest. God's blood! Twenty-five years of it. My lady Idonea is ill again, by the way. She has taken to her bed, I fear; otherwise she would be pleased to welcome you. We don't often get neighbours calling.'

Sir John's voice trailed off sadly and Harcla, in silent mirth, was forced to look away, sipping his wine.

'How is your father Sir Michael?' Crumbwell enquired.

'Tolerably well, Sir John, I thank you. But he does not go abroad so much these days; he reads a lot. He has become quite old in the last two years.'

'Don't I know it!' the other exclaimed, 'I mean, speaking for myself, of course. I can barely get out of my bed some mornings for the pain in my legs.'

Harcla was determined to make no sympathetic noises and he remained silent. Crumbwell began again: 'What with Idonea abed, with my own indispositions and so few reliable servants...'

'Ah! So we come to it at last,' said Harcla to himself. Ketel remained in the corner gazing into space.

Sir John coughed and said: 'I have corresponded with my lord Clifford and he agrees that, unfortunately and with great personal sadness, I should not take up my command in the borders this summer.

'It falls therefore that you, Harcla, have been chosen to lead my company. Clifford has the greatest faith in your competency, as indeed I have. You leave for Wark in three days; that is on the morning of the feast of Saint Mary Magdalena. The company musters at Brough under Stainmore. Everyone has been informed.'

'What of Sir John de Castre?' Harcla asked.

'Castre? Well, as keeper of Carlisle, his force will remain based in that city. You, with Clifford hold the centre at Wark and Sir John de Segrave, Warden of Scotland, will have his headquarters at Berwick, and patrol the east. It's quite simple really. In any event, Sir Robert will be at Brough to provide the greater detail.'

The old knight paused, relieved to have completed an uncomfortable task without loss of face. 'If you should ever wish to come to me for advice,' he continued with some abandon, 'be sure I shall freely give it. You may always rely on that score, my boy. Now God go with you.'

When our two men had left the castle and were riding the green road back to Hartley, Andreas said: 'You go on Ketel. I am for Maulds Meaburn.'

PEREGRINES AT COCKERMOUTH

Antoigne de Lucy, the new lord of Cockermouth since his father's death, stood taking the air in the bailey of his castle. The morning was sunny and warm and he had dressed simply in a fine scarlet tunic. The tunic was brought in at the waist by a leather belt, which held a large silver buckle. This buckle, of which Antoigne was particularly proud, was imprinted with his device - three silver pike, called luces. His father had changed the family name, originally Multon, to match the fish; perhaps Sir Berthold had thought Multon soft and lacking bite.

He was standing with his falconer, a man called Eric, in front of one of three large fenced cages. In each of these cages, which Eric had constructed at the order of the late Sir Berthold, was housed a pair of birds; peregrines, goshawks and kestrels. Antoigne had stuck his thumbs under his belt and was listening carefully to the talk of the falconer beside him.

'You see, my lord, this young peregrine falcon. I purchased her for you three days ago at Whitehaven. We have bought birds from this same breeder before and not been disappointed. See the beautiful colouration on the side of her breast. There. And the noble way she holds her head. She is a fine animal.'

Antoigne nodded his head appraisingly. He could not admit to being an expert in falconry; the patient effort required was foreign to him, but he loved the savagery and thrill of the hunt. The kill held an atavistic fascination for him; much like the excitement that flooded him on the field of battle, although that was cleaner. Afterwards, the natural indolence of his character would soon reassert itself and, like Achilles, he was too self-indulgent to subject himself to discipline.

He then said: 'That's all very well, Eric. I admit she looks well. But is she a killer? How is her eye in flight?'

Antoigne pulled a piece of rabbit flesh from the bucket at Eric's feet and, pushing it on to a stick, placed it through the fencing. The falcon flew to the walls of the cage before swooping to grab the food. He watched the way the bird ripped the flesh and pulled at it with its beak .

'None better, my lord,' replied the other. 'I watched her before I bought. And she is fast.'

46

'Well, that is good of course. But what should I name her?'

'It was in my mind to call her Wingfast, if it pleased you, Sir Antoigne.'

'Wingfast', Antoigne mused. 'Hmm. We shall consider. Eric, I am eager to see her myself. I shall try her now.'

'My lord, she is a young bird; I do not know how well she has been trained. I myself have done nothing with her. I would rather leave the flight until I have had time.'

'Nonsense. Besides, I must leave for Carlisle today. You do not wish me to realise the poor purchase you have made. Is that not it, you reprobate?'

'As you command then, my lord,' said Eric, and he walked to the rear of the cages where, under the bailey walls, he stored the gauntlets, handling chains and other gear.

The peregrine watched as Eric clad himself and then handed a second gauntlet to Sir Antoigne. When he was ready he opened a fenced door and entered the cage, making gentle noises and calling her Wingfast by name. After a moment she flew down and settled on his fore-arm. He felt the strength of her talons as they tightly gripped the thick leather of the gauntlet. Wingfast, spreading her wings noisily in a rush of muscle and bright colours, moved from one foot to the other and pecked at Eric's hand as he attached one end of the long handling chain to her leg.

Antoigne was impressed by the beauty of the falcon and he stood back as Eric emerged from the cage and walked towards the outer gate.

'Come, my lord,' said Eric, 'we will make a try anyhow.' The peregrine, staring over Eric's shoulder, watched Antoigne with its unblinking gaze. Then the falconer dropped a leather hood over its head.

They stopped in the stretch of pasture beyond the castle walls; it was bounded, about one hundred yards distant, by the trees of Park Wood. Eric lifted his arm and then straightened his elbow with a sudden movement. 'Fly, Wingfast,' he said. The falcon leapt from the gauntlet and the coiled lengths of light chain unravelled at speed from his other hand as she soared upwards. She twisted in her flight, feeling the pull of the chain. Antoigne heard her cry, a harsh rasping kraah-kraah-kraah, as she soared again towards the trees.

'Come round, come round,' Eric shouted to Wingfast, encouraging her to fly in widening circles thirty yards above their heads. Her long pointed wings were outstretched as she glided through the sky and Eric, entranced, walked across the pasture guiding her flight.

Lucy said: 'Let me try her.'

Eric transferred the leather toggle bound to the handling chain and attached it to Lucy's gauntleted wrist. Immediately Lucy felt the muscular pull of the bird.

'Gently, my lord,' Eric instructed quietly.

'I know, I know,' Lucy said brusquely. Wingfast swooped downwards. The chain slackened, drooping in a concave arc in front of them.

'Go round, Wingfast, go round.' Eric called and he turned to Lucy in some agitation. 'Move back, my lord, move back. Steadily. That's it. Oh!'

Lucy had tripped on a tussock of grass and fell to the ground swearing. Eric retrieved the toggle chain from his prostrate master and the peregrine resumed her flight.

'Well, my lord?'

'I think Wingfast is a good name, Eric,' said Lucy, getting to his feet and gazing upwards.

'I had better bring her in now,' Eric suggested.

'It's a pity you cannot release her,' Lucy said, pointing to the wood. 'There are a couple of pigeons on the edge of that copse.'

'Next time, my lord.'

Lucy seemed to accept this and they walked back to the castle, Eric securing Wingfast in her cage. Lucy stood for a few seconds admiring his purchase. He turned to Eric, who was storing the handling gear, 'How much did you pay?' he asked.

'She is a wonderful bird, is she not, my lord?'

'How much, falconer?'

'Just eight shillings, Sir Antoigne. A great bargain.' The falconer had, in fact, paid six but thought eight an acceptable price.

'Eight shillings!' shouted Lucy and he punched the falconer in the chest. 'Christ's blood. What do I pay you? Two pounds a year, is it not? I wonder whether that's too much; equivalent to, say, two pence a day. Very well, I withhold one week's wages - one shilling. That is to cover your over-exuberance in dispensing my money to all and sundry.'

Eric picked himself up and looked suitably chastened but was privately content. Lucy, having made his point and vented some spleen, sauntered off to make his preparations for the journey, apparently forgetting all about his new peregrine, Wingfast.

Eric watched him go. 'Worse than his father he is,' he muttered.

Antoigne walked towards the keep. He had received his instruction from John de Castre to present himself at the castle of Carlisle and he would leave before noon, as soon as Threlkeld and the others arrived.

He was excited by the prospect of action.

'Mind you,' he thought to himself, 'anything to get away from home was a blessing. His mother's wailing these last three weeks following Sir Berthold's death had been more than tiresome. Anyone would think she had loved him. Old fools! His father for getting himself killed in that ludicrous fashion - Christ, he could still see Harcla smirking at that - his mother for bewailing the fact.

'Still, I am lord now,' and he smiled in satisfaction. 'I had better go and bid her adieu.'

My lady Marjory de Lucy was in her solar and gazing out to the distant mountains. Standing by the window she had watched her son as he walked from the falcons' cages by the western wall towards the gate of the keep. As he disappeared from view beneath the buttress of the tower she sat down and bade her serving-woman bring her needle-work. She pushed some grey strands of hair beneath the wimple she had taken to wearing and picked up the needle. She looked at her hands; they were still white and without blemish, her fingers long and slender, but the smoothness of youth had gone. As she ran a finger along the back of her hand her skin crinkled like thin parchment. She put down her work and thought of Sir Berthold. He had not been a loving husband, although she was unable to make any comparison, but he had provided well for her, she had her home and comforts; and she in turn had given him a son. She had lost her husband, what should happen if she lost her son too?

'Antoigne,' she said as he entered the solar, 'how tall you look. Surely you are not still growing!'

'I doubt it, my lady Mother. I had my twenty-third birthday last month, as you should remember.'

'Of course I remember. How could I forget? Your father came home with that lovely gift.' Marjory de Lucy stopped and began to weep.

'Mother, you must cease these tears. You will make yourself ill.' Antoigne couldn't help thinking she would make him ill too. 'Father would not wish that, would he?'

My lady Marjory dabbed at her face and looked up into the unlit eyes of her son.

'Oh! I am not thinking of him. I am thinking of you.'

'Of me? Why should that upset you?'

'Oh, Antoigne, what if anything should happen to you? If you are killed in those wastelands out there,' and she waved her thin arm behind her.

'My dear mother, I am not going to die; of that I can assure you. For one thing, I am worth far more to an enemy alive than I am dead.'

'I don't understand you.'

'Ransom, Mother, ransom.   Knights and lords get captured, not killed. It's better business.'

'And do these Scots understand this?'

Lucy burst out laughing; he had always thought his mother a little slow. 'Most of the Scots lords are no more Scottish than I am. They are of Norman stock, like us. They have lands there that is all. The only ones to worry about are the natives, the Celts.'

'You are saying all this to make me feel better.'

'Mother, it's true, I swear.' He looked down at her and placing his hand upon her shoulder he kissed her cheek. It was still damp and, unlike his lips, warm. 'And now I must go. My men will be waiting.'

'God keep you, my son,' she said.

8

CLIFFORD'S CONFERENCE

n the evening of the twenty-third of July Robert de Clifford's central border force of five knights, their vallets and twenty-eight men-at-arms were quartered at Wark Castle in Northumberland.

Clifford had received a letter from the earl of Pembroke before the company left Brough; it seemed from this that the Ordinaires continued to resist the King's summons for the September invasion. Clifford gathered that Pembroke was finding it increasingly difficult to remain on civil terms with Gaveston and Reynolds, which made relations with the King himself strained and there was no desire, on either side, to ease wounded vanities.

Clifford talked over these politics with Harcla on the second evening of their arrival at Wark. 'Pembroke also says,' he added abruptly, 'that Gaveston might put in an appearance.'

'To what end?' Harcla asked.

'A good question. Apparently he is keen, as one of the King's tenants-in-chief, he is the Duke of Cornwall of course, to judge the situation in the borders at first hand. I suspect, though, that there is more to the matter than that.'

Clifford paused, thinking, and drew his hand through his hair. He went on: 'Pembroke, who as you know is taunted by the nickname Joseph the Jew does not delight in the mockery Gaveston and his friends apply to him. By all accounts even Lancaster is not immune; I hear they call him The Black Churl. Imagine! The King's cousin! They call young Gloucester The Cuckoo's Chick, an allusion, it seems, to his mother's honour, or the lack of it; and Guy of Warwick is The Black Hound of Arden! Gaveston, a latter day Patroclus, and his accomplices have quite an array of grotesque doggerel for the amusement of the King. By all accounts they act out these parts in plays which Reynolds, the master dramatist, composes.

'Little wonder,' continued Clifford, 'the Ordinaires are driving the King to finish with Gaveston; to exile him, for the sake of peace in the realm. But he will not, of course. This sojourn to the Borders is a means of alleviating the pressure.'

Harcla was quiet, staring at the wall.

'I would not worry too much, Andreas,' Clifford said. 'I will see that he does not interfere with our plans; you remain in charge of day-to-day operations. But be prepared, he may wish to ride out with you.'

'Oh, I am easy on that score, Robert,' replied the other, 'but will he designate me a churl or a Jew?'

They both laughed.

'He is a meddler by nature; and one with a sharp tongue. But don't forget he is the favourite of the King. In fact,' said Clifford glancing across, 'he could be more than simply a favourite; there are some rumours that their relationship is...pardieu.. unnatural.'

'Good Christ!' Harcla exclaimed incredulously. 'You mean our liege lord and King, ordained by God...'

'You have not lived long in the world, my friend. There are probably worse things to encounter.'

'I'm sure there are, but dear Christ, the King!'

Clifford began to laugh, 'Ha, Andreas, your face is a picture. Yes, to quote a line from that bawdy poem we heard one night in York, "they have consumed the apple of Sodom". Do you not recollect?'

'I do, but I did not make the connection.'

'You were probably dreaming of Emma la Frraunceise. Much more wholesome. How is my lady, by the way?'

Harcla was taken aback. 'She is well, I thank you, my lord,' he said. 'But I did not realise you knew my cousin.'

'Well, I don't particularly. I was speaking with your brother.'

'Who? James?'

'No. John. We rode together for a while yesterday on the road from Brough.'

'Great God!' Harcla exclaimed with some warmth. 'Is there nothing sacred?'

'Sacred, Andreas?' queried Clifford, astonished at the word. 'You employ unusual language in discussing your cousin.'

'Robert, I do not wish to discuss my cousin at all.'

Clifford began to regret his chaffing of Harcla. 'Andreas, I am sorry if I have been indelicate,' he said.

'You have not,' the other replied. 'But I was with her at Maulds Meaburn three days ago. I had to say I would be away for some time. It was difficult.' But Harcla smiled across at his friend and the star-shape on his cheek was evident in the last rays of the sun as they filtered through the open window. 'We have become quite close,' he said finally.

'Quite close!', Clifford muttered to himself, 'I used to call it something else.' And then he said aloud, 'Well, Andreas, I think we should discuss our plans for the summer. But, wait, we should call the others.'

He looked towards the doorway where two men were standing in the dim light. He motioned to one of them and Henry of Appleby came forward. 'Henry,' he said, 'be good enough to ask my lords Richard de Musgrave, Walter de Strickland, Nicholas de Vipont and Robert de Leyburne to come to me.'

'Yes, my lord,' said Henry, bowing; he was about to withdraw when Clifford asked: 'Who is that there with you?'

'It is Ketel.'

'Good God!' the earl exclaimed, turning to Harcla, 'Does he ever leave you?'

Ketel, for whom some remarks had little purpose, stepped forward and said fixedly to Clifford: 'It is my duty and my honour to serve my lord Andreas. Where else should I be?'

'Assuredly so,' answered Clifford, laughing. 'But you may go now. I shall act as guardian in your absence.'

Ketel, pleased to have made his point, bowed, and he and Henry left the apartment. Clifford smiled across at Harcla. 'Well, my friend,' he said, 'you may safely trust your life with that man.'

'I have already, Robert, and will probably do so again.'

The two men were silent for a few moments. The evening had drawn on quickly as they talked, and they realised, as they looked around the room, that it had grown dark. Outside the walls of the castle the river North Tyne flowed down from the hills and here was already a wide stretch of water. The bridge was just visible one and a half miles away; this was the only river crossing for ten miles and the village of Wark was therefore something of a crossroads, a meeting-place where armies and warrior bands gathered to cross the Tyne.

Dere Street, the great Roman road to Scotland, ran straight as an arrow south-east to north-west six miles away. The company would become well acquainted with it soon enough.

Henry of Appleby, holding a lighted taper in one hand, pushed aside the hangings by the door and the four knights who had been summoned entered the chamber together. Henry walked behind them and went to light the torches upon the walls.

Clifford rose as they approached the long table. 'Good evening, friends,' he said cordially. 'Please, sit down. I trust your quarters are comfortable, or at least reasonably so.'

They all nodded their thanks except Musgrave, who said: 'My lord,

53

if it is possible I would prefer a separate room to my men. I have no privacy.'

Clifford's jaw dropped a little in astonishment. 'None of us have privacy, Sir Richard,' he retorted tartly. 'Pardieu, we are at war you know.'

Clifford sat down. 'I thought it would be appropriate,' he said, 'now that we are settled, comfortably settled here at Wark,' and he glanced coldly at Musgrave, 'to hold a council whereby we can decide on our individual roles this summer.

'The overall objectives, as you know, are twofold. First, to gather what information we can on enemy movements along the border; and, of course, their strength. That means frequent, co-ordinated missions into the border country. Second, to prevent any raids by the enemy into the northern marches of England - that, potentially, could cause us more problems because we are, after all, only a small force; and that is why mobility and discipline are so important to us; they are the factors, my lords, in which we need to excel.'

Clifford was a good speaker. In describing the tasks that faced them, he imparted an enthusiasm that impressed them all; the young knights, as they listened, became eager to begin.

Each of the five scouting parties was ascribed a particular corridor of ground of about ten miles in width and fifty in length running towards Scotland. They were put on a calendar of three days out and one day in; every fourth day a written report from each group was to be submitted to Clifford and he, on a weekly basis, collated similar reports from Castre at Carlisle and Segrave at Berwick. In this way it was hoped that a detailed and accurate picture of Scottish activity would emerge.

Two of the knights, Strickland and Musgrave, admitted to illiteracy. There was nothing greatly unusual in this and a scribe from the monastery at Hexham was allotted to each of those two parties.

'Andreas here is in overall command of day to day actions,' Sir Robert went on. 'It is crucial that everybody is aware, not just of the area of their own duties and responsibilities, but also of where their colleagues are operating. Do you have the map, Harcla?'

Harcla nodded and unrolled on the table in front of them a square of parchment. It was a chart depicting the north of England and the southern half of Scotland, from Lancaster to York in the south and from Glasgow to Berwick in the north.

Clifford leaned over the table. 'Most maps and charts that you may have seen,' he said, 'are useless for any military purpose because it is impossible to calculate the actual distance between any two points; and even whether those distances are uniform throughout the chart.'

Not all of the knights had seen a map before but imagined sagely that that would be the very difficulty in their practical use; they nodded their heads in agreement.

Clifford continued: 'This map is different, because this map has been drawn to a scale.'

'Ahh!' they said, looking at each other in some perplexity. 'A scale!'

'Scale means that, in this case for example, one inch on the chart is equivalent to three miles on the ground. Look here.' Clifford stuck his finger on a point in the centre of the map. 'What does that say?'

Walter de Strickland looked at Robert de Leyburne and said: 'Well, Robert, spit it out. You can read, can you not?'

Leyburne smiled and said, 'It reads Wark.'

'Excellent,' cried Clifford. 'Of course, Wark. Where we are comfortably settled, are we not? Now, look to this.' Clifford pushed his finger to the right along the parchment for a very short distance, stopping at a wavy line etched in a blue dye. 'What will that represent?' he asked.

There was a short pause before Strickland whispered: 'The river.'

'Bravo, Walter! The North Tyne.' Clifford laughed and turned back to the map; he traced his finger a further two inches to the right and halted at a thicker dark line that ran undeviating to the north west. 'And this?'

'Dere Street,' came the immediate reply.

'And if my finger has travelled two inches upon the chart, then how many miles must I ride eastwards before I reach Dere Street?' Everyone was laughing now; even Musgrave joined in the merriment. Harcla poured some more wine.

'Well?' asked Clifford again.

'Six, of course,' said Nicholas de Vipont.

'Oh, it is "of course" now, is it? Pardieu, I am obviously too good a teacher. Yes, six miles to Dere Street, you imbeciles. So, the point is, by studying this map we know that Dere Street is six miles, or say half an hour's easy ride, from Wark.'

Clifford stood up from the table adding, 'The cartographer from Hexham, a very clever monk called Ambrose, is drawing up copies for each of you. I hope that he will deliver them to us early in the morning. I want you to take great care of the maps you each receive. You will, perhaps, notice that there are parts of them which are devoid of any inscriptions at all - they are blank. That does not necessarily mean there is nothing there; there may well be a village missed or a track inaccurately drawn. Ambrose has told me this; his work really is at an early stage. It is in all our interests to make note of any major inaccuracies or exclusions and pass them to me as part of your reports. Does everyone understand that?'

The knights around the table smiled at one another and nodded their heads.

'Good,' Clifford went on. 'Also, although the maps note the high peaks such as Stainmore, here, and High Street, here, the gradual falling or rising of ground is not shown. Indeed, how could it be you may ask, but Ambrose, our clever and enlightened monk, is thinking of a system whereby even this could be accomplished.'

Clifford concluded his discourse with a repeated admonition: 'Guard these charts most carefully, my lords. For one thing the Scots do not have any knowledge of their existence.'

After the particulars of the following day's duties had been finalised Strickland, Musgrave, Leyburne and Vipont said their good nights and quitted the apartment.

Clifford got up from his seat and, stretching, walked leisurely over to the window. 'Well, that went well enough,' he said to Harcla. 'I must say, I am deeply impressed with Ambrose's maps. He first talked to me about his ideas four years ago, you know. He has been sending novitiates out all over the north this last year or two - armed with quill and parchment!' Clifford paused before adding: 'I hope, anyhow, they will be of practical use.'

'I'm certain they will, Robert,' Harcla said.

Clifford looked out over the pleasant hills to the north, dark now beneath the twilight sky. 'Do you remember that fat abbot at Boroughbridge?' he asked Harcla.

'Ah, yes. The letter to the King about Robert the Bruce's presence at Durham.'

'The very one. Well, it will not surprise you to learn that the letter never went. I corresponded with Pembroke on the matter; he says the King is unaware of any meeting between the Archbishop of Durham and Robert the Bruce.'

'Hmm,' pondered Harcla, 'what inference should we draw?'

'I don't think we can draw any - yet. Except that Abbot Malton of Boroughbridge is untrustworthy; and also I would be careful of the archbishop.' Clifford stopped, gazing into space. 'I wonder if there is anyone in his household we could use as er...an agent, an information-gatherer.'

'You mean a spy, Robert.'

'Well, yes if you want to use the term.'

'I might know of someone,' said Harcla. 'A man my brother Henry knew at the seminary in Belgium. I can't remember his name, but I know he is now at Durham.'

'That might suit, but find out more about him, if you can.' Clifford pulled the heavy wall-hanging across the window and moved back to the table.

As he sat down Harcla took a mouthful of wine and said: 'Robert, I have an interesting story to relate to you. Last week while I was at Pendragon with Crumbwell I met a man who called himself Uther. A strange fellow, a hermit I think; he offered to make me a sword! Can you believe it? He seemed to be knowledgeable enough - he could handle a sword well at any rate. He particularly wants to use my forge at Hartley. What do you make of that?'

Clifford laughed. 'Harcla, do not concern yourself with mad men. They are dangerous to know.'

'He did not seem mad to me.'

'Well, what do you know of him? Where is he from?'

'No one knows for certain. I asked Ketel to make enquiries. The most we found out was that he is from a place called Cavan - although I do not know where that is. He fought against Edward I twenty years ago before fighting for him as a mercenary in Flanders. It is said he was an archer.'

'Cavan is in Ireland,' said de Clifford, thinking hard, 'how old is he?'

'Oh, I don't know. About forty.'

'And an archer? With a knowledge of sword-forging? An unusual mix.' He paused for a moment. 'My father used to tell me of a man he had known; an Irishman who claimed to be a king, or a chieftain. I actually met him once or twice during campaigns in Holland. He had become notorious for his distinctive method of fighting. Some called it dishonourable. He made his own swords, which was odd. My father said they were lighter, designed for thrusting rather than sweeping. And he was a crack shot with the bow; that was the funny thing - he fought with both. On horseback. Not knightly, you see.'

Harcla's eyes lit up as he heard Clifford describe this warfare, mirroring so closely his own ideas. 'It can't be the same man, can it?' he wondered aloud. 'If he has been in Mallerstang these ten years why would he not make himself known to your father.'

'I don't know. They would be separated by birth and rank, of course. Old Simon at Appleby might remember the name; he served as vallet to my father in Flanders. I shall ask for you.'

'Thank you, Robert. Although I don't suppose it is of any consequence.' The nonchalance of this remark was not real, for Harcla was exhilarated at the thought of the hermit Uther and the lost Irish warrior being one and the same.

'By the by,' Clifford asked, grinning, 'how did you get on with Crumbwell?'

'Well enough,' Harcla answered. 'He is getting old; a fact he was at pains to point out. He has no desire.'

'I cannot really blame him for that. Of course, it suited my purpose to allow him to relinquish his command. He is better off out of it - and we are better off without him.

'Did you see my aunt, the lady Idonea?' Clifford asked again.

'No, unfortunately she had taken to her bed.'

'Yes, I had heard she was ill. My mother has visited her recently. What a miserable promise long life holds for us. Eh, Andreas?'

Harcla nodded his head. Clifford looked at the empty flagon upon the table and thought about calling for Henry.

'I sometimes wonder what we should most prize,' Clifford said.

9

EMMA LA FRAUNCEISE

arcla left Clifford and made his way to the southwest tower of the castle, to where he and his men had been billeted. As he approached the apartment he overheard the sounds of laughter and lively conversation. He paused at the door, listening; he concluded that the wine flagon had been a few rounds of the table.

Alexander of Kelleth was speaking loudly, 'Christ's blood, James! I tell you - it's the absolute truth.' There was a pause, a loud expectoration and then he said: 'You were there, Conan. Tell him!'

Conan was laughing. 'Yes, Kelleth is right,' he said, turning to James, and he continued the story: 'We had just pulled into the courtyard when a pack of bloody great dogs, wolves more like, started snarling round us and biting. Look I've still got the scar.'

He rolled up the lower arm of his tunic to display a long red weal and James nodded his head in admiration. 'Then,' Conan went on, taking a huge slug of wine, 'we saw seven or eight of the bastard's archers crouching behind the windows of the house. I felt my insides churning, I tell you. Christ, I thought I was going to disgrace myself.'

'You did, Conan, you lump of lard,' shouted Alexander in huge merriment. 'Your face was the colour of wet ashes.'

'You did not look too composed yourself,' retorted Conan.

'Alright, alright,' said Ketel.

'Anyway,' Conan continued, 'Ketel here pulled down his horse to kneel behind its body. This we all did - except your brother, of course. Threlkeld had appeared at the doorway by this time, shouting and swearing, the ugly bastard. Then the air was whistling with arrows but your brother just walked straight through them, as though it was a stroll with his love in sunlight. He whacked Threlkeld a huge swipe on the head and stepped over his body and into the house.'

He added, a little shamefacedly: 'Then we got up from behind our horses.'

Everyone started laughing again and Harcla could hear the rough pouring of wine. Conan took a noisy draught, wiped his lips and said: 'James, if you ask me to talk about your brother then I will tell you: I believe he is guarded by angels. As for me, well, I will follow him through fire and earth and water!'

Harcla pushed open the door. 'There will be nothing but water left to drink in the whole castle shortly. Good God! Have we won the war?' He looked around the disordered table with severity. 'We rise at first light, you know. We should be sleeping.'

His elder brother John was sitting a little apart from the others, closer to the fire. He asked: 'Where are we going, Andreas?'

'Roxburgh,' came the reply.

The men looked at each other in solemnity, digesting this news, and quietly they began to arrange their beds for the night. Harcla walked across the chamber to the small adjoining solar and settled himself. Ketel appeared in the doorway and spread his cloak on the floor. 'Goodnight, my lord,' he said.

'Goodnight, Ketel,' Harcla answered and he closed his eyes.

It was the action of sunlight through trees that he remembered most clearly. He had stopped at the top of the hill, looking down on the township of Maulds Meaburn. The water of the Lyvennet sparkled as it ran through the village meadows and he saw, standing on the far side of the river, the manor house of Fraunceise with its large walled garden. He stood there for some few minutes gazing on the scene and then he saw a figure, a horse and rider, emerge from the gateway of the house, three hundred yards away. The figure, riding swiftly, took the track leading towards him; it was Emma. She rushed from a small copse at the bottom of the hill, urging her horse upward. Her hair was loose and shining in the sun; it flew around her shoulders. Harcla watched and the heart within his body, which he was about to make a gift of, thudded against his chest.

She was still moving fast as she approached and she shouted to him: 'Come on! There is something I want to show you.' She sped past him and looked back over her shoulder, laughing. 'Come on, Andreas!' she said again.

By the time he wheeled his horse to give chase she was fifty yards ahead and breaking to her right where the ground rose towards a wood of beech and oak. Harcla, spurring his horse, gradually gained on her and Emma, glancing back, realised this. She leant further forward in the saddle and kicked the sides of her horse.

'Emma!' he shouted, wishing her to slow.

She looked across at him and said, breathing hard: 'We are nearly there now anyhow. I win.'

Harcla burst out laughing as they slowed to a walk. He was unable to follow the paths her mind seemed to take and he said: 'How do you win? I have been gaining on you this last mile.'

'Is that all you can say?'

'That is all I need to say, is it not?'

'Hardly, Andreas! I arrived first. I win.'

'Oh! We have arrived, have we?' Harcla said, looking around the empty spaces. 'And where exactly have we arrived at?'

'Secret,' Emma replied. 'But, come, I shall show you.'

She jumped down from her horse and led him by her free hand into the trees. They walked on a little way in silence, the sound of a running stream becoming louder as they went. Emma seemed to know the path and eventually they reached a beck in a small clearing. On the edge of the clearing the beck disappeared in a fall of water and the ground dropped away sharply to a steep gorge far below. Above them the branches of huge oak, beech and chestnut intermingled and through the greenery bright beams of sunlight shone. It was a beautiful place.

Straight ahead, beyond the precipice, the world opened before them and they gazed across the wide valley floor to the massive bulk of the Pennines, a darker blue beneath the clear sky.

'This is my secret place,' she said.

'It is beautiful.'

'I come here often; or at least, as often as I can. It is good for thinking.'

'I have never been here before.'

'No one has, except me. I don't even know if it has a name; but I just call it Eden.' Emma leant against a huge granite boulder, eight feet in height, that stood on the edge of the cliff. 'You can see this rock from the tower of Appleby Castle,' she said, standing back from it. The sunlight caught and danced on the flakes of quartz embedded in the stone; the rock itself seemed to sparkle.

'Do you not see the shape they make, Andreas?' she asked him.

'Shape? I don't understand.'

'Look!' Emma said, and very slowly she traced her fingers over the smooth surface, following the glinting particles of quartz.

Harcla stood and stared at this girl; first at her face, a little to one side, a determined set to the muscle at the corner of her mouth, and then at her hand, her fingers as they glided along the granite. He saw she had traced the image of a heart.

'A heart,' he whispered at last.

61

'Yes,' she said and looked at him. Their eyes met as had happened once before.

'Emma, I came today to make you a gift.'

'Did you, my love?' she answered softly.

'Yes,' he said, gazing upon her. 'I am disinherited of a part of me - because it beats only for you.'

'Oh, Andreas, I know, I know!' she cried, happy yet unsatisfied. 'But I want your soul as well. And you are to have mine; for I belong to you heart and soul.'

'Yes, always,' Harcla murmured and he moved unconsciously towards her, living in the beauty of her eyes.

'Wait!' she said. 'Listen to me! I wanted you to become a part of this place so that, in your heart, and wherever you may be, it will always be a remembrance. And that in your heart, therefore, I will always be.' Emma la Fraunceise gazed upon her lover with an intensity in which they were both engulfed.

'What worlds do you inhabit?' he asked her.

Harcla was woken by Ketel. 'My lord,' he said, shaking Harcla's shoulder, 'My lord, it is time.' Ketel threw back the wall-hangings surrounding the window and a grey light entered the chamber. The others were rising.

Ketel, thinking he had heard a murmured question from his master, turned to him and asked: 'I beg your pardon, my lord?'

Harcla woke up, and in waking he lost the last trails of the sweetness of the scent of her. He said: 'Nothing, Ketel. All is well. I was dreaming, that is all.'

10

DERE STREET

n the morning, after the dawn mass to celebrate the Feast of Saint Christopher, the Bearer of Christ, Harcla and his men departed from the castle at Wark and rode up the left bank of the North Tyne to the ford above Redesmouth. They crossed the river as the rain came down and cantered the four miles to Habitancum, the old Roman fort by Dere Street. Here they stopped for a few minutes examining the ground for signs of a recent encampment. There were none and Harcla and his group, looking like peculiar hunched creatures underneath their heavy over-cloaks of waxed hide, mounted the stoned causeway that was Dere Street and headed northwards.

The wind gusted and they looked up to see the flying clouds and the swaying branches of trees. The rain came in heavy bursts and left puddles and rivulets of water on the broken surface of the dark road. Up on the fells the peat hags filled and the once dry gills rushed with water and tumbling stones. In between the showers the big black crows came to scavenge for food in the wet fields. The horses picked their way unwillingly, both they and their riders were wet and cold.

Towards the middle of the morning they came down from the road. Harcla consulted Ambrose's map. 'Otterburn should be about two miles north-east of here,' he said confidently, 'a short distance beyond the River Rede. Let us hope it is not a torrent after this rain.' He regarded his men, who looked like Trojans in wet misery. 'Follow me,' he said heartily, 'we shall get hot food in the village.'

The riding formation they had adopted was one in the shape of an arrow-head, or a solid chevron. Harcla considered it to offer better protection in defence and greater scope for manoeuvrability in attack. He led, being the arrow-tip, in the second rank were Ketel and Fraunceise, and side by side in the third, being the base of the arrow-head, rode James, Conan and Alexander; behind these, in the centre rear, the stump of the arrow shaft, was John de Harcla.

They rode into Otterburn, the horses' hooves splashing in the muddy pools along the street. They could see the church, their object, at the far end of the township. As they approached a robed figure scurried around the corner of the church and slipped through the doorway of a small steading beside it. They heard the door-nail bolted.

'That's our man,' said Fraunceise.

They came to a halt in front of the house. 'God's greeting,' Harcla called out.

His men gathered around him and the horses fretted in the rain. 'Pax tecum,' he said again, 'we mean you no harm.'

After a few seconds a small voice from within said: 'What do you want?'

'Shelter for an hour, Father, and a bite to eat. I am happy to recompense you.'

'I warn you, I am well armed,' returned the voice.

'You will have no need of that,' said Harcla, smiling to himself. 'Let us in, I beg.'

The door opened and the resident curate, a solid peasant, appeared before them.

Harcla questioned his host as they ate. The priest told him of a small band of Scots who had passed through a week before, going south. 'There were about fifteen of them,' he said.

'Who was their leader?' Harcla asked.

'He called himself Sir John de Soulis, from Eskdale. They stayed overnight in the church. We didn't have much choice, of course.'

'Did he say where he was going? Or for what purpose?'

'No. But I imagine his purpose is much the same as yours.'

Harcla laughed and said: 'And what is that, Father?'

'To hold control of the Marches, I suppose,' replied the priest. 'You should know, my lord, that the people are frightened - the law of the land is not upheld. An army of Scots marched through last November and killed all the cattle and sheep they wanted; they stole our grain. The winter was hard for many of us after that.'

'Who is lord here?' Harcla asked him.

'Leonard of Elsdon. But he is powerless.'

Harcla nodded, powerless himself, and rose to depart. 'Thank you for your hospitality,' he said. The priest thought to ask of his guests' destination but decided that ignorance was, perhaps, the better policy.

Harcla and his men, refreshed and newly dry, continued their journey into the borderlands. The heavy dark clouds of the morning had passed and the brightening day imparted a lighter mood to the company. Their over-cloaks, now lying across the rear of their saddles, flapped to the motion of the horses and dried as the fresh breeze caught them. Once they were clear of Otterburn they halted and Harcla opened his tablet to write there. He now had two inscriptions on the first sheet of his book; it read:

25 July   *Habitancum*   *VIII hr*   *no sign*
         Otterburn   *X hr*   *enemy party XV*   *enemy army CCC*
                                  I night   *I night*
                                  S. VII days   *S. Nov III yr*
                                  Soulis   *sltrd cattle, stole grain*

The tablet and map he kept in a deerskin pouch beneath his jerkin and, having studied the map once more, he returned them both to their place. Alexander of Kelleth, who had been looking over Harcla's shoulder, said: 'My lord, what does "III year" mean?'

'I did not know you could read at all, Alexander,' replied Harcla.

'I cannot, in truth, but some fashions of letters I can pick out.'

'It means, clodhead,' Fraunceise interrupted, 'the third year of the reign.'

'What? King Robert's reign?'

'King Robert, my backside. King Edward's, you clown. You know, the King of England.

'Ahh!' said Alexander a little sheepishly.

The others jostled him, laughing. 'Do you not know the King you serve?' they said.

'Here we are, in the middle of Christ knows where,' said Conan, 'and Kelleth doesn't even know which side he is supposed to be fighting on!'

'Alright, enough,' said Harcla, 'at least Alexander tries to take an intelligent interest in our projects.'

'But sadly fails,' said John.

This riposte set everyone laughing once more.

'As for Robert the Bruce,' stated Harcla, 'it is actually his fifth year; and I doubt it will be his last. But come, we have some miles to cover.'

It was in his mind to follow Dere Street into the hills of the Cheviots and camp there that night before striking north to Roxburgh. In this country Dere Street had been superseded as the main road to Strathclyde by the King's highway, which continued further to the north-west and travelled upper Redesdale before dropping into the valley of the Jed Water and so to Jedburgh and St Boswells. Harcla intended to return to Wark by this lower western route of the highway, estimating enemy strength around Jedburgh as they headed south.

The castle of Roxburgh, held by an English garrison under the command of Sir Henry de Beaumont, lay ten miles to the north-east of Jedburgh. The exchange of intelligence with Sir Henry in his lonely outpost was an important element of the mission and Harcla was anxious to arrive there before noon the next day.

Five miles up the valley from Otterburn, at Horsley, Dere Street broke northwards from the King's highway and climbed out of Redesdale. According to Harcla's map there was a pele tower some way along this stretch of road, above the western banks of the Rede.

'Ambrose's genius is sublime,' said Harcla, as the tower came into view on a small hilltop.

'I don't suppose though, he can guess the mood of the inhabitants,' said Fraunceise, as, two hundred yards away, a dozen men ran shouting towards the tower, pointing out the approaching horsemen to others within; the running men entered the pele and slammed the gate shut.

Harcla's company rode up the grassy banks at an easy canter; several men appeared on the walls of the tower amid some background movement.

'Andreas, there is something wrong here,' John de Harcla shouted from the rear. Harcla, staring hard to the tower, slowed the company. He was about to shout up to them when suddenly a flight of seven or eight spears was cast down.

'Holy Christ!' Conan yelled, as the spears started to drop.

'Get back!' ordered Harcla. 'Get back, for Christ's sake!'

The horses wheeled quickly but smelled the fear and two or three panicked and collided with one another. James and Alexander struggled to right their horses as the spears fell.

'Mary Mother of God!' cried Alexander, as a spear thudded into the ground, just grazing his leg.

But James was hurt, hit in the top of the shoulder; the eight foot spear shaft wavered upright in the air and then, as it fell, its weight brought the spear-tip upwards ripping through his flesh and widening the wound. James swooned and fell from his horse, the spear wrenching itself out of his back.

'Ketel, Conan,' shouted Harcla, 'unleash, unleash! Get the bastards back from the walls.'

Ketel and Conan had already dismounted and, with feverish fingers were stringing their bows. The first arrows whistled towards the tower as Fraunceise and John rode back quickly to their two comrades; but Alexander was already kneeling beside James and he threw him upon his own horse, leapt into the saddle and galloped down to the others, now standing a safe distance from the walls of the tower.

They drew James down and laid him upon the wet and muddied turf. Fraunceise pulled a knife from his belt and, cutting around the torn jerkin, lifted the pierced mail shirt from James' shoulders. James groaned and opened his eyes, making a movement to rise.

His eldest brother, John, knelt by him. 'James, you must lie still,' he said.

'Can you tell whether the spear-tip was poisoned?' Harcla asked Fraunceise.

'I do not have that knowledge, Andreas. But we must surely clean the wound.' Fraunceise turned to Ketel and said: 'Pass me your water bottle; and I need a strip of cloth. He got to work and Harcla looked towards the pele tower.

The men on the ramparts were shouting again. 'Do not come near us,' they yelled. 'We shall shoot you again. Go back to your own country.'

'The stupid peasants think us to be Scots,' said Conan, beside himself with anger. 'Hola! Hola!' he shouted over to them, 'Castrati! Imbeciles! Which King do you think we serve?'

'We do not care,' came the answer, 'go your way.'

Harcla rode forward a few steps to more closely see their faces. 'My name is Andreas de Harcla of Westmorland,' he called in a clear voice, 'If you have killed my brother, who lies here amid the mess and shite of your cattle, then, as God witnesses this, I shall return to kill thee.'

After a small silence they shouted again, although with less conviction, 'Go your way. You cannot harm us.'

'Tell me your name, you who is speaking,' Harcla persisted.

'My name is my own affair,' replied the other, and said again, 'Go your way.'

'Your vocabulary is as limited as your brains, you cur,' Harcla cried in his frustration. He knew he was culpable in allowing this danger on his men.

'Come, my lord,' said Ketel, 'I think James can ride. Sir Richard has cleaned and bandaged the wound.'

They put James in front of Alexander, who was the lightest of the group, and rode down to the road. Derisory cheers followed them as they went. Harcla felt the awful tide of humiliation rising over him.

They followed Dere Street into the hills and rode at a good pace as the afternoon wore on. They reached Coquet Head two hours before sunset and made their camp there. The summit of Brownhart Law sheltered them from the north-westerly wind and in the lee of the Roman earthworks, close to the infant Coquet, they made their bivouacs. Conan, the expert with a tinder box, produced a fire and they made James as comfortable as they might close by.

Fraunceise said to Harcla: 'I am worried about him, Andreas. He has a fever, and Alexander says he has lost a lot of blood.'

They watched as Kelleth scrubbed himself in a small pool by the beck. The light from the evening sun, filtering through the gaps in clouds, caught the falling water from his arms and chest and glistened as the pale crimson droplets fell into the stream.

'We shall leave him at Roxburgh in the morning,' Harcla decided. 'He will receive good care there and a week or two of rest. We can pick him up on our next sortie.'

Fraunceise nodded his agreement and went over to sit by John de Harcla, who was carefully unpacking his gear. Ketel had shot a couple of hares earlier in the day; these he had skinned and dressed and now they were roasting nicely over Conan's fire. They made a broth of oats, water and strips of meat for James, who was able to sit up against the bank and sip his meal. The rest of the company chewed on their supper and discussed pleasantly what they would do to the men of Horsley Pele – or, more precisely, which few dismemberments they would not perform.

Harcla turned to Alexander of Kelleth and said: 'You did well today, Alexander. Thank you for saving my brother.'

'It was my honour, my lord. Anyone would have done the same.'

'No, some would have thought of their own life.'

'In truth I did, my lord,' said Kelleth with artless candour.

'But you thought of James too. That is the difference.'

Alexander sat back in happiness and finished his supper. The sun slid down behind the rounded tops of the Cheviots and in the firelight Harcla withdrew his deerskin pouch to make the third entry in his tablet.

They passed a bad night. James' voice, distorted by feverish dreams, rose and fell throughout the hours, calling on his dead mother. Some showers of rain came before the dawn and in the first grey light of day, tired and in poor humour, they broke up the camp and rode out. Kelleth insisted that James ride with him as before.

The company made slow progress for the first half dozen miles through the mountains. The surface of the one thousand year old road was broken badly and in places it disappeared completely under old falls of rock. Thereafter they were able to increase their pace and they came down to Teviotdale, having met with no one, friend or foe.

The town of Jedburgh, which they had neatly by-passed, now lay three miles to the south and they forded first the Jed Water and then the Teviot, just above their confluence, before leaving Dere Street and riding north-east for Roxburgh.

~ 11 ~

A NEW WARFARE

Harcla and his men were ill at ease as they followed the Teviot river northwards for there was a curious stillness about the country. After a while it came to them that no birds sang. In silence they passed through the deserted village of Nisbet. The company had not before witnessed such scenes of desolation: a number of steadings were burnt out, cattle byres empty or destroyed; no crops of wheat or oats grew in the charred stubble of fields and solitary blackened trees stood leafless and dead in the pale summer sun.

'War has been here,' said John grimly.

The men looked at one another in disbelief. They went on quickly and after half an hour, by the middle of the morning, rode into Roxburgh; war had been there too. The castle stood before them, to their right, above the banks of the Teviot and they approached the outer wall with caution, watching from behind the side building of a partly destroyed town house.

The tall gates of the castle were shut and on the ramparts above no guards were visible.

Harcla stood quietly; Fraunceise and the others stared about them. Alexander said: 'We must get James inside, my lord.'

Ketel trotted his horse down the street, away from the castle, and disappeared around a corner.

Harcla said: 'John, ride back to the edge of the village and keep a look-out. Stay in sight.' Harcla rode forward a few paces to be in full view of the castle gates.

Ketel returned. 'I have seen nobody, my lord,' he declared. 'The place is deserted.' He paused then and asked the question all were thinking. 'Who holds the castle, I wonder - English or Scots?'

Harcla was dismayed and he stood by the gate considering this. 'It must be Beaumont still,' he said to himself and he scanned the ramparts once again.

A voice came down to them in the silence: 'Who goes there?'

Harcla relaxed; it was a trooper's voice, of distinct Anglo-Saxon origin.

A THEORY OF BORDER WARFARE

'We are friends.' Harcla shouted up: 'I am Sir Andreas de Harcla of Westmorland, here under orders of my Lord Clifford.'

John rode back to the group in haste. 'Andreas,' he panted, 'there is a band of horsemen to the south, twenty or thirty, riding hard.'

'Send for Sir Henry de Beaumont,' Harcla called to the trooper on the walls. 'Quickly, man.'

John circled his horse, gazing behind him. 'Andreas,' he called out, his voice breaking with tension, 'we have two minutes, no more.'

'For the love of Christ, open the gates,' Conan muttered.

'Henry de Beaumont!' de Harcla shouted desperately. 'Henry de Beaumont!'

'Qui va la?' called a different voice.

'Sir Henry, I am Andreas de Harcla, sent by Robert de Clifford, Lord of the Marches. Open your gates; we are pursued.'

'Show yourself, Sir Andreas,' came the voice.

'I am here, Sir Henry,' Harcla returned. 'Look, my crest,' and he pulled back his cloak to reveal the red cross and martlet. 'Open your gates.'

Beaumont, a war-hardened Gascon, smiled at this naïve gesture; but he nodded to his men at the gates. 'With pleasure, friend,' Beaumont called down to him. 'But hurry, they are on the street.'

Harcla's company rushed forward as the gates were pulled open and they rode safely into the bailey of the castle. Beaumont, having placed a dual line of archers above the gatehouse, was taking no chances on his visitors being other than they whom they claimed to be. Harcla and his men rode this gauntlet to the middle ground of the bailey and dismounted. Harcla jumped up to the gatehouse and joined Beaumont.

'How many are they, my lord?' Harcla asked as he peered around the crenellated wall.

'Dispense with the formality,' Beaumont said, leaning against the battlement, 'My name is Henry.'

'Andreas de Harcla at your service.'

'To answer your question, my friend,' said he, glancing down, 'I should say twenty-five, or thereabouts. I recognise most of them. It might interest you to know that Edward de Bruce, Robert's younger brother, is stationed somewhere near Melrose at the moment; we have seen a lot of him recently. That's him there, to the right of centre, in the brilliant blue tunic.'

Harcla looked down eagerly. 'Edward de Bruce! Good God!' He saw a dark haired man a few years older than himself, clean shaven and bright-eyed, sitting upright in the saddle. His first impression was one of solidity, of unseen strength. He watched Bruce's men, with Edward in their midst, circle the ground in front of the castle gates; some others were simply riding fast up and down the street.

'What do they wish to achieve?' Harcla asked.

'It's a show of strength, nothing more.'

'Why do you not shoot at them? They are easy targets from here.'

Beaumont looked over to Harcla and asked: 'Have you seen much border warfare? I ask, not out of disrespect, but because it is different here. I think we should talk over dinner, say an hour?'

James de Harcla was placed in a large lower chamber which the men of the castle called the hospital; six other wounded soldiers lay there also. They enjoyed a reasonable comfort, lying in clean linen on thick straw mattresses, and watched over by an old physician, a monk from Dryburgh Abbey.

The rest of Harcla's men were quartered in the keep among a number of Beaumont's retinue of forty men-at-arms. Harcla himself was resting in a corner of the crowded apartment when John came over to him.

'The priest says James will live, Andreas,' he said.

'Yes, of course he shall.'

'The spear was not poisoned, as we had feared, and the wound is clean. His mail shirt reduced the impact - otherwise he should be dead.'

'Do you think I do not know that?' Harcla replied.

John, the eldest living brother, looked at Andreas and wondered how to frame his question. Eventually the words came out. 'Andreas, what were you thinking of at Horsley?'

Harcla stared stonily at the wall. 'Christ, John, do you not know I blame myself? He is my brother too, you know. I am still learning.'

'Well, do not experiment on your brother,' John replied. But he immediately regretted his words and, unable to hold Andreas' gaze, he looked away, abashed.

'You should not expect me to display emotions,' said Harcla, 'even to those of my blood; I think you are over-critical. We have done well thus far. This is a new warfare and we do not always know what to expect from it.

'I do not wish to argue with you John,' Harcla went on.

'Nor I with you.'

'Come then, brother,' Andreas said, and they embraced. 'Let us go to James and display some fraternal affection.'

72

A THEORY OF BORDER WARFARE

They both laughed and walked down to the hospital; James, awake but a little delirious, seemed to look straight through them as they entered. Harcla explained to him that he must remain at Roxburgh for a couple of weeks while his wound healed.

'We shall collect you on our next trip,' Harcla said. 'Get well.'

James, his face fixed in a sick smile, closed his eyes.

After their visit to the hospital the two men went up to Beaumont's room on the highermost storey of the keep. Harcla introduced his elder brother and all three sat down to eat.

'Well, Henry,' Harcla began, 'first tell me about your border warfare, which in truth I know nothing about.'

Beaumont laughed. 'I do not know where to begin,' he said.

'Well, why did you not engage Bruce this morning?' Harcla asked.

'Reprisals.'

'Reprisals? What do you mean?'

'You must understand the situation,' Henry began, in between mouthfuls of his dinner. 'In the Lothians we, the English, hold the major strongholds, running west to east, of Buittle, Linlithgow, Edinburgh, Roxburgh, Wark, Norham and Berwick. Rutherglen, near Glasgow, fell to the Scots eighteen months ago. All very well, you may say. But, although the leading families and knights remain mostly loyal to the Crown, the Scots are growing stronger. They ride the highways of the country in bands of say, anything from twenty to fifty light horsemen; these forces are commanded by knights such as Soulis, Lyndsay and Boyd - good men and effective leaders - and sometimes you might see Douglas, Randolph or, as this morning, Edward Bruce. In other words, Andreas, outside of these English castles, they are the masters and we do not have the strength in numbers to contest that supremacy.

'Some local lords have already switched allegiances, not always because of a moral or patriotic conviction - although that is also true - but to protect their families and lands. You must have seen the destruction, even here in Teviotdale.'

'We could not believe it.'

'Well, you should,' continued Beaumont, settling himself back in his chair. 'It is far worse further up country around Biggar and Lanark. If I had attacked Edward de Bruce this morning then, mark my words, someone else would have suffered, their lands spoiled or their families injured. And then they would join the enemy; there is no choice.'

'This is lunatic!' Harcla exclaimed. 'You cannot even fight them!'

Henry stopped to take a swallow of wine, and smiled. 'If they attack our castles or our baggage-trains - which they do incidentally, and successfully, for supplies from the south are intermittent to say the least - we defend ourselves.   That is different for then we have no choice; other than to surrender, of course.   We fight a war of appeasement, nothing more.

'I have been here just a few months,' he continued, 'a place forsaken by God, if ever there was one.   My predecessor told me I should soon learn the habits of the country – I did, it's a matter of survival.   The people up in Norham and Berwick must be in worse straits: the only good thing you can say about Berwick is that it's on the coast and can be victualled by sea, although I hear that Scots privateers are becoming more active – easy pickings, you see.'

The two Harcla brothers sat back in their chairs, dumfounded.   'Is my Lord Clifford aware of this....this mess?' they asked incredulously.

'That's your job, I imagine.   He knows the situation is deteriorating, of course; but not to what extent.   So does the king; and his Chancellor - who is it now?   Some bloody play writing prelate.   What's his name? Reynolds, that's it.   They don't always acknowledge my letters, so really I have no idea if the couriers are getting through.'

'I'm sorry,' he went on, 'I don't often get the chance to speak like this.   As you may imagine, it is difficult to maintain morale, and discipline.   I have thirty-four able bodied men-at-arms, the other six being in the hospital; luckily for me they are all English and less likely to desert.'

He paused as Harcla smiled in disbelief.

'You think I am joking?   I assure you I am not.   Many of the garrisons have a Scottish contingent, obviously enough; it didn't matter a few years ago, but now that Robert the Bruce is King Robert the First and winning the war without even breaking sweat, it makes a difference.'

Sir Henry got up from the table and walked to the doorway.   'What news of the Scots?' he asked the guard standing there.

'My lord, they left the town an hour ago, riding south.'

'Well,' said Beaumont, returning to his guests, 'that probably means Jedburgh.   How long are you planning to stay?   I have to say to you, Harcla, that although I welcome the extra men, it will put a strain on our resources - food, I mean.'

'Do not worry, Henry.   We are due back in Wark tomorrow; we are leaving now.'

'Now?   I would not advise it, Andreas; wait till dawn.   Do you not believe in circumspection?   They know you are here and will be watching for you.'

'That may be, but we cannot stay. Anyway, I want to have a look at Jedburgh on the return journey.'

'Oh, you do, do you?' Beaumont said in awed scepticism. 'The place will be glutted with Scots. Talk some sense into him will you, John?'

'It is a part of our mission,' John admitted.

Beaumont shrugged his shoulders.

'Thank you, Henry, for your help and your hospitality,' Harcla said, smiling. 'We shall return in two weeks, perhaps a little less. Look after our little brother.'

Beaumont nodded his head and said: 'God speed.'

~12 ~

THE WALLED TOWN OF JEDBURGH

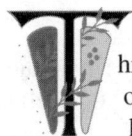

hree hours after the gates of Roxburgh Castle had been pulled open in haste for Harcla to enter, with Edward de Bruce and his Scots horsemen on a close chase through the town, they were re-opened more sedately for his company of six horse to depart.

Where they could they rode the higher ground to Jedburgh, and always avoiding the road. They halted on the edge of a wooded hill overlooking the town and a little to the south of it. The gates were open and as they gazed down in the pale afternoon sunlight they saw the market-place emptying of farmers, merchants, journeymen and peddlars as these men and women, sitting in their carts or astride their ponies, shouted to the bridled asses and oxen to pull them away homeward. These sounds drifted up to the Englishmen, a quarter of a mile away, as they waited quietly on horseback in a broken line behind the first of the trees.

Harcla watched the Scots troopers walking the tall timber walls that surrounded the township. There were perhaps half a dozen on guard, chatting amongst themselves and joking with the departing peasants and traders.

The town was roughly rectangular in shape, about one hundred yards wide and three hundred in length, with the Jed Water running slowly through it on the western side. In an open space within the walls was an encampment of a dozen tents; outside of these fires were burning. Further around, directly abutting the western wall, was a line of recently erected wattle and daub shelters running half way the length of the town.

Groups of riders were leading their horses to and from these new buildings beneath the wall, as they entered or quitted the gates. Harcla's men pointed out to each other this great activity.

Fraunceise, who was standing next to Harcla, said in some astonishment: 'If those lean-tos are stables, which I cannot believe, then there is room enough for one hundred horses!'

'Yes,' Harcla replied, 'and it is time we undertook a little espionage. Ketel and myself shall ride slowly down to the town. The four of you must remain here; if we have not returned in two hours you are to ride hard for Wark. Here, John, keep this pouch for me,' and Harcla passed him Ambrose's precious map and his writing tablet.

The two men unslung their shields and dropped them to the ground, threw their dark riding cloaks about their shoulders and, bareheaded, rode away skirting the wood northwards, to come to the town from the Saint Boswell's road in the heart of the valley.

'If anyone should challenge us,' Harcla said to Ketel as they gained the road half a mile from the gates, 'then we are Irish troopers from beyond the Forth, from Perth, say, making our way to Whitehaven for a ship home. Agreed?'

'Agreed, my lord.'

They passed a number of carts, lately at Jedburgh for the trading, and entered the gates. A guard, not recognising their dress, shouted down to them: 'Who are you and what is your business?'

'We are Irish soldiers,' Harcla called back, 'lately in the pay of the Earl of Lennox, on our way home. We seek food and lodging for the night; can you direct us?'

The guard looked at his mate who shrugged his shoulders and walked back into the gatehouse. 'Look for the sign of the White Peacock,' the Scots guard told them, 'It's in Abbey Street, straightaway along there,' and he pointed to the middle of the town.

'Thank you, friend,' Harcla said with a wave and he and Ketel rode at a walking pace into Jedburgh.

The guard watched them as they went.

'That was well done, my lord,' said Ketel with admiration.

Harcla laughed and replied: 'That was the easy part, Ketel; we shall need to be greater actors yet; do not forget we require to get out also.'

'Hmm.'

'Come, let us use our eyes and ears,' he said. 'Let me do any speaking, Ketel; your accent betrays you.'

'Very good, my lord,' said the other, content with his role.

'How many, do you think?' Harcla asked, gazing to his right at the booths and tents of the encampment.

'A hundred?'

'Matching the new stabling, then. Let us see what strength they have in the town.' The abbey towers rose before them and the bells rang out for the evening service. They approached the market-place, which they had previously seen distantly from the wooded hill, some traders were there, townsfolk of Jedburgh, and still shouting their wares. Small groups of people strolled the streets around the market, and leant against the walls of houses talking amongst themselves; some parties were of townsmen and women and some of soldiers with the bright crest of

Edward de Bruce emblazoned upon their tunics.

They looked uncuriously on Harcla and Ketel as they walked their horses past them and towards the abbey. At the lower end of the street, a hundred yards away, a company of horse was gathering. The knight at their head was distinctive in a bright blue tunic.

'Mother of God, it's Bruce,' whispered Ketel in agitation. They had come to the outer dormitory walls of the abbey; a lane led off to the right, to a courtyard and above its gate a dirty sign showed a white peacock.

'Down here,' said Harcla, 'do not rush.' They ambled their horses into the yard and dismounted as Bruce's men cantered past them up the street.

'Are you hungry, Ketel?' Harcla asked. 'Now that we are here we should avail ourselves of Scots hospitality.'

They pushed open the door of the ostlery and entered a long dimly lit room of high vaulted arches. A group of a dozen men, two in white surcoats, were gathered around some tables.

The master of the house who was attending them, a small fat man wearing a soiled apron, glanced back over his shoulder as the new arrivals sat down beneath a window nearer the door. 'One minute, my lords,' he called to them.

A burst of laughter came from the Scots as they leaned together to drink and eat.

'As it pleases you, my lords,' the ostler said in reply to some question or jest, and he left them to go to the kitchens.

The merriment of the party of soldiers increased as one of them, under some duress, got up embarrassed from the table and cleared his throat to recite.

'Come, Mauchline,' his friends cried, 'Astonish us with your singing. Get up on the board so we may hear you the better.' And they all laughed.

'I learned this,' Mauchline said, standing on the table and swigging at his beer, 'at the English court in Carlisle; when I was there with King Robert - before he became king, of course.'

'Of course,' said one of the men in white, toasting him, 'now give us your song, troubadour.' Mauchline coughed and spat, and then began.

I have a yong suster
Far beyondin the se;
Many be the drouyris
That sche sente me.

JEDBURGH

Sche sente me the cherye,
Withoutin ony ston,
And so sche dede the dove,
Withoutin ony bon.

Sche sente me the brere,
Withoutin ony rinde,
Sche bad me love my lemman
Withoutin longing.

How shulde ony cherye
Be withoute ston?
And how shulde ony dove
Ben withoute bon?

How schulde any brere
Ben withoute rinde?
How schulde I love my lemman
Without longing?

Qwan the cherye was a flowr,
Than hadde it non ston;
Qwan the dove was an ey,
Than hadde it non bon.

Qwan the brere was onbred,
Than hadde it no rind;
Qwan the maiden has that sche lovith,
Sche is without longing.

'Well sung, Mauchline,' cried the tall knight, and his men clapped and praised him also. 'Truly spoken is that last, by Christ. There is no understanding them.'

'Alas, no,' replied Mauchline, as he got back to his seat, and they all laughed and sat to resume their supping.

The ostler emerged from the buttery and came to Harcla and Ketel. 'How can I serve you, my lords?' he asked, standing before them.

'Food and lodging for the night, if it please you,' Harcla said.

'Food I can do but not the lodging,' the fat man said, speaking quickly and panting a little. 'By Our Lady, I haven't stopped to draw breath for three days. My lord Edward has commissioned my rooms.'

'What! All of them?'

'Indeed - there are thirty of his men here presently. That's some of them over there,' and he jerked a thumb behind him. 'Shall I introduce you? Perhaps you don't mind sharing?'

'No, no, we would not wish to impose,' Harcla said hastily.

'You could try the abbey,' returned the ostler, 'although I believe the guest rooms are for my Lord Edward and his captains. Sir John de Soulis could tell you; he has just come from there to sup with his men. They are half-boosed already, as if you couldn't tell. That's Sir John there, the taller of the two knights in white.'

John de Soulis looked up as he heard his name spoken. He saw the ostler attending the two men but the light from the window behind them prevented him seeing them clearly. Harcla raised his head and his eyes picked out Soulis easily.

Ketel whispered in his ear: 'Soulis? Is not that the knight who passed through Otterburn eight days ago?'

Harcla nodded his head. 'Holy Mother of Christ!' he murmured, and the colour drained from his face, 'It's the tall knight I unhorsed at Pendragon last November. He knew me then; he will recognise us now.'

'Well, my lords,' said the ostler cheerily, 'will you have a bite to eat? We have broiled venison, or perhaps a chicken?'

Harcla rose from the table. 'Thank you, my friend. I think we shall try the abbey.'

Soulis, watching Harcla idly, was arrested by something in his movements. 'Who is that there with you, Ostler?' he called, 'Ask them to join us.'

'Just as I was saying, Sir John,' replied the fat man smiling.

Harcla moved towards the door and out unwittingly from the shielding window-light. Soulis advanced a few yards down the room, wiping his lips with the back of his hand. He stopped then and his mouth fell open. The chatter and laughter of his men had ceased as they looked around them from their tables.

There was perfect silence for a second as the two knights gazed on each other, and then Soulis said: 'Well met, Andreas de Harcla,' and with great deliberation he withdrew his sword from its sheath.

Harcla undid the clasp of his cloak and let it fall over his left arm. Ketel, one hand on the hilt of his dagger, rose to stand beside him. Soulis shouted to his troopers and motioned to them to spread themselves out in a concave arc to surround the two men.

He was eager and he lunged at Harcla who leapt back easily and evaded the sweep of his sword; he drew his own.

One of Soulis' men, who had approached the closest, was eyeing them with malignity, his face bloodshot, and he stepped forward again. Ketel, with a practiced flick, withdrew his knife and threw it spinning in the air. It entered the man's chest to the hilt and he fell to the ground dead; his sword clattering among the rushes on the stone-flagged floor.

'Give me your knife, my lord,' said Ketel urgently, as Soulis paused and looked down at his fallen trooper. Ketel, sword now in one hand, reached for Harcla's belt and grabbed the dagger.

The ostler, at this point, ran shouting to the kitchens, his apron flapping.

Harcla sprang towards Soulis and brought his sword down with terrible violence. Soulis attempted to parry but the force took him to his knees and the edge of Harcla's sword thudded into the back of a chair and splintered it, missing Soulis' head by inches.

As Soulis staggered to his feet another trooper engaged Harcla as he tried to regain the door. Simultaneously two of the Scots ran toward Ketel but he threw Harcla's dagger and one of them, a dead shout on his lips, was halted in mid-stride and almost decapitated as the blade buried itself in his throat. The blood spurted as he fell and it splashed against his comrade. Ketel ran at this other, who had slowed in awful fear, and hacked at the man's neck and downed him.

'Ketel, get the horses,' Harcla shouted. Ketel hesitated, for the blood-lust was upon him.

'Go on!' Harcla said again. 'Get out!'

Ketel bolted for the door and disappeared into the courtyard. Harcla, guarding the door, hit his man a great blow in the ribs and the wound opened and the air left his body in a loud rushing sound from his mouth.

Soulis, holding his sword now in his left hand, for he feared his right wrist was broken, shouted to those behind him: 'Mauchline, send for my Lord Edward. Go.' Mauchline, looking around him at the bodies strewn amid the rushes, required no second bidding and he went.

Soulis came at his adversary once again but Harcla said: 'I give you quarter Sir John. Your arm is broken.'

'I fight as well with my left arm, Harcla,' he said with courage, as though he were the living Diomedes; and he came forward strongly, pushing Harcla against the wall and their swords crossed at shoulder height.

'My lord, my lord,' came Ketel's shout from the courtyard, and mixed with it was the clattering sound of their horses' hooves on cobbles. Ketel swung up on his horse, holding the other bridle with difficulty as the horse jumped and reared. He saw two of the Scots emerging from a rear doorway of the ostlery ten yards away.

'Andreas,' he shouted again desperately.

Harcla thrust Soulis back, pulling his sword away and, in the same movement, hitting him across the right fore-arm. Soulis let out a cry of pain and fell back, slipping in the bloody floor. Harcla turned and sprinted for the open door as the remaining Scots tried to reach him.

Outside, Ketel kicked his horse and set off, still holding the other bridle, and shouting: 'Come, my lord. Jump.'

Harcla leapt upon the back of the second horse as they flew out of the courtyard. They were halfway up the street before he safely gained the saddle and grasped the reins. The people of the town, still mingling around the market, jumped out of the way of the flying hooves.

'Which way, my lord?' Ketel called over his shoulder as they burst through the market-place scattering the flimsy stalls. They were heading for the gates, one hundred yards distant. But they saw then that they were closed, with an array of guards upon the walls about the gate-house. Soulis' trooper, Mauchline, had already arrived there and Edward Bruce, not yet having left the town with his thirty horse, had turned his men around and was riding directly at Harcla and Ketel.

'Not this way, that is certain,' replied Harcla and they broke away to their right, towards the new stabling beneath the western wall. They splashed across the Jed Water, riding hard. Bruce, in turn, cut through the tents of the encampment and was now sixty yards behind them. Two or three tents collapsed as the galloping horses caught at the hangings and ropes and Ketel looked back to see some horses tripping as they became enveloped in wreaths of tent-cloth.

'There is chaos behind us,' he said and smiled grimly. 'But I think we shall soon be engulfed.' Some men were running from their tents towards the stabling and others strung their bows and prepared to loose.

'Mary Mother of Jesus!' Ketel shouted out, and he pointed to the right as some more riders appeared from the town and crossed the river fifty yards downstream. 'There is no way out, my lord,' he said.

'Stay with me, Ketel. It should take the weight,' and Harcla, crouching over the neck of his horse, pointed to the sloping roofs of the animal housing thirty yards in front of them.

'My lord, it is madness,' called Ketel in disbelief, 'We will never do it.'

The roofing came down to within four feet of the ground and then ran upwards for some three or four yards to the top of the wall. Harcla whispered gentle words of encouragement in the ear of his horse and the animal, twenty yards from the leap it needed to make, began to measure its galloping stride. He glanced across at Ketel. 'Come on, my friend,' he said, 'Have faith.'

'Holy Jesus!' Ketel yelled and the two horses took off, flying for an eternity, and hit the thatching of the timber roof with their front legs and, with a huge effort, brought themselves and their riders up. With great urging from the two men the horses clambered the twelve feet to the edge of the rampart and leapt skywards.

The ground outside the wall rose benignly to meet it here and they dropped just eight feet to a grassy pasture; the horses struck the ground cleanly but their front legs, as they landed, buckled, throwing Ketel and Harcla over their heads. All four bodies, riders and horses alike, rolled headlong in the grass.

The two men got to their feet and looked anxiously upwards; some Scots were running northwards along the rampart from the gate-house, armed with bows and spears.

'Come, Ketel,' Harcla called, 'the horses.' But as they looked around to them they saw that only one, Ketel's, was walking. The other lay on its side whinnying piteously; its near front fore-leg was broken and grotesquely twisted. Harcla reached for his dagger, but realising the sheath was empty he stopped.

'Jesu,' he muttered then, for he remembered that both their daggers were gone. He drew his sword and plunged it into the courageous heart of his horse. Then he slowly wiped the blade upon the grass.

Ketel had mounted the other horse and he called to Harcla: 'Come, my lord. Quickly.' And Harcla ran to Ketel as the arrows came down around them and, unscathed, they galloped off westwards away from the walled town of Jedburgh.

'Have they opened the gates, my lord?' Ketel shouted over his shoulder. Harcla, with one arm tightly around Ketel's waist, swivelled around to look. 'Not yet,' he said breathlessly, 'but they will.'

'They probably can't believe it,' Ketel panted out, 'Christ have mercy, I can't believe it.' Harcla smiled and glanced back once more. Still no sign.

'There is one thing I shall endeavour to do henceforth.'

'What is that, Ketel?'

'Carry two daggers. Or maybe even three.'

Harcla laughed. 'I think that to be an excellent plan,' he said.

'Are they coming yet, my lord?'

Harcla looked again. 'Yes,' he said. 'Mort de dieux! There are dozens of them. They have an army chasing us, Ketel!'

'Well, at least we know their strength, my lord.'

'Break to the south, Ketel,' Harcla said, pointing to their left. 'Just there where the ground falls away. We have a good half mile on them anyhow.' They dropped down into a little valley and rode southwards for a mile before turning east, making for the base of the wooded hill where the others of the company were waiting.

ANTOIGNE DE LUCY LAYS A SNARE

hile Lord Clifford's central border force was engaged upon its first sortie of the summer his western division under John de Castre was executing similar forays into the southwest of Scotland. Clifford, sitting at Wark and eager for news from Castre, had dispatched a rider to Carlisle to collect his report; Castre had not yet compiled it and, discomposed, he told the trooper to stay overnight and he should have it on the following morning.

Castre, the Custodian of the Castle and City of Carlisle and short of cash as the king's lieutenants always were, had then made a late and ultimately unsatisfactory visit to one of his own tenants in an attempt to secure some monies owing to him. Now, having returned to the castle and shortly finished his supper, he stood unhappily by a window in the Great Hall, wine in hand, looking eastwards out over the city.

This tenant, who did not supply his Lord Sir John with a knight in service, had been arguing over the fee in lieu that Castre demanded. It was sometimes less troublesome for a landowner to pay a fee rather than submit to the rigours and discomfort of regular military duty himself. While there was a general understanding regarding the amount the fee should command, often extenuating circumstances were begged.

This was increasingly the case now, in a time of war, when the revenues from individual farms were greatly reduced, not only on account of raids by the Scots but also by higher taxes exacted by the Crown to counteract those very raids; a perplexing and deteriorating situation for which there was no obvious solution.

The tenant, who happened to be the Abbot of Holmcultram Abbey, which lay some ten miles from Carlisle, had written to Castre asking his forbearance in the matter and hoping for some charity. Castre was furious; the Abbot was known to be wealthy, far wealthier than Castre himself and he resolved to ride out to Holmcultram and gather the monies due to him. The abbot received him cordially enough but was adamant that the whole question of knight's fees in the borders was under discussion between the bishop and the king himself. Castre left empty handed, in a rough and poor humour.

The chamber in which Castre now stood looked out over an angle of the great Keep. Far below, the dark waters of the moat glinted fitfully by the light of torches. Immediately beyond lay the ruins of Hadrian's Wall and what had been, in more peaceful times, the castle orchard. A few trees still stood but they were dead, blackened by fire, their stark branches a dismal reminder of mortality. Castre made a mental note to instruct a working party to clean up the orchard. The scene was too morbid.

Raising his eyes a fraction more, they rested on the walled city of Carlisle. It abutted the southern ramparts of the castle and ran southeast, roughly trapezoid in shape, some five hundred yards long and two hundred and fifty yards wide, the east and south curtain walls of the city converging on a narrow point - the English Gate.

Occasional lights mapped out the thoroughfares, Fisher Gate, Castle Gate and Abbey Street; all three of them fanned out from the transverses of the wall. The narrow lanes of the city crossed the main streets neatly at right angles. And there, in that labyrinth, beat its economic heart: the houses and shops of bakers and butchers, brewers and tailors; the merchants who dealt in gold and precious stones, spices and silks. There also the craftsmen lived, the carpenters and masons, important men in these days, for the walls and defenses of the city had ever to be maintained and strengthened.

Castre counted the torches along the curtain walls of the city, and the clusters of them at the gates: the Caldew Gate, leading out to Rose Castle; Scotch Gate, facing northwards towards the fortifications at Ricards Gate, two hundred yards away by Eden Bridge; and lastly, looking south-east, the English Gate. Each torch illuminated two square yards of parapet. No man visible but when he passed through that brighter circle of light on the journey from gate to gate. Each man had his vigil to keep, his path to follow.

'Why can I not see my own path as easily?' he asked himself fretfully, and, troubled in mind he swung his gaze across to the right, southwards, and there, hard by the Caldew Gate the church of the Minorite Friars was a glowing yellow of light. It was the hour of compline and Castre could hear the sound of chanted psalms coming to him through the night.

When I call thee answer me, O God of my justice
I shall thank thee, Lord, with all my heart.

There was a movement at his back and Castre turned to the opening door. Antoigne de Lucy, having returned with his company from a largely uneventful trip to Loughmaben and Annandale, had arrived to make his report to Castre. Lucy, carrying a document case under his arm, entered behind a servant.

'Christ Almighty,' Castre bellowed at him, seeing his deerskin wallet. 'Clifford is obsessed with these damned reports! What difference will it all make in the final reckoning anyway?'

Lucy, nonplussed, was silent. Castre, an uncomplicated hard-fighting knight, took a large swig of his wine and said harshly, 'God, it makes me want to puke.'

He sat down heavily and Lucy, his face expressionless, said, 'Would you like to hear my report now, my lord?'

'Damn your report, Antoigne. Have some wine. Your father and me passed a few pints together, you know. Ha!' and he laughed in a moment of dialectic inspiration as he added roughly, 'Perhaps I should insert a different vowel there!'

Lucy smiled in a close, ribald fashion and accepted a goblet of Castre's red Bordeaux.

'Well, you had better tell me, I suppose,' said Castre resignedly; and then he paused before adding, 'You might as well collate the whole damned thing. The others are here, look.' And he pointed to the table where the reports of Curwenne, Penrith, Mulcaster and Moriceby lay scattered. ' Can you do that for me, Antoigne?'

'With pleasure, my lord,' replied Lucy, interested to study the formal, written versions of what he had heard in casual conversation with his fellow-knights since their return.

'I hope your news is not as complex as Curwenne's appears to be. God, that man sees half a dozen peasants with pitchforks and scythes and thinks an army is mobilising. He is a creature of Harcla's, of course - part of the whole pernicious family, a cousin, I think. You need to watch him, Antoigne.'

Lucy nodded his head; he was being told nothing new.

Castre continued: 'Sir Michael de Harcla is not long for this world, I hear. Your father hated him, as you know, and with good reason. That business over the manor at Culgaith galled him. Christ, it makes me angry to think of it. But of all his proud sons the one they call Andreas is the danger. He is with Clifford at Wark. It wouldn't surprise me to learn that all this damned detail about Scot movements and strengths and intentions and Christ knows what are his own ideas. The man is an awkward nuisance.'

Lucy, having always thought Castre brutish, now saw in him a potentially useful collaborator.

Sir John went on in exasperation: 'Clifford appears spell-bound by him and is seeking favours on his behalf from the King. Harcla works to his own ends, and at a cost to others, I guess. I would dearly love to know his heart, and his ambition.' Castre fell silent and in those moments Lucy's clever mind sped along a series of gambits he might offer to Castre.

Eventually he said, as though disinterested: 'His ambition, albeit simple, is exalted. It is the command of Carlisle and the Lordship of the Marches.'

'What! To be keeper of my city and castle?' Castre cried, amazed, 'and of the Marches? This rustic sycophant?'

'Do not be deceived by his apparent nonchalance in these matters, my lord. His self-interest, as you rightly guess, is evident and paramount - and in Clifford he thinks he has the ideal benefactor.'

'Bah! Clifford, the high-born bastard!' cried Castre, deep in his cups. 'My family traces back to those who came with the great Duke William when he destroyed the Saxon oath-breaker Earl Harold. I care not that for Clifford,' and he snapped his fingers under Antoigne's sensitive nose.

Lucy brought back his head and sipped at his wine, nodding in agreement. 'I think, my lord,' he said carefully, 'we should determine a course of action whereby King Edward understands their avaricious nature. Avarice at the cost of the King's realm, its safety and its well-being.'

Sir John de Castre peered at Lucy, his countenance palely lit in malice and envy, like Thersites of old. He said, rubbing the side of his face: 'Show me the way, Antoigne.'

'It is quite simple, my lord,' Lucy returned slyly and his dark gaze slid along the papers on the table. 'We must expose this nonsense about reports and show it to be useless, or worse than useless; in that, military decisions based upon them are proved to be wrong at the cost of lives and livelihoods - and the discontent of the King's own lords.'

'And how do we do that?' asked Castre, his eyes gleaming dully.

'Again, simple, my lord. We enter some judicious under-estimates of Bruce's strength in Annandale, or, say, the manning of the pele tower he has taken at Liddesdale. An assault or a foray is planned, led by Clifford or Harcla; a military disaster ensues. The result? Disgrace and ignominy of the highest order ascribed to our enemies.'

'Our enemies?' asked Castre, a little fuddled. 'The Scots? Or our local English? Bah! They are each alike, the one a whore the other a cuckold.'

'My lord,' Lucy went on, made uncertain by Castre's drunken dissembling, 'I meant our greedy and power-hungry nobles Clifford and Harcla. Of course Clifford's fall from grace would necessitate the King turning to a more trustworthy and loyal right hand in the marches.'

Castre struggled to bring his thoughts to a coherent whole and then, gazing into the starlit distance, beyond the city of Carlisle and into greater realms, he said: 'He would look to me. Of course, it would only be right.' He got up from the table and poured some more wine. 'You paint a pretty picture,' he said to his conspirator.

'A realistic one, Sir John,' Lucy replied disingenuously, 'and readily achievable - if you give the word.'

'I give it,' Castre said thickly, swallowing his wine. 'And take these damned papers with you. Go, I'll see you in the morning.

~ 14 ~

THE DUKE OF CORNWALL IN THE BORDERS

t eleven o'clock in the morning, the day after the escape from Jedburgh, Harcla's company, tired and saddle-sore, rode through the gates of Wark. They had seen no sign of Bruce as they flew southwards along the road by the Jed Water. Whether this was due to their superior speed or to the Scots simply giving up the chase, they were not certain; whatever the reason was, in truth they were completely indifferent to it.

They had rested for a few hours overnight near Rochester and, after Harcla had set a watch and they were making their camp, Ketel, looking troubled, had walked across to him and said: 'I felt a sorrow for that second. The one I killed with your dagger.'

Harcla looked at him surprised, in some perplexity. 'Why so?' he asked.

'He seemed so full of life, when they were singing there, you know. I don't know, my lord, it troubles me. He did not see it coming.'

'A lucky man,' said Harcla presciently. 'Death was swift.'

'But I would like time, I think,' Ketel replied in meditation, 'to prepare myself to meet the God who made me.'

'It is not always granted, Ketel. The fore-knowledge might be too much to bear.'

Ketel looked away, towards the others grouped around Conan's fire. Harcla followed his gaze and said: 'Look at Alexander there.'

Ketel's eyes flickered and he nodded his head.

'How do you think Alexander would have felt had he known the men of Horsley Pele would shoot at him and nearly kill himself and James? Would he have liked to know he must dismount as the spears were falling and run to James in that wet field? I tell you, Ketel, no one would wish to know what destiny must bring. Again I say, your man was lucky.'

Ketel looked to the others joking amongst one another at the fire. Fraunceise shouted across to him: 'Ketel, you have not shot us any hares today. What about our supper? Very ungrateful, do you not think, friends?'

'We must make do with oats,' said Alexander in mock misery.

'You were sitting on the edge of that forest all afternoon,' retorted

Ketel. 'Useless as usual. What were you doing apart from making daisy chains?'

'Ah! The boy has spirit.'

'He has been on a quiet jaunt in Jedburgh,' said Conan. 'admiring the Scottish ladies.'

'You could at least have brought us a nice fat pheasant from the market.'

'He spent all his money on the Scottish ladies,' cried Fraunceise. 'Is that not right, Andreas?'

'I wish the chance had availed itself. Eh, Ketel?'

Ketel laughed and rose to join the others. Harcla put a hand on his arm and said: 'If our lives are ordained by God, which surely they are, then we should question none of it; but live and love as best we may. Yes, and fight too.'

As soon as the horses of the company were settled in the stables of the castle of Wark Harcla's men made for their quarters in much need of sleep. Harcla himself walked towards Clifford's apartments in the keep of the castle. On his climb up the stairway he almost collided with Walter de Strickland who, having just left Clifford, was carefully descending the narrow spiral stairs.

'Helloa, Andreas,' Strickland cried happily. 'How went your holiday in the country?'

'Quiet enough, Walter, I thank you,' Harcla replied. 'And you?'

'Ha! Morpeth is a fine town,' he said with irony. 'Full of welcoming Northumbrians. It is only as you'd expect up there, of course. Life is not pretty; the people are grim and untrusting.'

'You were not appreciated as their noble guardians, Walter?'

'Far from it. We struggled to find a decent meal, or even a kind word.'

'I did not realise you had such a thin skin, my friend,' said Harcla smiling, and he made as if to go.

'Ah, Andreas, it is not a question of skin, or the thickness of it. It is a question of money.'

'Explain yourself, Walter.'

'Well, one small bribe procured us some interesting information. We had word two days ago of a Scots party riding north through Redesdale. North, mark you.'

'Was their leader a knight called Soulis?'

'Yes, that was the name,' answered Strickland in considerable sur-

91

prise. 'You know him?'

'I have come across him twice. The second time was in Jedburgh yesterday.'

'You are on friendly terms with the enemy, Andreas?'

'I do not think he cares much for me, Walter,' Harcla replied laughing, 'which is unfortunate for he is a good knight.'

Walter de Strickland leant back comfortably against the wall and, in great thought, brought the finger and thumb of his right hand down his cheeks; then bringing them together under his chin and pinching the flesh he said: 'Do you ever think, Andreas, of the strange situation we find ourselves in? Take me, for instance. Here I am a knight of Cumberland serving my king with a clear heart; and then, on the other side, a friend of mine since boyhood, Soulis of Eskedale, (yes, the very same), serving his king, Robert the Bruce, also with a clear heart. There is something wrong there somehow.'

'You may be right, Walter, but I cannot fathom it.'

'Nor me either,' Strickland said with finality and continued his way down the stairs. But then he shouted back to Harcla: 'We dine in the Hall tonight, Clifford has arranged it. Will you be there?'

'Doubtless. If he is paying it should not be missed.'

Harcla carried on his way and entered Clifford's chamber. The earl looked up from his work and waved his lieutenant to a seat. He was reading from one of several documents on the table in front of him.

'Give me a few moments, Andreas,' Clifford said briefly.

Harcla smiled and nodded. He sat down on a high-backed chair standing by the window-space; the chair was cushioned and covered with sindon, a fine dark linen. Harcla stretched out his legs luxuriously and his feet rested on the window-seat before him. He settled back in the cushions and gazed into the blue sky of the summer day. The warmth of the sunlight, magnified through the white glass of the window, disposed his eyes to close and he allowed his head to fall back against the soft linen of the chair. He could sense the heat and light dancing through his eyelids and travelling the channels of his body as though it were an action of restoration and replenishment; it was blissful and he fell asleep.

After a few minutes Clifford put down the narratives he had been studying with a suppressed snort of displeasure and walked across to the window saying: 'Some of your colleagues, Harcla, have less wit than they were born with; which I doubt is very much. My God....' He stopped, looking down on the sleeping form of his lieutenant.

THE DUKE OF CORNWALL IN THE BORDERS

'My God,' he said again, 'the sleep of youth that surpasses all.'

Sir Robert de Clifford, thirty-six years old, sometimes gave the impression of an ancient sage. He picked up Harcla's deerskin pouch, which lay by the edge of the chair and returned to his desk, leaving his friend to his slumbers.

'Well, well,' Clifford muttered to himself as he opened Harcla's wallet, 'what have we here?' From the hard back of the tablet a carefully coiled loop of hair fell into his lap. Clifford put the tablet on the table and picked up the twirling length of hair; it was fair in colour, of thick strands and held in one piece by a scarlet thread, which had been tied in a knot around it.

'Ah! My lady Emma,' he whispered, 'for I take this to be yours, you are inescapable! And if you are as pretty as Alice, your mother once was, for I remember her well, then you are a prize indeed.' Clifford brought the lock of hair to his nose and breathed in deeply; but he could catch no scent except perhaps a slight sweetness of honeysuckle. He did not know whether to be disappointed or not, for the small smell he detected might as easily have come from the pressing of the parchment in its making, and not from the flowered-water in which my lady had washed her hair.

'I am losing my touch,' he said, worried at these notions. He put down the coil of hair and, carefully replacing it, he opened Harcla's book at the front. He read the first words without comprehension as the image of Alice la Fraunceise came before him. He had known love then, and the shock of returned love; in all these years nothing else had gripped him similarly. But his father had thought the match beneath the family and would not hear of any marriage; after some time it became known that Alice was carrying a child and William la Frauneeise, the father of Alice and Richard, in a paternal rage, quickly married her off to an elderly knight from Annandale. This knight, at the time, supported William Wallace in his wars against the First Edward and was uselessly killed in an English ambush near Loughmaben. Alice, heavily pregnant, immediately travelled home to Maulds Meaburn where she died in her childbed. Clifford often thought of this and sometimes tried to reconcile his actions and the events of two decades ago to the world he inhabited today.

He searched again for the words Harcla had written:

26 July, Roxburgh, Beaumont secure but defections increasing. Supply convoys attacked. Local sentiment turning against the King. Bruce commands the King's highways west and east

Henry of Appleby entered the chamber a little precipitately and announced: 'My lord the Duke of Cornwall.'

Clifford jumped up. There had been some noise and disturbance in the bailey ten minutes before but he had given it no thought. 'Christ's blood, Henry,' he said in an aside, 'where was my warning?' And he looked keenly at his vallet, who stood abashed and flexed his hands a little as though to say, 'I could do nothing, my lord.'

Piers Gaveston strode into the apartment resplendent in a purple mantle. It was lined with ermine and the cut of the cloth extravagant. He paused in the centre of the room, one leg prettily in front of the other, as though asking a question.

'My lord,' he said and bowed graciously.

'My lord Duke,' replied de Clifford, 'this is a great pleasure.'

Gaveston bowed again.

'I had not expected you so soon, my lord. Please sit down.' Clifford attempted to clear the papers from his desk. 'Forgive me, I am in the midst of deciphering these reports from the Marches.'

'Deciphering, Clifford? I hope there is nothing to conceal.'

'Ha, my lord!' said Clifford, laughing weakly. 'Only from the Scots - I refer to the illegible scrawl of some of my knights.'

Gaveston, despised though he may have been, had a charismatic power and an authority that was only partly endowed by the King. He sat down at Clifford's desk and casually picked out one of the papers. He read for a few seconds and then exclaimed: 'What's this? "sentiment turning against the King; Bruce commands the highways." Who wrote this?'

There was a movement in the sunlight by the window and Harcla emerged from behind his chair.

'I did,' he said simply.

Gaveston, amazed at the apparition, turned to Clifford and asked: 'Who is this person, my lord?'

'Allow me to introduce Sir Andreas de Harcla of Westmorland, my most trusted lieutenant and the new Captain in the Western Marches. Harcla, may I present my lord the Duke of Cornwall.'

Both men bowed.

'Harcla?' Gaveston mused, 'an unusual name. What is it? Some Saxon village?'

'Not Saxon, my lord,' Harcla replied, 'Viking. Icelandic Viking.'

'Ah! Cold and northern.'

'The country may be, although I do not yet allow myself that distinction. Whereas you, I believe my lord, could be classed as warm and southern.'

Clifford winced, but Gaveston laughed: 'I am from Gascony, if that is what you mean,' he said.

Harcla shrugged his shoulders.

Gaveston was quiet for a moment and then he asked: 'Why do you say our people gather to the traitor Bruce?'

'That is a big question, my lord.'

Clifford interrupted: 'Let us leave these debates awhile, my lord. You must be tired after your journey. Let me call for some refreshment.' He motioned to Henry. 'Harcla,' he continued, 'Musgrave was asking for you. He wished for your advice on a disciplinary matter.'

'Very good, my lord,' said Harcla bowing, and he left the chamber smiling, certain that Musgrave would never consult him on that or any issue.

'A man of accomplishments,' Gaveston remarked when Harcla had retired, 'although a touch too duplicitous for one so young. His wings may need clipping; but I do not wonder you trust him in your counsels.'

'Thank you, my lord. I like to think my judgement good,' Clifford said with paternal pride, as though he were Priam standing on the strong walls of Troy. 'But tell me, how can I be of service to you during your time here? How long do you think you shall stay?'

'Well, Sir Robert, I shall tell you,' the Duke replied cordially. 'I promised King Edward that I should return to York after three or four days with some intelligence, not only of the state of the border lands but also of the state of Bruce's mind. I mean in regard to the September invasion. You know, better than I indeed, that he has been indeterminate in the past.'

'I think that then Bruce was weighing his chances,' Clifford said, 'first with one, and then the other. Not very honourable, I freely admit.'

'Not honourable? I would call it traitorous.' Gaveston paused, framing his next words carefully, 'Would he not turn his coat once more, in fear of our strength?

'It has gone beyond that now, my lord,' said Clifford.

'You do not think the prospect of an English invasion, with ten thousand men, might disabuse him of any notions of superiority? His majesty the King would still welcome him into his peace.'

Again Clifford said: 'It has gone beyond that. On his own ground, where we must fight him offensively, he believes himself indestructible.

And, judging by our clumsy strategies, by the way in which we fight our wars, he probably is.'

Gaveston was discomfited by Clifford's direct manner and he said: 'Sir Robert, this is precisely the sort of talk and argument that I wish to check. I did not expect to encounter it in our northern tenant-in-chief. There is no place for defeatism in King Edward's vocabulary.'

Clifford began to grow angry, struggling with the same impotency he had felt at York earlier in the year; he decided he could not accept this latest barb from Gaveston and he declared: 'I am the last man you should accuse of defeatism. By Christ, I have lived the reality of war in the Marches these fifteen years. I know the brutality of it, the squalor of it, and yes, some glory too I have known. But I also know how Bruce fights; and I tell you, my lord, that trailing aimlessly through Scotland with ten thousand men in search of an elusive enemy who will not even give battle is pointless in the extreme.'

Gaveston's face darkened and his mouth clenched unpleasantly. He was not pleased to hear his grand strategies for the defeat of Bruce dismissed as fantasies.

'You do not think, then,' he said, mocking the Lord of the Marches, 'Bruce as frightened of our strength as you appear to be of his.'

Clifford, insulted and exasperated, almost lost his composure. The dignified and confident manner had gone and he rose agitatedly from the table, his fingers twisting nervously about the grip of his dagger.

Gaveston must have thought the explosion of wrath, when it came, would be violent and directed at himself. He said in an attempt to appease: 'What I mean, Clifford, is perhaps we should explore all the ways. Bruce must know he cannot hold Scotland against us. He may be looking for a way out himself.'

Clifford, calmer now, said sarcastically: 'Do you expect me to ask him?'

'Ah, my lord, how blunt you are. I would call it a testing of ground. But yes, I think you should. We would travel together, of course; Bruce is at Melrose presently. Our good friend the bishop of Durham is acting as my emissary. The King's emissary, I should say. He has ridden to Dryburgh Abbey this last week, ostensibly on church matters.'

'The bishop of Durham, my lord?' Clifford interrupted.

'Yes. What of it? His name is Anthony Bek, perhaps you are acquainted?'

'I only know him by reputation.'

'Very good, Sir Robert,' he said. 'Well, I received news today from the bishop.' Gaveston warmed to his theme and went on, 'I knew Bruce would meet us; he has agreed to it, with some conditions. He is afeared, I'm certain.'

'What are the conditions?' Clifford asked dryly.

'Oh, nothing of any import; just that he chooses the ground and that we be no more than four.' Gaveston waved his arm airily, 'There are one or two other minor points but they escape me.'

'I cannot leave Wark, my lord,' Clifford rejoined. 'The King commanded me to hold the Marches this summer. All news comes here, almost daily. What if any dispatches should go astray?'

'Leave Harcla here in your absence. You spoke yourself of his capabilities; and, after all, he is one of the King's captains.'

Clifford considered this and then said: 'Of course, you are right. And it should prove instructive to see Bruce again. You have the letters of protection, I take it?'

'Everything is arranged, Clifford, do not worry. Your name is here already, but I shall need to add the names of those knights who accompany us. Which two shall they be?'

'Sir John de Harcla for one.'

'Harcla?' queried Gaveston.

'The elder brother, my lord.'

'Very good. And the other?'

'Sir Richard de Musgrave,' Clifford said after a moments thought.

'Ah, Musgrave,' said the Duke, smiling. 'A loyal knight, I have heard favourable reports.'

Clifford raised his head a little, wondering where these reports might have issued.

'And now, my lord,' Gaveston concluded, 'thank you for your attention. I should like to rest.'

'Of course.'

'Do we dine tonight?' he asked as he walked to the doorway.

'Yes, my lord, in the Great Hall; there should be quite a gathering.'

'Good. Is there any entertainment planned?'

'Well, my lord,' answered Clifford, wondering what Gaveston would consider an entertainment, 'it depends what you mean.'

'I should be pleased to recite for the company,' Gaveston said, his eyes brightening. 'A scene from one of the ancient wars might be appropriate. My "Aeneas before Agamemnon's Tent" is particularly good.'

The Duke of Cornwall sailed out of the room, guided by Henry, leaving Clifford with his mouth agape, not knowing whether to laugh at man's vanities or weep for his spirit. 'I care not for that man,' he muttered, 'clever and powerful though he be.'

15

BY THE NORTH TYNE

hen Harcla left Clifford's chamber Henry of Appleby approached him and said: 'My lord Andreas, these packets arrived for you; they were in part of Sir Robert's delivery of correspondence from home.'

Harcla, in good humour and still smiling at his display of verbal dexterity with Gaveston, said: 'Thank you, Henry, you are a jewel among men,' and he glanced at the sealed papers.

Henry bowed and returned to his post.

Harcla entered the large room where his men lay sleeping and he walked across the rush-strewn floor, avoiding the prostrate and snoring bodies, till he reached the small solar at its south-western end where his own mattress was unrolled upon the rushes. He stepped over the recumbent form of Ketel who, wrapped in his great campaigning cloak, was blocking the doorway. Harcla settled himself on his bed and, lying beneath the window, he turned in his hands the three packets that Henry had given him.

'Is all well, my lord?' Ketel asked, half-awake and aware of some movement about him.

'All is well, my friend. Go back to sleep.'

Harcla broke open the seal of the first. It was instantly recognisable to him and he knew the letter to be from his father. It read:

To Sir Andreas de Harcla, Captain in the West Marches, serving the King under my Lord the Earl of Westmorland, Sir Robert de Clifford, at Wark Castle in Northumberland.

Filium salutem

It is not many days since you left us yet there has been an occurrence I should relate to you and would be glad of your response. I know Sir Robert is in regular contact with his reeve at Appleby on matters concerning the barony and other things of import and I send this letter by way of there.

I trust you keep in good health and continue to serve well our king and his Lord in the Marches. Do not forget, as I am sure you never shall, that there is an order in life and it is this: God first, blood second and king third; although I always hope that the first two are inseparable, or at best should be, by their sacrosanct nature.

While I speak on family matters, your brother John is, of course, capable of looking after himself, but James is still a boy; take care of him, Andreas, and bring him home safe.

De Harcla's mouth hardened in self-recrimination as he read this, but then he thought: 'My father grows old and other-worldly, he forgets what war is.'

Sir Michael's letter continued: *The occurrence I need to acquaint you with regards a beggar with a lordly mien who walked into Hartley three days ago. He calls himself by the name of Uther and on his arrival he immediately demanded to see you. He said you were acquainted, although I find that difficult to believe; he also mentioned Sir John de Crumbwell. On learning that you were away in the king's service he declared to me, in his outlandish accent: 'No matter, my lord. Sir Andreas was anxious that I make a start anyhow.'*

'Make a start?' I asked him in some perplexity; you may readily understand this as I know nothing of him. 'Make a start on what?'

His answer startled me in the extreme. He said: 'On the training of thy light horsemen in bowmanship and the forging of a new sword for thy son.'

Harcla smiled as he read this, picturing his father's face as he re-lived the interview through his writing of it.

Andreas, you know I view some of your military ideas with scepticism. I could relate to you this conversation in much greater detail but it would tire you in the reading of it as much as me in its writing. I simply ask for your reply as quickly as you may; ordinarily I would turn to one of your brothers but you are all away from home and Godfrid our reeve at Kirkby is, as you know, useless in matters outside his immediate remit.

This man Uther has, by some accounts, come down from a cave beneath the stone image of Saint Thomas in the mountains of Mallerstang. He is now temporarily residing with the priest Thomas in Kirkby Stephen, and acting as his pig-man. He comes up here twice daily asking for my instructions. Give me word, Andreas, I beg.

Your lady sister and myself are well and in God's keeping. God keep you.

Written by Sir Michael at Harcla, this day the Feast of Saint Anne, 26 July 1310.

THE NORTH TYNE

I attach a communication from your brother Henry; it arrived from Dacre this morning.

Harcla re-folded the letter, resolving to ask his father to allow Uther the use of his forge now, but to await his, Harcla's, return before undertaking any military exercises; he would tell Sir Michael to expect him at Hartley for a short visit in ten days or so. In the meantime, and as well as having the forge, Uther could employ one or two workmen of the manor in the making of say, three dozen bows, of a type and design to be decided by Uther. He hoped his father would find this acceptable. He also determined to speak with Clifford on his query to the household at Appleby respecting Uther's identity.

Having decided on his course of action in response to his father's letter, Harcla put this to one side and picked up the second epistle, the one from Henry.

Harcla was surprised that his brother should reply so quickly to his own letter, sent just three days ago via Appleby as part of Clifford's diplomatic and military packages; Henry de Harcla did not always react so promptly to worldy messages, leaning as he did to those of the spirit.

Henry, the third son and some ten years older than Andreas, was recognised as the cleverest and most inventive of the Harcla family. His intelligence and quick wits directed him to the Church where he aspired to a successful career, although, by his own admission this had somewhat foundered: he had taken Holy Orders with great ambition but was currently the resident rector at Dacre, a small village near Penrith. Henry did not believe his talents were fully recognised.

Years ago Henry had taught Andreas to play chess – a game that demands clear thinking and teaches caution. 'Unfortunately, you do not excel in either,' his brother used to say as Andreas lost one game after another.

What impressed Harcla most about Henry was his ability to take a theoretical concept and translate it into something practical. The episode of the smoke signals on Stainmore, using a code ascribed to certain commands was a good example and, as it came to Harcla's mind, he smiled in remembrance. Harcla had been sitting in the top-most tower of the castle at Brough-under-Stainmore while Henry and the others rode off towards Bowes.

The message he eventually deciphered from the smoke of the last station above Augill Beck read, as the reader may remember, "Eva Ceaser". For a while afterwards the two brothers hailed each other, whenever they met, with: "Eva Ceaser". Sir Michael their father thought them both foolish.

Harcla would not have been surprised if Henry's letter were written in cipher. He broke open the seal and read:

Hail Brother,

I should not yet, in truth, call you Caesar although you appear to be well on the journey in that glorious pursuit of temporal adulation. As for me, I am, as you know, more concerned with matters of the inner man and his Creator, which pre-occupation has led me so far to the indescribably tiny village of Dacre where I shall be ensconced for only some small time longer, Deo volente.

I was delighted to receive your message and gathered from it you were anxious to see again our old friend Peter Claxton of York. You will remember him as discreet to the point of inscrutability and completely trustworthy in his friendships. He is now Dean to the Chapter House at Durham and attached to the Palatinate of his highness the lord bishop. I am certain he will be pleased if you can visit him and will offer you his generous hospitality.

Remember me in your prayers. Henry.

'Ah! My brother,' Harcla said to himself as he put down the letter, 'how clever you are!' Henry had neatly apprised him of all the information he required in respect of his potential spy in Durham.

He now had two issues that he should discuss with Clifford. This second would, in all probability, necessitate a two-day trip from Wark; Gaveston's presence was unfortunate in that a credible pretext for his absence would have to be discovered.

However, that invention could wait, and he brought to his hand the third packet. This last bore the seal of his brother-in-law Fraunceise; he broke it open and searched eagerly for the signature. His hand trembled as he found it.

Dear Cousin,

At whiles I think on how you may be faring in those northern parts by Scotland. My uncle Sir Richard always promised me that you and he should be safe and return to those who love you. I pray that this shall be and confidently await it.

Your sister, the lady Sarah, has been to see us and we spent together a happy day, marred only by the advent of some ruffians of Threlkeld (he is at Carlisle with Sir Antoigne, I believe) who troubled us as we rode out Crosby way. But this is of little matter, young John from the house was with us and they did not approach too closely. We spoke of Robert de Leyburne, her fiance and your friend; he is a most lucky man, and you should tell him so, for Sarah has the sweetest nature, of which I am jealous. We have become fast friends.

You may remember our day in Eden. I mean, of course, our Eden, where I dwell most happily; that, most naturally, is the answer to the question you put me as we parted. I had thought it plain, but I remember your face wore a puzzled look as though you had miscomprehended something that was obvious to others. It made me want to laugh, I confess; but I did not wish you to think me frivolous. You looked so solemn, Andreas! Ah, dear friend of my heart, come home soon. I count the hours as they pass.

Your loving cousin, Emma.

Harcla was affected most by this the last of his letters. It worried him that sometimes his mind should be so taken up with thoughts of Emma la Fraunceise that his primary duty was obscured. He considered then his father's injunction of God first, blood second and king third. 'Where, he asked himself, 'should Emma appear in that ranking, if at all?' Harcla was inclined to place her in between the first and second, in some debatable region of divinity. Or perhaps Sir Michael's third category of duty and love for kingship should be extended by some sophistry to include sexual love for a queen, or a princess.

He felt unqualified to take the argument any further. 'There are many kinds of love,' he concluded unsatisfactorily and, with a simple pleasure, he read Emma's letter once again.

The chapel bells rang out the afternoon office and, about the chamber, some of his men stirred, cleaning and repairing their war gear, and waxing their swords and daggers.

Henry of Appleby came up to Harcla and said: 'My lord, Sir Robert requests your presence, if you please. He is gone down to the bailey.' Harcla nodded his thanks and rose, stowing the correspondence in his pack.

He found Clifford walking up and down the line of thirty-odd horses in the heat of the stabling. A couple of grooms of the castle, who had been sprawled on the hay in a cool corner, were now industriously brushing away the mire and dirt from the horses' legs.

'It is not good enough, Harcla,' Sir Robert said to him irritably.

'These animals are as important to us as the men who ride them. The cost of replacement, even for these ponies is eight or ten marks apiece. I know we say: "Well, the king pays", but ultimately, of course, we pay. I want these beasts treated like visiting nobility.' Clifford smiled. 'Please ensure that all our knights are aware of this and that they delegate the responsibility as appropriate.'

'Yes, my lord,' Harcla replied.

'Well, Andreas,' Clifford said, wiping some drops of sweat from his brow as he moved toward the stable door, 'come with me. I thought we could manage a walk by the river; I am told it is quite pleasant at this time of the year.

'We can take a couple of dogs with us,' he went on. 'I am sure we are entitled to kill a bird or two, or some other game. Ah! Here is Henry.'

Henry met the two men at the gate. He was armed with a long bow and a quiver of arrows that he bore across his shoulders; he carried a short sword in his belt and two hounds were straining at the leash he gripped in his right hand. He was sweating.

'Here, Henry,' said Ketel, appearing from around the corner of the wall, 'let me help you.'

'Good,' said Clifford, and he burst out laughing, 'so we are four. A nice number for an afternoon stroll.'

Henry and Ketel walked ahead leaving the knights to begin their discussions. Their way followed a grassy track that fell, steeply at first and then more gently, towards the bridge over the North Tyne. The party crossed the bridge, stopping for a few moments to stare into the clear streaming water, and then they continued northwards up the left hand bank of the river.

'I have heard from Appleby,' Clifford said, 'about your man Uther.'

'Yes, my lord,' said Harcla expectantly.

'His name is Richard le Bret, an Irish warrior; a chief in his own land. Why he left Ireland I do not know for certain, some family quarrel probably; or perhaps it was for purely mercenary reasons. Anyhow he fought with Wallace at Stirling Bridge and Falkirk. He did not agree with Wallace's tactics at Falkirk; he thought they deserved defeat. Well, then he adopted the First Edward as his paymaster and served for two or three years in Flanders – the story of which I have mentioned to you before – and subsequently disappeared without trace to re-surface in, of all places, Mallerstang.'

Clifford stopped and looked across to Harcla, who was walking in thoughtful silence. 'That is your mysterious anchorite, Andreas,'

Clifford said, 'I wish you well with him.'

'Thank you, Robert, for taking the trouble.'

'No trouble,' Clifford replied. 'But look there!' He pointed fifty yards ahead where Ketel was notching an arrow at two pheasants the dogs had flushed. They flew in a whirr of heavy wings towards a copse of alder and birch and Clifford ran like a boy as Ketel took aim and loosed. One of the birds dropped ungracefully in weird arcs and hit the ground amid the trees. The dogs bounded forward and one came back a minute later with a skewered pheasant neatly in its jaws.

'Bravo, Ketel,' Clifford cried, 'a fine shot. That shall be yours tonight.'

Ketel, all smiles, bowed.

They walked on and Sir Robert said: 'Andreas, we need to speak about this Durham business. I have not opened my mind to Gaveston for I do not hold him close enough. I have doubts of this enterprise all the way through; treachery and assassination are as like to be familiars in these murky places, which I am glad not to inhabit.

'We need to obtain some air and light; to ascertain the facts, hard facts and thence deduce our course.' They halted by a grassy sward close to the bank and rested, leaning against the trunk of a large beech.

Clifford had come prepared and he withdrew from his tunic a paper which he handed to Harcla. 'Study that,' he said.

Harcla opened out the parchment; it read:

Factor ~ first	Bruce interrupts with ease our convoys and messengers in Scotland and the Marches.
Infer ~ first	to strike one convoy, its direction and schedule, is credible; to strike them all, or nearly all, is impossible without aid.
Factor ~ second	my lord the bishop of Durham entertains Bruce in his Palace, and without the knowledge of the king or his ministers.
Infer ~ second	albeit tenuous, there is a link between factor second and inference first
Factor ~ third	the bishop, as an Ordinaire, is fully cognisant of the destinations and schedules of relief convoys.
Infer ~ third	he is a possible informant
Factor ~ fourth	(most recent news) the bishop is, at this moment,

		acting as Gaveston's emissary to Bruce regarding a possible truce or political agreement.
Infer ~	fourth	there is a close relationship between the bishop and Gaveston/the king.

Harcla read the document twice through and then looked up to Clifford.

'Do you understand the argument, Andreas?' Sir Robert asked.

Harcla nodded.

'Good. Then we can destroy the paper.' Clifford retrieved the parchment and tore it into many small pieces, dropping them into the streaming water; they floated away heavily, like little submerging boats. He turned back to Harcla.

'Our objective therefore,' Clifford said, 'should be to either confirm these connections or discount them. My hope is that any discovery we make does not embarrass or discredit Gaveston; because the King's mind may, in that instance, turn not on the perpetrator but on the messenger, *videlicet*, ourselves.'

'Did you receive any communication from your brother?' Clifford asked.

Harcla smiled and said, 'Yes, my lord, today. The priest's name is Peter Claxton, he is the Dean to the Chapter House. My brother Henry tells me he is completely trustworthy and that I should visit him.'

'I agree, and that immediately. I shall supply you with funds when we get back to the castle. Durham will be what distance, perhaps thirty-five miles by Dere Street? Ha! - you should consult Ambrose's chart, of course. A three hour ride I should guess; you will arrive well before dusk anyhow. Take Ketel; and aim to return by late morning tomorrow. I will tell Gaveston, should he ask at dinner tonight, that you have been called away on urgent family business, which in a way it is.'

Clifford laughed at his joke, and then pulled at his ear in thought. He added: 'You must be back, Andreas, by noon at the latest, for I travel then with Gaveston to Melrose; and he has suggested I leave you in command during our absence, which will be one night, or perhaps two.'

'Gaveston made that suggestion?' queried Harcla.

'Indeed. He thinks you accomplished, although somewhat clever. Take care, my friend,' said Clifford gravely. 'He is a snake, Patroclus reborn.'

Harcla's face was solemn as he looked at Sir Robert.

'Good,' Clifford thought to himself, 'I have made him think.'

'But, come,' Clifford cried heartily, rising to his feet. 'This hunt is over and we must now commence another.'

16

A SPY AT DURHAM

ithin half an hour of that conversation by the North Tyne Harcla and Ketel rode out from the gates of Wark and made for the south and the road to Durham.

They forded the river at Chollerford, above the ruins of the Roman mile-castle and, riding westward at a great pace, they reached Port Gate on the Vallum where Dere Street crosses it at right angles. They climbed onto the road and stopped, resting for a few moments.

Looking north they saw the road easily in the great rolling uplands; at once shining like a dull metal and then like a sea-green emerald, darker than the fields it divided. For the afternoon sun, still hot on their backs, played through high white clouds and the road was bright and then slowly darkening in a swelling swathe northward in those fields of wheat.

Harcla let loose the reins; he undid the clasp of his cloak and, pulling it from his shoulders, he folded it carefully and placed it beneath the saddle-pack behind him. 'It is warm,' he said as Ketel looked across. He fastened the sleeves of his tunic at the wrist and tied at his chest the cord of his doublet.

'That way lies Jedburgh,' Harcla said, following Ketel's gaze towards Scotland.

'So soon, my lord?' Ketel asked.

'No, Ketel,' he laughed. 'We are for Durham tonight.'

Ketel considered this then said, with some disappointment in his voice: 'What about my pheasant?'

'If you wish to return to Wark and eat it, you may.'

'It is not that important,' Ketel said, but then thinking of his friends at supper in the great hall, he added: 'Conan and Alexander claim they have forgotten the taste of wine.'

'They intend to make a re-acquaintance at dinner, do they?'

'In no small measure, my lord.'

'Ah, Ketel! But look at us,' said Harcla, gazing at the open spaces. 'God's blood! Here we are in God's own country with no one but ourselves the masters. We drink the ambrosial wine of heaven now and tonight the Bordeaux wine of the archbishop. Now which course do you favour?'

'The one you travel, my lord.'

'Good,' Harcla cried, 'then let us go.' The two men spurred their horses southward and raced to Corbridge. They arrived some fifteen minutes later and, paying their penny toll, they clambered onto the bridge that spanned the blue waters of the Tyne.

'It is bigger than the Eden,' Ketel remarked, looking on the wide movement of the river.

'Wait till September and you see the Forth,' said Harcla. 'It makes the Tyne look like Hartley Beck.'

Later, as the sun began to fall from its heights they dropped steeply into Ebchester, a straggling village of afternoon shadows and snarling dogs who would not leave them be, and they climbed swiftly out of the narrow valley and on to Lanchester. After a little while they came down from Dere Street and followed, more gently now, the track through Broom Park to Neville's Cross. At vespers, two and a half hours after leaving Wark, Harcla and Ketel rode into the great palatial city of Durham.

The castle and cathedral lay in magnificence on a hill-top within a huge loop of the Wear. As they climbed up Harcla asked directions for the Chapter House and they walked the horses towards the vast cathedral and its steepling central tower, beneath which, both men knew, lay the incorruptible body of Saint Cuthbert.

'We should make a pilgrimage,' Ketel said, 'now that we are here. People travel hundreds of miles to be at the very spot on which we are standing.'

'If we have the time, Ketel, we shall pray over Cuthbert's tomb and, for good measure,' he said with some sarcasm, 'we can also make our intentions at the Shrine of Our Lady.'

'Yes, my lord, you are right,' Ketel said reverently, oblivious to Harcla's raillery, for he was, at times, taken by a great piety. 'This town, like Appleby, is dedicated to her.'

'First,' said Harcla briskly,' we must find my brother's friend. If that building to our left is the Chapter House, for I think that was directed to us, then our journey is over.'

Harcla halted his horse and swung to the ground. They stood by the edge of a handsome garden close to the southern abbey walls. A large double doorway opened to the south-facing transept and the garden, at some distance, was neatly enclosed on its other three sides by two-storied buildings housing a refectory and kitchens, storage chambers, dormitories and guest-rooms.

Two young men in the habit of minor canons emerged from the kitchen doorway. Harcla walked up to them and said: 'I am looking for Monseigneur Claxton the Dean. Where may I find him?'

'In the House,' said one, pointing over his shoulder. 'Come, I shall show you,' and he led them around the corner of the garden. The other offered to take their horses and took the two animals through an archway to the stabling.

The door to the House was still standing open after the heat of the day and the novice paused in the cool dark hallway and called: 'Sylvester. Sylvester, here are visitors for the Dean.' He smiled at Harcla and Ketel. 'Sylvester is Monseigneur's secretary. He will serve you now.'

'Thank you,' Harcla said. 'You have been kind.'

The novice again smiled and bowed a retreat as the Dean's secretary walked down the hallway to meet them. He was of middle age and dressed in the manner of the Premonstratensians; the white cloak he wore, which had not been tied, ruffled a little in the draught his passage made and the outline of his face was softened by the darkness.

'How may I help you, my son?' Sylvester asked.

'We should be grateful, Canon, for an interview with Monseigneur the Dean. My name is Andreas de Harcla. The Dean is a close friend of my brother, whose name is Henry. He is the Rector of Dacre in Cumberland.'

'It is a little late, my lord,' said Sylvester slowly. 'Vespers is complete but....well, I shall ask for you. Please wait here.'

'Thank you, Canon.'

The white cloak retreated and Harcla kicked his heels impatiently; the spurs jingled loudly in the quiet of the House.

A minute later Sylvester re-appeared and called to them: 'Come, my lord. This way.' He led them into a large chamber, a study, with a fire recently lit in one wall and a series of tall windows overlooking the garden in another. An enormous desk stood in the centre of the room and leaning against it, side on to fire and window, was a tall man of about thirty-five years dressed in white. He stepped forward and placed his hands on Harcla's shoulders.

'Andreas, is it?' he asked smiling broadly.

'At your service, Monseigneur.'

'Pax tecum, Andreas.'

The Dean turned to Ketel and Harcla said: 'This is Ketel Ormsson of

Nateby, Monseigneur.'

'Pax tecum, Ketel,' said he, placing his hands on Ketel. 'Please, sit down. Have you eaten? And my name is Peter, by the way; there are over-many "monseigneurs" in this place.'

Ketel did not know whether to sit or not. In the end, after some internal debate, he stood behind Harcla's chair.

'I can see Henry in you, Andreas,' said the Dean. 'No doubt of it. But you are much the younger? Yes, I thought so.' Peter Claxton drew his chair around the table. 'You must tell me about Henry,' he said eagerly. 'But first, may I ask where you are lodging tonight?'

'We intended to find a place in the town.'

'Oh! No, you must, of course, stay here.'

'We thank you, Peter, but we cannot. It would be too great an imposition, believe me. If you can recommend to us an inn, that is all we need.'

The Dean was puzzled at this refusal; but, anyway, he asked Sylvester to send one of the novices to the Durham Ox and secure a room.

'I know the man there,' he said to his guests. 'He will look after you well.' He looked at Harcla as he spoke but found nothing in the dark grey eyes. He found his gaze drawn irresistibly to the curious scar on Harcla's cheek. 'It is like a star,' he thought, 'like the star that drew the Magi. This man is no man's liege.'

'You are too kind, Peter,' said Harcla, courteous with his thanks.

'Think nothing of it,' the dean replied, jerking his mind to attention. 'Although I am disappointed you do not stay in the House. We have a curfew now, you know, and you must leave in an hour or so.'

'Peter, I realise that and I think you have guessed that I need to speak with you confidentially.'

The Dean sat back in his chair and, pulling at his robes, he stretched his legs to the fire. 'I am listening,' he said.

'Henry may have told you,' Harcla began, 'that I am recently appointed Captain in the West Marches.'

The Dean nodded and poured some wine for his guests. 'Take some Bordeaux with me,' he said.

'I am serving in the borders this summer with Sir Robert de Clifford,' Harcla continued, sipping from his cup. 'We are to hold the borderlands against any raids of the Scots and maintain our lines of communication with English garrisons in Scotland. It was regarding communications that I wished to speak.

'Our strongholds in Scotland rely heavily on our supply lines; for the victualling of the castles and the continual re-manning of the garrisons. Robert the Bruce is gathering greater strength and support from the Scottish nobles and consequently the militia he has at his disposal is growing, almost week by week. Increasingly he is able to disrupt our supplies and attack our convoys doing us great damage.

'That, of course, is a major concern in itself. But we believe we have a more serious problem which contributes to this dangerous situation.'

'And what is this problem, Andreas?'

'I need to be frank, Peter. Over the last few months the Scots have had, inexplicably, advance knowledge of our movements. Not in all cases, but in enough. I refer in particular to the schedules of the convoys and the manning of the garrisons. Also you may have heard, for it is no longer a secret, that the king is planning an offensive in September; this, obviously, will generate considerable activity in the Marches as the army mobilises. There are concomitant issues of the soundness of our intelligence there as well.'

'Why are you telling me all this?'

'Because I think you can help us,' Harcla answered. He looked closely at the dean and then dropped his thunderbolt into the air. 'Military information is being revealed to the enemy,' he said. 'It is possible that Durham is the source.'

'What!' the Dean exclaimed, aghast. 'Who in Durham? You cannot mean the church?'

'Robert the Bruce has visited the Archbishop at least once this year,' Harcla said quietly.

'The Archbishop!' the Dean's face was ashen as he got to his feet and walked rapidly to the door; he leaned out for a moment, scanning the corridor, then straightened up and pushed the bolt across.

'Dear God in heaven,' he cried. 'Bruce was here at Pentecost, I know. His lordship and he have been friends for many years – but this cannot be true.'

'Peter, it may not be,' said Harcla soothingly. 'But we must ascertain the truth of the matter. The malefactor may be someone in the household with access to his lordship's papers. We need to establish two things: one, *who* it is and two, *how* the information is transferred. The security of the northern kingdom is at stake.'

Harcla sat back in silence and looked at his brother's friend, who had leant forward and was staring into the fire. 'Now, will you help us?' Harcla asked.

111

Monseigneur the Dean watched the flames unhappily; he did not wish to become embroiled in this, he thought it would be a dirty warfare. But then he supposed that, in these times, he had a duty to Caesar as well as to God. Besides, there was something compelling about his friend's brother.

After some time he asked: 'How do I relay any findings to you, Andreas?'

Harcla relaxed and said, smiling: 'Do not worry about that. I shall send a rider to you every seven days.'

'Mmm. I have a better plan, I think. A friend of mine is at Hexham Abbey, an Austin Friar called Ambrose.'

'Ambrose the cartographer?' asked Harcla in amazement.

'Ah! You know him?'

'Only through his maps.'

'Good. Well, there are always travellings between Durham and Hexham; I can direct my packets under cover to Ambrose. Would that suit?'

'Perfectly,' Harcla replied, impressed by the Dean's suggestion. 'Henry said you possessed a quick intellect.'

'Did he?' said Peter, laughing. 'Well, I always beat him at chess.'

'Do you indeed? Then I would be no match for you.

'It is a game of stratagems,' said Monseigneur, 'that demands clarity of thought. You should practice, that is all.'

'I shall endeavour to do as you say,' said Harcla, smiling. 'Thank you, Peter, for this interview. I am glad you are to help us.'

'We shall see what transpires, Andreas. All I can do is watch and wait; I may discover nothing, of course.'

'Of course, that may be. And you must take care; do not speak overtly to anyone on this matter.'

'I understand that well enough,' replied the Dean assuredly.

'Good,' said Harcla, 'and now we should go.'

They said their goodbyes and, as the Dean escorted them to his door, he gave them directions to the Durham Ox. Ketel went ahead to fetch the horses while Harcla and Monseigneur stood in the doorway for a few minutes, enjoying the evening air and chatting amicably about Henry. Sylvester, who had been abroad on some business, returned then and, murmuring an apology, he edged past them into the House.

17

SUPPER AT WARK CASTLE

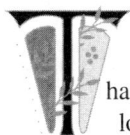

That same evening, as Harcla and Ketel rode down to seek their lodging in Durham, the knights of Clifford's company, their men-at-arms and some of the household and tenants of Wark gathered together in the Great Hall for Clifford's well-advertised supper.

The places at high table were reserved for Clifford himself, Gaveston, Robert le Ros the Warden of the castle, and Harcla's colleagues Musgrave, Strickland, Vipont and Leyburne - although none of these seven had yet made an appearance. All the others, some forty men and a dozen women of the manor, were mingling freely about the long trestle tables in the body of the hall.

The fireplace in one wall was aglow as the huge logs caught in the grate and opposite, beyond the dining-boards, the heavy wall-hangings were being pulled across the window spaces. Some of the men stood in small groups about the ingles of the windows and looked out to the darkening sky as the curtains were drawn.

The castle servants, together with the knights' vallets who had been pressed into service, brought up from the kitchens a great number of flagons of ale and baskets of bread, which they placed on the tables.

John de Harcla, Fraunceise, Alexander and Conan stood together by one of the window spaces. They were classically dressed in doublet and burnet hose with a short white tunic over; this they had taken in at the waist with a leather belt which held one or, as with Kelleth, two short daggers. Emblazoned on their tunics was the red cross and black martlet of Harcla. All the men of each knight carried their own distinctive crests and it made for a colourful gathering in the growing light of the fire and the dancing light of the wall-mounted torches of reed and tallow. The younger women, brilliant in their blue and scarlet gowns, looked around them at the young men of war.

The smell of the freshly lit torches was acrid in its waxy smokiness and the dark trails of smoke rose before falling like an incense over the guests. It was almost impossible, because of the draughts from fire and windows, to escape the reek.

'Christ,' Fraunceise said to Conan, 'this stink is worse than the one you produced for us at Coquet Head; and that was bad enough.'

'My lord,' Conan replied equably, 'you do not realise when you are fortunate and in good hands.'

Fraunceise laughed and took a swig at his ale. 'I beg pardon, my lord,' he said as he bumped into a local tenant who was passing through the crowd with his wife and daughter.

The man nodded his thanks as he squeezed past; the girl smiled at Alexander.

'Now there's a pretty minx,' said Conan.

'Feline, certainly,' Fraunceise said jocularly, following Kelleth's gaze as she disappeared in the throng moving towards the tables. 'But inclined to shrewishness when she's older.'

'Who cares?' said John de Harcla.

'John,' Fraunceise said profoundly, as he turned to him, 'you have a wonderful gift of conveying much when saying so little. You should have been a Stoic in the mode of Zeno.' There was some shaking of heads among his friends as he continued: 'Zeno proclaimed that the truly virtuous are indifferent to the vicissitudes of fortune and maintain a constant harmony with Fate and the Gods. So like you, John,' Fraunceise concluded, sighing.

'I do not know what you are talking about,' replied John. 'I thought we were discussing women.'

'Oh, it was a discussion, was it?' said Fraunceise affably. 'I did not realise your simple question, rhetorical I think, would merit that description.'

'At least people can comprehend me when I speak,' John retorted. 'What's all this Greek nonsense?'

Conan and Alexander lost interest at this point and, hearing a sound like a low droning of pipes, they looked up to a small gallery that projected at second floor level above the far end of the Hall. Some five or six minstrels, distinctive in green and yellow tunics, were gathering on this balcony with a variety of musical instruments and preparing the evening's entertainment. Two of the players were grappling with a large stringed contrivance that looked like a violoncello but had a spoked wheel, which abutted the strings, attached to it. From the centre of the wheel a wooden handle extended and one of the performers was furiously cranking this handle, through which action the resinned rim of the wheel spun against the strings. The other was busy at the neck of the instrument pressing strongly on the frets, over which the strings passed, in a repeated and rhythmical sequence.

'This is strange music,' said Alexander as the low droning grew louder and more resonant in a tune that made him think of things broad and slow and of a deep loveliness like a river come down from the fells and running in bracken, but slowly, magisterially, with mossed boulders in the streaming water as strongholds against the current, like ancient things; and the willowy greenness of ferns at the water's edge, and the small feet of birds there, like youth.

'It is called a vielle a roux,' said Fraunceise.

'In English if you please, my lord,' said Conan.

'A wheel-fiddle, a hurdy-gurdy.'

'It makes a powerful sound,' said John quietly.

A whispering silence descended too on the rest of the company in the Hall as, in the lambent light of the torches, the people listened to the sweeping melody. In the glimmering of the window spaces, also, men stood and the music reverberated there in an assonance with the shadows on the cold walls.

There was a movement at the doorway and the crowd parted to allow passage to the high table for the lord of Wark, Robert le Ros, and his guests Clifford and Gaveston. Clifford nodded to John de Harcla and Fraunceise as he passed them by.

In the gallery the other minstrels, who had been at their ease while their two companions sweated, took up their own mandolins and flutes and the sound grew fuller now, like a symphony, as the great lords took their places at the table. Robert le Ros raised his hands and the music slowed, leaving only the deep drone of the hurdy-gurdy as the wheel made its last few revolutions. 'My friends,' he shouted out, 'you are welcome. Please take your places and eat and drink with me.'

There was some cheering at this and a noisy scuffling as the guests sat themselves down; and then a small silence for the priest as he said a grace. Our friends, perhaps as Zeno's Fates intended, found themselves sitting close by the local tenant and his wife and daughter; pleasantries were exchanged and introductions made. The girl's name was Gytha.

The supper began and, amid the toiling of the servants and vallets who brought great quantities of meats and wine to the Hall, the hubbub of the diners rose again. Clifford and Gaveston surveyed the assembly at times from their place at high table.

'Northern culture is still based upon the Viking, I see,' Gaveston said derisively as he picked at his grouse.

'I do not understand your meaning, my lord,' said Clifford.

'Barbarous oafs at barbarous food is what I mean,' he replied pushing his bowl away. 'Have you nothing for a civilised man to eat?'

Clifford called to Henry: 'Be pleased to bring my lord duke a Tyne salmon. With your permission, Ros?'

The lord of Wark expressed his delight at offering his magnificent, almost royal, guest a dainty of the country.

'Good,' cried Clifford and he turned to Gaveston saying: 'The dish is delicious, my lord; Ros' cook is one of the best. The flesh of the fish melts in the mouth.'

'I am pleased to have something to look forward to,' said Gaveston sourly and he looked around to Musgrave, who was sitting at his left. 'Tell me, Sir Richard, how you think our policies go against Robert the Bruce.'

Clifford, although engaged in conversation by Ros, overheard the query and tried to hear the reply.

'My lord duke,' replied Musgrave in a low voice, 'I am pleased you ask me the question.'

'The clever bastard,' said Clifford to himself, but smiling at Ros. 'What is he saying?'

'We have him running like a fox to his burrow,' said Musgrave almost in a whisper. 'He is frightened of our strength.'

'Speak up, man,' said Gaveston, 'I can't hear a word you say. Are you ill?'

Clifford gurgled into his wine at this.

'We should run him to ground,' said Musgrave more clearly, 'and kill him in his earth.'

'Stern words, Sir Richard,' said Gaveston, 'but bravely spoken.'

'And how, Musgrave,' Clifford said, breaking off his conversation with Ros, 'would you accomplish that fine act?'

The knight coloured a little at his words overheard. 'We should bring an army to Scotland,' he said 'as quick as we may'.

'There are plans afoot, Sir Richard,' said the Gaveston, 'that you shall hear more of tomorrow. Have you told him, Clifford?'

'No, my lord, not as yet.'

'Well, now is as good a time. You, my lord,' he said to Musgrave, 'along with Sir John de Harcla, escort us to Melrose in the morning. We parley there with Bruce. Ah! My salmon.'

'I do not know the way,' Musgrave said in an aside to Strickland, the knight on his left. Clifford snorted in disgust as he heard this and said: 'Consult your map, Sir Richard.'

Gaveston broke into the flesh of his salmon and the minstrels up above broke forth again on the vielle a roux.

'I love this music,' said Kelleth to Gytha. 'I have never heard anything like it. It makes my blood surge, but quietly, if that is possible.' He felt warmed by the wine he had drunk and he looked at her candidly.

'It is a sound not unlike our Northumbrian pipes,' said Gytha, 'but less raucous. I like it too.' She smiled at him and then asked: 'Where are you from, Alexander?'

'A village called Kelleth, near Hartley.'

Gytha laughed. 'What strange names! They sound like mythical places, like those we are told of in old books. But I am none the wiser,' she said. 'Is it far from here?'

'No more than a day's ride. Have you heard of a town called Appleby?"

'Yes, of course,' Gytha replied. 'My father says that the Lord Clifford has his castle there.'

'Well, my village lies ten miles to the south of it.'

'I have never been farther than Hexham,' she said. 'Who is your lord?'

'A great warrior whose name is Andreas de Harcla.'

'Ah! That mythical place!'

'He is gone away tonight on business of Sir Robert, although no one is supposed to know that. That's his brother over there.'

Gytha lifted her sleepy eyes toward John who, she saw, was talking with her father. 'He looks sad,' she said. 'Is your lord sad too?'

'Not usually,' said Alexander laughing. 'He is severe sometimes, and sometimes easy. He is never content.'

'I do not like to be sad,' said Gytha. 'There is too much of it in the world; our lives are over short.'

'Perhaps that is the reason,' he said thoughtfully. Gytha's glance moved away from him for a moment and Kelleth said: 'There will be dancing later. Will you dance with me?'

She returned her gaze to him and she said: 'Surely.'

Fraunceise gave Alexander a nudge with his elbow. 'The father thinks you spend over much time with his daughter,' he said. 'Have you discovered where she lives?'

'No, my lord, I haven't.'

'Poor fool!' said Fraunceise. 'You should learn first things first. It is a summer night after all.' Upon which Fraunceise smiled and he turned to Gytha's mother, a handsome woman of thirty-five years, and said to her, offering his arm: 'Come, my lady, I think they wish to clear the tables.'

There was indeed some activity at the lower end of the Hall as the servants began to lift away the trestles and benches. A light music descended from the gallery; it was the flautists displaying their own dexterity. After a few moments the mandolins joined the melody and in the rising sound Gaveston strode through the empty spaces in the centre of the Hall. He called out in a clear voice:

"Trumpet, blow loud,
Send thy brass voice through all these lazy tents;
And every Greek of mettle, let him know,
What Troy means fairly shall be spoke aloud."
(Gaveston motioned to the gallery and the noise of a trumpet sounded)
"We have, great Agamemnon, here in Troy
A prince called Hector - Priam is his father -
Who in this dull and long-continued truce
Is rusty grown: he bade me take a trumpet,
And to this purpose speak. Kings, princes, lords!
If there be one among the fair'st of Greece
That holds his honour higher than his ease,
That seeks his praise more than he fears his peril,
That knows his valour, and knows not his fear,
That loves his mistress more than in confession,
With truant vows to her own lips he loves,
And dare avow her beauty and her worth
In other arms than hers - to him this challenge.
Hector, in view of Trojans and of Greeks
Shall make it good, or do his best to do it,
He hath a lady, wiser, fairer, truer,
Than ever Greek did compass in his arms,
And will tomorrow with his trumpet call
Midway between your tents and walls of Troy,
To rouse a Grecian that is true in love:
If any come, Hector shall honour him;
If none, he'll say in Troy when he retires,
The Grecian dames are sunburnt and not worth
The splinter of a lance."

Gaveston concluded his recital and, awaiting the applause, he raised his head and gazed around the company. There was some cheering and banging of pots upon the benches and he smiled and bowed to all.

Sir Richard la Fraunceise, who had been standing unobtrusively in the shadows with the local tenant's wife, left her arm and stepped forward. He did not care that Hector's chivalrous challenge, brought to the Greeks by Aeneas, should be announced by such a dainty as my lord Gaveston, the Duke of Cornwall. The words of Ulysses to Agamemnon, describing the cowardice of Achilles and Patroclus, came to him, as though in counterpoint, and he shouted out to the people:

"The great Achilles, whom opinion crowns
The sinew and forehand of our host,
Having his ear full of his airy fame,
Grows dainty of his worth, and in his tent
Lies mocking our designs: with him Patroclus
Upon a lazy bed the livelong day breaks scurril jests;
And with ridiculous and awkward action,
Which, slanderer, he imitation calls,
He pageants us......
All our abilities, gifts, natures, shapes,
Severals and generals of grace exact,
Achievements, plots, orders, preventions,
Excitements to the field, or speech for truce,
Success or loss, what is or is not, serves
As stuff for these two to make paradoxes."

Fraunceise dropped these last words with slow contempt into the ears and hearts of the crowd; he did not look at Gaveston. He had couched his speech in the northern vernacular, thus making it readily comprehensible to the greater number of guests and who, then, were able to distinguish more easily the honour of one and the knavery of the other.

'Brava!' cried Gytha, clapping her hands.

'Encore!' called the guests. 'Again! Again!'

'Give us Hector,' shouted Conan from the fireside, 'to be our leader.'

Clifford walked down into the body of the Hall. 'You already have him,' he said to Conan. 'Do you not know it?'

Conan was abashed. 'Yes, my lord,' he said with great humility. 'I do.'

'Then do not forget it.'

'My lord,' replied he, sorry to have made such a poor picture for Clifford, 'I would follow him to Hell and die there unloved.'

119

'I know,' Clifford said relenting, and he smiled. 'You all would, it seems.'

In truth Clifford was annoyed with himself for having upbraided Conan of Askham; more properly, Gaveston himself, should have been abused. 'God,' he said to himself, 'he is like the worst of strutting players, and with a gargantuan conceit that is barely credible.'

'Tell me, Conan,' Clifford asked, 'have you enjoyed our supper?'

'Indeed, my lord.'

'Then let us have some wine. Listening to recitals always makes me thirsty. Where is the rest of your company? Henry!' he called. 'Henry, bring me two or three quarts of that Bordeaux, if you please, for Conan and his friends.'

Conan was delighted. 'I hope Henry is generous with his master's wine,' he thought, 'and brings the three, a much nicer number.'

'Where is Sir Richard?' Clifford asked. 'I must compliment him upon his discourse; I did not realise he was such a scholar.'

'He often regales us with philosophies of an ancient type,' said Conan, with a touch of resignation. He glanced around the room. 'But I am afraid, my lord, I cannot see him.'

'No matter,' Clifford said. 'Conan, you did well in Scotland, I hear.'

'We are Trojans, my lord.'

Clifford's face broke into a wide grin and he laughed freely. 'Well said, Conan. But here is your wine. Drink my health, will you?'

'With much pleasure, my lord; and thank you.'

Clifford nodded and moved toward a group of knights with Gaveston at their centre.

Conan gazed contentedly upon his wine and took a great draught. He stepped away from the fire, for its heat was making him uncomfortable. He wondered where were his friends that they may share the wine; he thought he saw John chatting with Vipont and Leyburne beneath the gallery, but Fraunceise and Alexander seemed to have disappeared. 'Ah, well,' he said to himself and smiling, with only a little regret, 'theirs is the loss.'

Some of Musgrave's men were standing close by and swigging at their ale. It seemed they had overheard Conan's conversation with Clifford and thought it laughable, for they jeered him in voices that rose above the music and the chatter of guests.

'Who is this soft ninny,' sniggered one, 'sipping so dainty at his master's wine?'

'It is a fat capon waddled up from the kitchens,' said another, gurgling into his pot.

Conan looked around him for his friends.

'Do you feel lonely, Sir Capon?' they asked him.

'I do not care much for present company,' he replied, as he searched the hall.

'Oh ho,' smirked the first. 'Well, tell us what company such a fat oaf should enjoy?'

'One devoid of clowns like you,' said Conan resolutely. He saw Kelleth at last, in the shadows of a window space, on the far side of the crowded Hall; but he was talking quietly to Gytha and Conan could not catch his eye.

'Here, you clever swine,' snarled the first, 'I shall wring your neck for you.'

'Let us truss him,' said one, still joking light-heartedly, 'and return the bird to the kitchen, ready for basting.'

'Oh, no,' said the other ill-temperedly, 'we can have better sport here and still drink his wine! Here, boys, pin him against the fire. Capons should be roasted, should they not?'

Two of the men grabbed Conan by the arms; one of the quarts of wine was dropped and it crashed to the floor as Conan struggled. They pushed him up against the lintel above the fire, slipping in the dark pools of wine.

'Christ! He's a strong bastard,' panted their leader. 'Here, get his legs.'

Conan screwed up his face as he began to feel the dry, tight pain from the heat of the fire.

A few guests looked around at the commotion. 'Some tomfoolery,' they said disapprovingly. 'They are drunk!'

The backs of Conan's legs were burning and he continued to writhe against the brawny hands that grasped him. John de Harcla broke into the group, pushing them apart, and swung his fist at one who was holding Conan. He caught him on the nose, squashing it flat; the blood ran freely and the man, nursing his ruined face, fell blubbering to the floor.

Conan brought back his freed right arm and, twisting his body toward the other who still checked him, he struck fiercely into his gut. The man, their leader, doubled up as the wind left him and he made a grunting sound.

'You bastard,' said Conan venomously into his ear.

Before Conan could hit him again he was thumped in the kidneys from behind by a third and he lost his footing on the wine-red floor and fell.

The melee attracted a greater attention now and the men of the manor together with their women-folk, backed away from the fight. Some others of Clifford's men, among them Leyburne and Musgrave, came in to separate the brawlers.

'Hola, John,' Leyburne shouted to John de Harcla, grabbing him by the arm. 'What are you at?'

'Nothing at all, Robert,' replied he somewhat out of breath. 'These loons of Musgrave were roasting young Conan there; they had him over the fire. I thought he needed some help, that is all.'

'Is this true, Musgrave?' asked Leyburne.

'I shouldn't think so,' answered he. 'We ought to welcome youthful high spirits, do you not agree?' Musgrave stopped then as he caught sight of his fallen trooper. 'But look at my man's face! Good God! I can't make out where his nose ends and the mouth begins.'

'Put it down to youthful high spirits,' said John de Harcla quietly, and he walked away.

The leader of Musgrave's troop turned to Conan and, speaking in a hoarse whisper, he said: 'I know you now, you cur. I shall repay you.'

'You are not man enough,' replied Conan.

The crowd around the fire gradually dispersed and they led Musgrave's injured trooper toward the door. Conan retrieved his unspilt quarts of wine and, walking gingerly from the searing of his skin, he followed John to a quiet corner of the Hall as the dancing began.

18

THE PELE OF LIDDESDALE

ndreas de Harcla stood on a small eminence. He halted the company with a wave of his gloved hand and Ketel rode up beside him. Together they gazed up the valley to the Pele of Liddesdale and the cluster of dwellings beside it. The castle river, a shallow stretch of water that shone blue in the sunlight, lay immediately below them and they saw the bouldered shores of the stream lapping close by the tower's southern wall.

In the airy heights above the keep, but still below their line of sight, two standards were displayed. One was the blue saltire of Saint Andrew, the protector of Scotland. The breeze was not strong and both banners flew stutteringly but the whiteness of the other could be clearly seen against the sunlit sky and the saltire embroidered upon it was red, not blue, and across its wide breadth a firm bloody band ran; it was the crest of Robert the Bruce.

Antoigne de Lucy, fidgeting in the background, then came forward and looked upon the tall walls of the castle below. 'They can have no great strength,' he asserted.

Harcla was silent. He saw the massive gates of the pele slamming shut behind their returning scouts; the ones Harcla's men had constantly seen – always in the distance as they marched up the valley. The oaken cross-bars of the gates were metal-rimmed and the clanking sound they made as they fell into place rose on the summer air to the Englishmen as they watched on the hill-side.

Harcla looked keenly toward the crenellated walls of the tower; the sun was behind his left shoulder and he saw the bright metal of armour, spear and arrow-tip, glinting at every gap.

Before the pele, in a wide circle of raised ground, a fence of sharpened stakes was drawn; a neat array of twenty foot-soldiers stood behind this outer defensive wall and each man projected over the stakes his twelve foot pike.

Harcla let his gaze fall farther out to where the slope was easiest, some distance from the gates. He saw an arc of ground about four feet in width that seemed less lush than that around it; the turf here was brown and scattered with brush.

As he watched, the men upon the walls defiantly clashed together their weapons in the certainty of their strength, and the turbulent, mocking shouts travelled triumphantly to where the English stood.

Ketel, following Harcla's eyes, said: 'They are well prepared, my lord; and why is that stretch of pasture brown, when all is green around?'

'I do not know,' Harcla replied; and with a growing dismay then he said: 'There is something not right about this.'

He swivelled round to face to Antoigne de Lucy, who had moved his horse slightly to one side. 'Sir Antoigne,' he said, 'your report to my Lord Clifford spoke of an under-manning of this pele, and that the Scots were over-confident, not only in their capabilities but also in our resolve.'

'We were not referring specifically to Liddesdale Pele,' Lucy answered defensively, 'but rather to the valley as a whole. We had word they took men to strengthen Ayr. I am sorry our information was mis-interpreted.'

'Mis-interpreted?' Harcla said angrily. 'By Christ, Lucy, the wording seemed plain enough to me.'

'They must have had notice of our intentions,' Lucy said, clutching wildly at any straw in the wind. In truth, he was as much shocked as Harcla at the Scots force before them.

Of course, and unbeknown to Lucy, his frantic claim made some sense. 'But is it possible?' Harcla asked himself. 'And so quickly!' His mind turned to the Chapter House at Durham; and his brother's friend, Monseigneur the Dean. 'I cannot see through this fog,' he muttered.

He raised his eyes to Lucy and he seethed; the two knights stared at each other in enmity.

'By God, Lucy,' Harcla shouted, 'just look down there! There must be four or five score of garrison crammed in that bloody tower; not counting the two dozen pikemen on the outer fence. Good God! We have less than half that number at Roxburgh Castle itself!'

Lucy, uncertain of what else he could do, stood his ground. 'We await your commands, Sir Andreas,' he said calmly, and he brought down the vizor upon the bright steel of his helmet.

'Be patient, Lucy,' replied he brusquely. 'I, for one, do not wish to be skewered on those pikes. We must discover our advantage, if one exists, and then fight.'

Sir Walter de Strickland, who, with his own troop of six horse, had ridden from Wark with Harcla, came alongside these two as they argued. 'What goes, Andreas?' he asked.

'A pretty mess, Walter,' he answered. 'They out-number us more than two to one; our intelligence is extremely poor (and he glanced at the hidden face of Lucy as he said this) and theirs is extremely good.'

'That is Bruce's crest,' Strickland said, pointing to the eight-foot banner above the keep.

'I know, I know that,' Harcla barked. 'But he can't be here. Clifford and Gaveston parley with him at Melrose. It must be his brother, Edward.' Harcla stopped then and looked once more to the strength of Liddesdale Pele.

'Jesu,' he muttered.

His orders were simple: he must take this tower. He had heard them from Clifford and Gaveston on the morning of his return from Durham, four days ago. This plan had been prompted by the arrival of Castre's report from Carlisle; it spoke of the weakness of the Liddesdale castle and urged an immediate assault. Gaveston, sitting with Clifford in his chamber and studying Ambrose's map, straightaway pointed out its situation; the military importance was manifest for it guarded one of the two western roads to Edinburgh.

'For the safety of our baggage-trains now –,' he said, 'and in September too, do not forget – we must take it! And if, as Castre says, they have withdrawn their strength to Ayr (although God knows why) it should not prove difficult.'

Gaveston paused for a moment.

Clifford looked at him in the silence; he thought he was observing a mutated form of himself, or as though Gaveston had usurped him and, in the changing, had stolen his powers of thought and speech.

'Twenty horse for the charge, I should say,' Gaveston continued, 'and forty foot for the escalade. Do you agree, my lord?'

Clifford nodded and found the use of his tongue. 'Yes, my lord,' he said.

'Leyburne can hold Wark for us, if you think Sir Andreas here can lead the assault.'

Clifford nodded again. Harcla was sitting by the window which had had such a soporific effect upon him the day before. He had not been spoken to and he kept silent. He followed Gaveston's argument and gazed out to the pleasant northern hills.

'We can postpone our departure for Melrose one day I think, Clifford. It will give you time to organise this affair with Harcla.' Gaveston glanced across to him and he rubbed his belly uncomfortably. 'Besides,' he said, 'I am somewhat indisposed today. It was that damned salmon, I'm sure of it. Will you excuse me, my lords?' he asked them, and he left the apartment precipitately.

Clifford turned to Harcla and said with violence: 'Even that man's back-end cannot hold the weight of shite his body contains.'

Harcla was amazed at the extraordinary ferocity with which Clifford made his joke. But both men laughed and sat together then to deliberate upon the course they must take and the orders that should be relayed to Castre, with the obligatory copy to the king.

It so happened then, that the following morning, six days after leaving Brough-under-Stainmore, the companies of Harcla and Walter de Strickland rode out from Wark. It was the Feast of Saint Martha, the Magdalena's sister, and they made their confessions and heard the dawn mass. The priest said: 'It is not the weight of our sins which drags us down but our proud refusal to allow Christ to carry them. The Magdalena came to learn this; we should too.' The war-like congregation received this admonition with equanimity and filed out of the chapel. The knights and men put on their chain mail, dressed their horses and quitted the castle.

They rode west along the Vallum to the foot of the Water of Liddel at Canonbie, to meet there with Lucy and Lowther coming from Carlisle. As it turned out Harcla was forced to wait there an extra day, and as he waited his impatience grew.

Sir John de Castre imparted the news of this plan to Antoigne de Lucy in the Great Hall of his castle at Carlisle. 'Harcla leads the assault and you, with Lowther, accompany him,' he had said, rubbing his face pensively. 'All may yet go our way.'

'It may, my lord,' Lucy replied, 'but do not forget I have my skin to consider.'

'Bah! You young ones are all ninnies!' Castre scoffed. 'It's the foot who carry the danger, poor bastards. Death and mutilation are their bed-fellows.'

'I shall remember your words, my lord, when I grow dissatisfied with my lot.'

'Clifford wants forty of them, foot-soldiers that is to say,' Sir John said, reading the order, 'fully equipped for an escalade.'

'Only send thirty,' Lucy offered. 'These are difficult times.'

'By God, you're a cunning one, Antoigne,' sniggered Castre. 'There is no chance that you will take this damned tower, is there?'

126

'None. Their actual strength is forty; that is, double our estimation to Clifford. One should not put the whole of one's trust in rumour and paid word, should one, Sir John?'

'Indeed not, Antoigne, indeed not. Here, have some of this wine, my friend. Old Gilbert, my victualler here, does a fine job, does he not?'

Castre raised his thirty foot from the county levies and it was two days later, not the one day specified in his orders, that these men, with their escalades, grappling hooks and ropes for the storming of the Pele, trundled out of Carlisle with their laden wagons. Lucy and Lowther, astride their great war-horses, followed them in knightly splendour.

There was a silence now among the Scots forces within the tower and upon the outer wall as they waited expectantly and with confidence for the English assault. Harcla brought up his company of five knights and twenty men-at-arms to a flat ridge below the hilltop. His thirty foot-soldiers stood in a line behind them.

The bright armour of the knights glittered in the sunlight and the plumes of their helmets were like rainbows, tumbling in the air about their heads. The huge war-horses, decked in their colours and crests, like garlands about their dark bodies, were motionless.

They looked down to the tower; about the outer fence the sharpened points of the Scots' pikes cast still, jagged shadows on the grass.

'Let us go back,' Harcla said into the silence.

No other made any response for a space of time, but Harcla sensed the sudden disbelieving twist in the saddle as each man turned. He looked up to see Lucy, Ketel and Fraunceise staring incredulously at him.

'What did you say, Andreas?' Fraunceise asked, finding his voice after an age.

'I said: "Let us go back." We can do nothing here.' Harcla pulled his horse out of the line and turned in a circle. Some others of the company, unhappy too at the odds against them, began to turn their horses also.

Ketel's face, as he looked at his master, mirrored the very image of despair and disbelief. The line was breaking up in places but some knights still held their ground. A few triumphant shouts came up from the Scots as they viewed this great indecision. Fraunceise, Alexander and Conan, in confusion as Harcla pushed roughly through them, swung their horses toward one another and, in the bumping, Conan's horse reared, biting the air, and sent him flying from the saddle to land in a tangle of legs, bow and spear. The horse bolted down the hill and the Scots roared from the battlements, bellowing their scorn.

Strickland, to his eternal credit, and in a moment of unvarnished courage, uncouched his lance and said: 'I am sorry, Harcla. I do not wish to be called a coward. I intend to charge.'

'Obey my order, Sir Walter,' Harcla shouted at him, incensed beyond words, 'or, by God, I shall run you through.' Harcla rode over to him. 'Turn around, Strickland,' he cried out. 'All of you, turn!'

The noise from the tower increased and, with the jeering, there were now raucous hoots of laughter at the confusion upon the hill. Harcla grabbed at Walter's lance and pulled it from him and threw it over to Ketel.

'By Christ, Harcla,' Strickland said bitterly, 'I shall never forgive you for this.'

The baying shouts from the pele and the strident clashing of weapons upon the walls grew to a fever pitch as Harcla's ragged and defeated company, in total disarray, fell back from the hilltop and, in full view of the tower, made for the road below.

Ketel looked again at Andreas as one utterly destroyed. Harcla could not bear this and, as they clambered in great disorder down the southern side of the hill, he drew Ketel to one side and whispered in his ear: 'Do you have no faith? All is not as it seems. But we must make a great show of retreat against their strength.'

Ketel's eyes opened wide, detecting hope where none had been and he watched Harcla ride, with drooping shoulders, to the front of the line. 'We said we should follow him through all,' he reminded himself, 'but, Christ in Heaven, I did not expect this path.'

They reached the road, gathered the foot and wagons and put them at the front of their retreating forces. There was no chase from the Scots; indeed, if there had been, Harcla's policy would have lain in ruins. But he had thought their numbers of horse to be few and they would not risk a skirmish in open country against his knights and men-at-arms.

After two miles, at a point where the castle river ran into the Liddel through a covering of trees, Harcla halted the company. He gathered his men; all of them together, and said: 'Well, my friends, there is light in the darkness. I have a confession to make to you.'

After midnight, in the dead hours before dawn, Harcla led his men, all on foot now, back to the Liddesdale tower. He left five of his troops at the waters' meet, which was to be their place of rendezvous, to watch the horses and carts. When his party had come to the road below the hill, the scene of their false cowardice earlier in the day, Harcla brought them over to the right northwards, following the lone star in that sky, and away from the castle river.

They crossed half a mile of rising ground and then turned due west. They crept slowly along an upland pasture and saw below them, to their left, two small lights glimmering like stars themselves through the darkness of the night; they were the watch-fires of the pele. He took them further still until these islands of brightness dwindled behind them and then they turned south with the fall of the land, and halted at the river, looking now from the west to the large bulk of the fortress before them. It rose in its greater blackness of stone three hundred yards distant.

'Keep your heads down as much as you can,' Harcla told them. 'When we arrive at the fencing wait for my word.'

They dropped themselves to the cold pasture, wet with the falling dew, and crawled on their bellies and hands and knees toward the outer wall of sharpened stakes. The men dragged with them the coiled lengths of their iron-runged rope ladders.

They passed over some raised banks and grassed ditches, the ruins of an old manor house, and then, on their left, out of the half-darkness the small stone chapel of the castle loomed; all was silent within and they crept past it, shivering with the wet and cold.

Harcla was in the first rank with Ketel, Fraunceise, Conan and Alexander. Lucy, with his group of six, followed at their heels. There was one watch-fire burning within this side of the wall, and one on the other. They could smell the warm smoke from them and see the loose sparks as they crackled upward in the quiet of the night.

The first rank was within twenty feet of the stakes when the texture of the ground beneath them was transmuted; their hands, as they crawled along, were on loose brushwood supporting cut squares of turf. They stopped and flattened themselves to the earth. Lucy's hand, as he came crouching forward in the darkness, landed on Ketel's calf and, unbalancing him, he toppled on to his backside with a low thud. Harcla looked back as Lucy righted himself and crept alongside him.

Ketel was leaning over and tugging at Harcla's jerkin; he muttered in his ear: 'My lord, it must be that arc of brownness we saw from the hill today. What is it?'

'They are called "pottis".' The whispered reply was from Lucy. 'They are freshly dug pits,' he said, 'covered with turf, to confound and maim our horses as we charge. By spreading our weight we can crawl over them alright.'

'Explain this to the men as they come up,' said Harcla. 'But they must wait here till we return.' He motioned to Ketel and his others to follow him and they crept over the broken ground and approached the fence.

Ten yards away three still figures lay huddled in blankets near the fire. Ketel and Conan wriggled between the stakes and, getting to their feet then, glided swiftly over the grass and withdrew their daggers. There was no movement from two of the sleeping men and they slit their throats; the third was half- awake at the disturbance about him when Ketel pulled back his head, muffled his mouth and killed him.

Ketel looked back to Harcla, his eyes gleaming in the silent light of the fire. Harcla waved him on and he and Conan sank back to the ground and followed the glow of the second watch-fire.

Fraunceise and Alexander gazed at the steepling walls of the tower where two Scots guards, silhouettes against the sky, walked the ramparts. Fraunceise counted the seconds until they reappeared.

'Two minutes, Andreas,' he murmured to Harcla. 'Alexander says he can do it.'

'Good,' he answered.

Ketel and Conan returned to the fence. 'All quiet now,' they said. 'Another three.'

Harcla said: 'Conan, tell my lord Lucy to come up with the others. Our thirty foot are to lie silently by the main gate – until we open it for them. Lucy and Lowther make their escalade upon the far wall. Strickland and ourselves attack here. Do you understand?'

'Yes, my lord,' Conan replied and he slipped away.

'Alexander,' Harcla whispered as he looked up to see the two retreating figures on the tower, 'go now.'

Kelleth stole across the pasture to the foot of the wall. In his right hand he held the grappling hook, wrapped in muffling layers of cloth, and in his left he gripped firmly the other end of the coiling rope. He measured the distance and swung the hook in widening circles as he took its weight. He let it go and it flew upwards and looped over the crenellations and caught in an angle of the embrasured wall. He climbed easily, in spite of the heavy rope ladder he had wound around his body, and vaulted on to the ramparts of the tower.

He glanced about him quickly; the guards were halfway on their circuit. 'Less than a minute,' he thought. Smoothly he unwrapped the ladder from him and attached its hooks to the foot of an embrasure; he lowered the rest of it down, holding the rungs away from the stone of the walls. He knelt in the darkness, fingering his knife. The two guards were ten paces away and chatting quietly.

Harcla's face appeared out of the night sky beside Kelleth, who pointed with his dagger to the Scots. Harcla raised himself at an angle, one arm around the stone battlement and his opposite foot in the next opening. He swung in the air from the ladder and with his right hand he gently withdrew his sword. The two Englishmen listened to the voices coming towards them.

'Aye, she's a tidy wench,' said one, concluding some libidinous tale.

'Lucky bastard you,' agreed the other.

Alexander sprang to his feet and sank his dagger in the throat of the first. Harcla's sword leapt in a huge arc and hewed the other's neck; the look of amazement, not terror, on this man's face as he saw his death was forever imprinted on Harcla's mind. He fell clattering to the floor, his head almost separate from his body, and the corpse rolled off the ramparts and dropped to a timbered roof below with a loud thud.

The others of Harcla's own party climbed now to the ramparts beside him. Walter de Strickland was first up the ladder. He had elbowed Fraunceise out of his way in a slight unseemly scuffle on the grass at the bottom of the tower. 'Give way, give way,' Strickland had said in a loud whisper, 'I must go next.' Eventually Fraunceise let him pass saying, 'Christ, Walter, there is time enough.'

Sir Walter, panting a little from the climb, watched Harcla look across to the far wall thirty yards away where, in the moon's eerie light, he saw Lucy's pale face rise cautiously above an opening and peer from side to side. Harcla walked a few paces around the ramparts and waved him on urgently. Lucy nodded and clambered up, followed by Lowther and the rest of their group.

Strickland, sword in hand, prowled the stone walkway. 'Where next, Andreas?' he asked, glancing impatiently around him. In truth he was like a dry piece of tinder looking for a spark.

'Through the trap-door to the gate-house,' Harcla answered him, and he pointed to some low timbered housing that protruded above the ramparts. 'It's over there.' Strickland began to walk away.

'But Walter,' Harcla called after him hoarsely, 'wait for Fraunceise and Lucy.' Strickland did not seem to hear and was moving ahead, almost at a run, to the trap door.

Fraunceise came up. 'Richard,' Harcla said, pointing to Strickland's receding figure, 'for Christ's sake, take the rest of the men and go with him.' He turned to Kelleth. 'Alexander,' he asked, 'can you drop down the inside of a tower as easily as you climb up its out side?'

Alexander laughed and replied: 'Of course, my lord.'

'Then do so, now if you please – and when you reach the ground open the gates. Our friends will be waiting for you. Ketel is with them.'

Kelleth repositioned the grappling iron so that its hook now caught on the outside of a battlement, and was gathering the coils of rope to him when Harcla spoke again.

'Wait,' he said, 'I had best come with you. The crossbars of the gates will be too heavy for one man.'

Alexander nodded and lowered the rope over the edge of the parapet. 'I shall go first, my lord,' he said, testing the weight. 'Watch me.' In the stillness of the night Alexander leapt backwards from the roof of the tower.

There were now though some noises of waking men and alarms within the buildings of the pele. The muffled sound of frantic voices came up to Harcla as he stood directly above the guard-room and peered down into the darkness that had swallowed Kelleth in his rapid descent. Alexander's hushed voice rose to him from the depths: 'Come, my lord, it is easy. Grasp the rope.' Harcla took the rope with his gloved hand.

In the lower buildings, where all had been black, a number of torches were lit and the flickering lights shone beneath his feet. 'Aux armes! Aux armes!' called a voice from below. 'We are attacked.' Harcla thought he recognised the voice to be Soulis' but the sound was disguised by the light tramp of his running knights and men as they rushed past him to follow Strickland and Fraunceise through the trap-door and into the body of the tower.

'My lord!' Kelleth called again from the ground, 'Quickly, my lord.' Harcla stood on the inner lintel of the parapet; his feet curled around the ledge and he leant back into space, holding the rope taut against his weight. He jumped backwards and allowed the rope to run through his palms. He fell for a long second and clenched again, bringing up his feet to push himself away from the wall. He thought the shock, when it came, to break his ankles; then he was in air again and he let the rope flow freely once more. Then another shock against the wall, less controlled this time and against his shoulder, and he fell to the ground. Kelleth ran to him. 'Are you hurt, my lord?' he asked anxiously.

Harcla got unsteadily to his feet. 'Good Christ! You said it was easy.' He took off his gloves and blew on the palms of his hands. 'My skin is burning,' he said.

'You fell too fast, my lord.'

Harcla looked at him and said: 'I shall remember your advice for the next time, from which may God protect me! But come, Alexander - the gate!' Harcla turned and, in the darkness, tripped against a body lying on the ground. Kelleth helped him to his feet once more. 'He tried to kill me, my lord,' Kelleth said, ' when I was calling you. He is dead.'

They ran past some stabling under the eaves of the wall to their left; a dozen horses were tethered there and fretting in the growing noise of the night. 'Bruce's horses,' Harcla thought as he raced ahead. He saw the gate now and two sleepy guards stirring at their post; these gazed in miscomprehension at the two men running hard toward them. And then, away to the right, in the wall of the tower buildings, a doorway was flung open and a flood of light illuminated the ground before it. Into this patch of brightness there stumbled a dozen men-at-arms of the pele; some had swords in their hands but others were unarmed or bore wounds to their heads and bodies. They stood in confusion as their blood dropped to the earth and they searched the greater darkness in which Harcla and Kelleth ran. More Scots troopers, some of them half-drunk and forced into the open bailey by Strickland and Frraunceise pressing from above, spilled out into Harcla's path.

'The gate, Alexander! The gate!' he shouted, pushing some of these men away from him. 'Before we are too late.' The two men put their arms to lift the great crossbars. They could hear the impatient fevered shouts of their comrades outside.

'Open the gates, you bastards!' they were shouting. 'Where are you?'

'We are here,' Harcla yelled back to them through the oak of the gate. 'For Christ's sake, do not push yet.' He heard Ketel ordering the men back a space from the gate.

'Get them away from the gate, Ketel,' he said. 'We must lift the bars.' Harcla turned quickly as he finished speaking; a Scots trooper was rushing at him from the bailey, his sword upraised. Harcla dropped to the ground as the steel thudded into the wood of the gate above him, then he sprang upward and thrust his shoulder into the man's chest, throwing him to the floor. He saw his face then; it was Mauchline, Soulis' singer at Jedburgh.

Harcla withdrew his sword and looking down at him he said: 'Ah! It's you, troubadour. Move away or I kill you now.' Mauchline lay still, staring terrified at the point of Harcla's sword. Harcla thrust into the flesh at his shoulder shouting, 'Get back!'

'The bar, my lord,' Kelleth cried. Harcla stepped towards him and they raised the bar and let it fall to one side of the gateway.

'Enter, Ketel,' de Harcla said loudly.

Twenty yards away in the darkness of the bailey Edward de Bruce was gathering his horses. He had woken five minutes earlier with the shouts of attack in his disturbed dreams; and now he heard the bloody cries of Harcla's thirty foot as they poured through the opened gates.

'Come, Soulis,' he called to his lieutenant, 'we can gain the gates, which our friends have kindly opened for us.'

'It is Harcla out there, my lord,' Soulis said.

Edward de Bruce nodded and leapt upon his horse. He unsheathed his sword and flexed the muscles in his wrist.

'What about my tower?' Soulis called to him.

'It has fallen,' Edward replied. 'I have been found a fool. But, come, Soulis, we must go. Do you wish to pay for your freedom?'

Edward de Bruce, Soulis and their ten men-at-arms came close together and the horses stamped and bit. 'It will fall again, Soulis,' said the Scottish king's brother, smiling; and he lifted his sword and spurred his horse violently, shouting: 'Bruce, Bruce!' They charged toward the gate.

As Harcla and Alexander stood back from the gateway Ketel and the thirty foot-soldiers of Carlisle leapt into the mouth of the tower. They were eager for blood and booty and they waved in the air their short swords and shouted out their cries of war as they ran to the enemy.

The Scots were discomfited now on all sides. Having been forced down from the guard room and second-floor chambers of the pele by Strickland and Fraunceise, they now met, as they gained the ground, the fierce onslaught of Harcla's bloodthirsty second wave. Lucy and Lowther, by their later descent through the trap door and the narrow passageways in the buildings, saw little action, merely watching and waiting as the way was cleared by their colleagues.

Strickland, having given many wounds, was finally hurt himself; one strike hit him in the ribs as he won the guard-room but then he received a second in the leg, fighting downwards on the stone spiral stairs. He reached a lower chamber then, the Scots stumbling out into the bailey from the opened doorway, and he fell to the floor in a faint. Fraunceise came to him and pulled away the slashed leather of his boot; he cut the hose from his leg and saw the deep wound in the muscle pulsing with blood.

He called to one of Strickland's men to come to him. 'Staunch the flow with this,' he told him, pulling some coarse linen from his wallet, 'and fasten it round with strips of hose. Like this, you see.'

The man nodded.

'Do not leave him,' Fraunceise said. He forced his way out to the ground of the bailey where he saw chaos: dozens of men were pushing and slashing against one another indiscriminately, no one easily knew friend or foe in the half-darkness.

But through it all, through all the noise and shouts and screams, a clearer harder sound of hoof beats on packed earth came to him and with these the cries of horses and the curses of their riders as they cleared a path to the gates. He looked to the gates and saw Harcla there, alone, sword in hand, in the middle of the open passageway, as though guarding the doorway to heaven.

'Andreas!' Fraunceise called in great fear. 'Andreas!' And he began to run.

Edward de Bruce rode at the gap to freedom.

Harcla stood immobile. 'Do you wish to fly, Sir Edward?' he shouted at the wild approach.

'As you did at Jedburgh!' Edward answered, laughing, as his horse rushed past. He swung his sword then and Harcla, with the shock, fell back against the gatepost and Edward de Bruce's small company galloped out from the Liddesdale Pele.

'We shall meet again, Sir Andreas.' Edward de Bruce's farewell drifted slowly in the air of the summer night and reached Harcla's ears as he slumped against the gates.

19

THE SEEDS OF GREATNESS

Sir Robert de Clifford dined alone in his apartments at Wark. He was a man who enjoyed occasional solitariness; he thought these periods helped keep his mind sharp. Clever ideas and strategies sometimes came to him when alone and he liked to indulge himself in this pleasure – when he was not constrained to be attentive to the conversations and desires of others.

He also believed these periods of remoteness made easier the tolerance and respect he should more often display to his fellows, creatures of God too; although this Christian virtue was one he found difficult to practice. Clifford was not unlike most men of his time in that he had one eye firmly fixed on eternity.

He was doubly gratified now, as he sipped at his wine and chewed on his duck, for he was quit of his companion of the last week, my lord Gaveston; he was like Priam delivered from the taunts of the Greeks. He felt unable though, even at the distance of one hundred miles – for Gaveston was now travelling back to York and the King – to offer any feeling of sympathy to this particular brother in Christ. But Clifford was forced to concede that Gaveston had never exhibited anything other than total devotion to the cause of the King; in that sense he was honourable. Clifford felt some rumblings of guilt as he thought of his private conversation with Robert the Bruce, of which we shall presently hear. Of course the fact that this cause – and Edward's well-being and security – was inextricably linked to Gaveston's own, was also true; for without the protection of the King he would be destroyed by his enemies, men who, originally mere foxes, had been metamorphosed into howling wolves through his acid tongue and derogatory manner.

Surely Gaveston was aware of this and, if he had cemented his fortune with that of the King, he must do all in his power to ensure the second Edward's success. But that fortune was unclear at the very best, and downright hazardous at worst. Could he not see the worthlessness of his military plans?

Clifford sat back and thought of their interview with Bruce at Melrose. Gaveston had delivered his argument with great self-assertion, as if it were unanswerable. He talked as though he had dice in his hand that would all fall as sixes. He told Bruce plainly of the planned invasion; he mentioned, with profound gravity, the number of ten thousand men. Bruce was impassive. Gaveston then spoke of the ruin that would come upon the land of Scotland and the impoverishment of the people. Bruce smiled a little but said nothing; Clifford thought this deliberate manner was exasperating to Gaveston. Gaveston could not have known, indeed no one in heaven or earth could have known, through what extremities of desolation and destitution Bruce was preparing to lead his new country and its people.

Lastly, and most weakly, Gaveston discussed the difficulties Bruce would meet materially as an excommunicated monarch in western Europe, with a powerful enemy, England, on his borders. Bruce laughed in his face; he knew now that Gaveston's dice all had the figure one engraved upon each of the faces.

Then, as the parley broke up, Bruce had drawn Clifford to one side.

'Robert,' he said, 'I should not say this, for the clown helps my cause greatly, but why do you not rid yourselves of him? How do you, the most honourable of men, bear it?'

Clifford shook his head. 'I have no choice,' he replied. 'It is my duty.'

'I found a choice,' Bruce said slowly, 'and took it. The way is there for you too.'

Clifford looked at him, as the meaning dawned; he saw his former friend smiling a deep smile he remembered well. 'Robert, you do not know what you ask,' he whispered.

'You think not? I could not ask without knowing myself – it is a great thing.' Bruce leant back in his chair and fingered the curls of his beard. One of his captains, Thomas Randolph, the Earl of Moray, stood behind him listening. Bruce tilted his head backwards. 'You made the choice, Thomas, did you not?' he asked of him.

'I did, Sire,' said Randolph.

'We welcome friends,' Bruce said to Clifford, facing him once more.

'And destroy our enemies,' said Randolph.

'Come, Clifford,' Gaveston called from the doorway. 'We should go. There is nothing to be done here.'

John de Harcla and Musgrave were following Gaveston outside when Bruce rose suddenly, put a hand on John's arm, and restrained him. 'Are you Harcla?' he asked.

Randolph started at the name, remembering the skirmish at Pendragon; involuntarily, he rubbed a hand along his shoulder.

'I am John de Harcla,' answered he, surprised.

'You were not at Jedburgh five days ago?'

'I was with my brother, Andreas – he was in Jedburgh, for a short time, I was outside it.' John smiled a little.

'Andreas,' Bruce mused. 'I thought to meet him here. Where is he?'

'Away on business,' Clifford interrupted.

'Why did you not bring him, Robert?' Bruce asked. 'He is your right arm, they say. This business he travels on must be of great value to you.' Bruce's eyes were hard and chill, like the frozen surface of a loch. 'I hope he rides well-armed,' he went on. 'This is dangerous country.'

Clifford was confounded. 'Come, John,' he said brusquely, 'my lord duke awaits us. Adieu, Robert.' And the two men bowed and parted.

Clifford finished his meal and drank his wine, calling Henry for more. His eyes creased as he thought of Bruce's interest in Harcla; it was almost as though he guessed their intentions. Was he, Clifford, right to think their intelligence was intercepted? Of the treachery of two of his own, Clifford was incapable of guessing. He frowned and wondered about the Liddesdale Pele; he had expected news from Harcla the day before at the latest. What if Bruce had learnt of the orders and strengthened the pele, or worse, had planned an ambush?

Clifford sweated in grave fear; this would be the end, he knew, of all his hopes – if Hector were to fall. He felt the cold drops falling from his armpits to the linen of his tunic.

And then, what of Harcla's spy at Durham? There had been no message as yet from that direction either. Clifford considered this and when Henry returned with his wine he asked him to send to Ambrose, the cartographer at Hexham, for any packets that may have arrived there for Sir Andreas.

He walked over to the seat in the window-space and gazed out to the hills, darkening now in the early evening. A heavy mist covered their tops and swirled in the light breeze; the mist became rain in the valley and fell gently by the banks of the North Tyne.

He looked down the valley to where the great Roman wall ran west to east in the rolling uplands and saw a rider moving very fast along the road from the south. He was hunched forward over the saddle, his grey cloak billowing out behind him. Clifford watched his approach for a few minutes, until the horseman clattered through the open gateway and into the bailey-ground of the castle. He saw it was Conan of Askham.

'News at last,' he muttered, full of dread.

THE SEEDS OF GREATNESS

Conan glanced up to the tower as he jumped from his horse and, seeing Clifford standing starkly in the window, he waved his arm victoriously and ran to the doorway. Clifford unclenched his hands from their grip upon the chair-back and saw the tears his nails had made in the sindon cloth. He breathed again. 'I knew, I knew!' he said to himself.

Henry entered the apartment with Conan at his heels.

'Well?' Clifford asked impatiently, walking toward him.

'My lord,' said Conan, breathing deeply, 'we have taken the Liddesdale Pele. We attacked early this morning, before dawn.'

Clifford punched his right fist into the palm of his other hand and shouted into the air: 'By Christ, now they taste it themselves!' He laughed loudly. 'An escalade by night!' he exclaimed. 'Bravo, Conan!'

'My lord,' said Conan. 'It was against all odds. The castle was heavily defended.' And Conan told his story.

When he had heard all, or nearly all, Clifford asked: 'And where is Sir Andreas now?'

'Ah, my lord, he lies at Carlisle, hurt.'

Clifford sat down by the window. 'Tell me the rest, Conan,' he said.

Conan related the last frantic moments of the attack and Harcla's vain stand in the gateway. 'Sir Walter fought bravely in the tower, my lord; he also bore a wound. He is at Carlisle too.' Conan finished then and, leaving the earl to his thoughts, he made his way to the kitchens.

Clifford stared into the wet night. The fells had disappeared in the gloom and small distant lights marked out the lonely steadings among their foothills. On the ramparts about the bailey his troopers trudged in silent misery, their torches spluttered and threw a dingy light on the stone walls.

'A hundred of garrison at Liddesdale Pele!' he muttered. 'Jesu! The fool! The great fool!'

Henry of Appleby entered the room. 'Sir Robert,' he said, handing him a sealed packet, 'Ambrose received this today at Hexham. It is addressed to Sir Andreas.'

Clifford leapt to his feet and ripped it open. The writer was Monseigneur the Dean, Peter Claxton. He read:

Andreas, I do not know that there any solid facts I can tell you of. I mean in respect of the matter we discussed four days ago. Two of our friars travel tomorrow to Hexham and I thought, anyway, I should avail myself of the opportunity to send to you.

My lord the archbishop returned from Dryburgh last night. He is in good spirits but spoke unhappily of the plight of our kingdom in the north. (Damn Bek and his spirits, Clifford thought. He had not seen the bishop at Melrose, nor had Bruce mentioned him.) *I think he knows Bruce well enough to admit of no volte face on his part. He will not turn now from his path.*

On the question of the informant, I am beginning to feel uneasy and harbour suspicions. I do not know how this mistrustful state could ever be and I feel unsuited to the task you laid upon me.

There are two of us here with access to the archbishop's desk and papers – you are, of course, aware that in his capacity of Lord Ordinaire he receives from the King's office copies of all the orders, letters of protection and reports from the Marches. The order and report regarding the Liddesdale Pele, for example, (de Clifford's breath caught in his throat) *issued by Sir Robert de Clifford and Sir John de Castre, arrived on his desk two days after you left here (the feast of Saint Martha, July 29). I have to tell you the document had already been opened when I saw it. While there is nothing greatly unusual in this, there then occurred a related circumstance that I freely admit has worried me.*

I cannot though find it in my heart to bring any false accusation, and I shall not divulge the name until I am sure of my ground. I shall send you again soon. God keep you.

Clifford finished the letter and threw it upon the table. 'What should we expect from a priest and his conscience!' he fumed. 'Pardieu! He has the name but is shocked to the core. He cannot believe his own eyes, I guess, and means to confront the man he suspects. Bah!'

20

THE INFLUENCE OF THE IRISH

n a hot summer's day one week later, when the only clouds were high and white and the only sounds the curlews and larks, two horsemen rode into the valley.

Before them, half a mile away in the rising of the land, Hartley Castle stood. Its lime-washed walls gleamed a brilliant white in the sun – dazzling to look upon.

Around this loop of land a river tumbled like a bright necklace adorning a woman's breast. The water fell white and shining in small leaps as it broke upon the limestone rocks that formed its bed. The two riders halted and knelt to drink. They cupped the cool water in their hands and splashed their faces. A few paces below them the horses lapped noisily at the stream's edge.

Harcla - for he was one of the two - leaned back and settled into the softness of the dry bracken; he was discovering a trouble in easing the aching bone in his shoulder. The flesh there was still tender and the broken skin a dark yellowing purple. His upper arm and chest were bound in linen strips that protected a compress of crushed comfrey root lying against the wound. Edward de Bruce's sword, as he swung it downwards in the gateway of the Liddesdale pele, had been turned by Harcla's defensive parry and the thick edge of it, thudding into the hauberk, the short mail tunic he wore, had distorted and fractured the chain rings at the base of his neck. It was these shattered rings that had pierced the skin and bruised the flesh and bone.

'I shall not do that again,' he had said to Walter de Strickland as they lay side by side in the house of the Minorite Friars in Carlisle.

'Courage cannot be defeated,' said Walter from his bed.

'Perhaps not; but idiocy may.'

'You saw a glittering prize, Andreas,' Strickland returned. 'How much would King Robert have paid, I wonder, for the freedom of his brother? One thousand marks? A fortune, my friend. But I was glad not to meet my friend Soulis – he escaped with Bruce, I think. I do not know what I should have done.' Strickland rubbed his cheek in his characteristic, thoughtful way.

'He might have been worth a few hundred marks to you, Walter,' said

Harcla, laughing. 'You could have spent a few happy days, as you awaited the ransom, talking of old times and drinking wine.'

'Yes,' smiled Walter, 'that may have been. But, still, what you did
was foolhardy.'

Harcla glanced toward him. 'How do you know?' he asked jovially.
'You were lying on the floor of that lower chamber at the time, I think.'

'I have heard reports, Andreas,' Strickland replied, tapping his nose.
'You were lucky. Your man Conan insists you are guarded by angels.'

'I hope we all are,' Harcla had said.

The apothecary at Carlisle had given him a quantity of oil of comfrey,
a decoction of the root and leaves of the plant, which he was to apply frequently to the wound. He lay back on the heather and, unwinding the
linen bands with his right hand, he poured a few drops on to the compress. He groaned.

Ketel looked over to him. 'It still pains you, my lord?' he asked.

Harcla uttered a low grunt in assent and stared up to the sky. His eyes
met the blue sky, peerless in its beauty, and he breathed deeply of the fragrant river air.

Some distance away, on a long stretch of pasture below the castle, a
line of a dozen horsemen appeared; they stood by a hazel pole pitched
upright in the grass. They were in a single column, one behind the other;
short swords dangled at their belts and each carried a bow with a quiver
of arrows slung at their backs. Two hundred yards from them, at an angle
to the right was a large target stuffed with straw and dyed distinctively in
reds and blues. Standing midway between the riders and the target was
a solitary figure who seemed to be shouting orders or directions. His
voice did not carry clearly to where Harcla and Ketel were resting by the
beck and these two got to their feet to better view the exercise.

The instructor, for so they assumed him to be, raised his arm and then
let it fall. On this signal the first rider kicked his pony and charged
toward the target. The thudding of hooves into the earth cast in the air
behind him flying clods of turf. When he was fifty yards short of his goal
he brought up his horse abruptly, leapt to the ground and, crouching on
one knee, he rapidly let loose half a dozen arrows into the target. There
was some cheering from his fellows as they watched.

The same signal was given then and the second rider set off; he was
equally successful with all six flights finding the mark. Harcla looked on
as all twelve men took their turn. When this was done the instructor, who
Harcla now realised must be the extraordinary Uther, gathered them all

together in a circle where he spoke to them; there was some shaking of heads among the men as they listened. However, after a few moments, they broke up and returned to the hazel pole that marked the starting point. This time, on the signal, they charged together in a single column but, as they approached the target, did not dismount to shoot but dropped the reins and let loose, from the saddle as they flew past, three arrows apiece.

Twelve flights of the thirty-six thudded into the straw.

'Good! Good!' Uther shouted to the horsemen as they jogged toward him. 'Now you are trying!'

The men jumped down from their small ponies and went in search of the lost arrows amid the grass and gorse bushes at the far end of the field.

'We see a betterment on yesterday, do we not?' Uther said to them in his strange accent.

The riders, all young men from Hartley and near-by manors, were excited by the prospect of war and the invasion of Scotland, of which they hoped to be a part. They would be summoned by the king, probably for forty days, as part of the feudal levy. Each was eager to be chosen by Harcla as a light horseman, a hobelar, for the pay was better – sixpence per day rather than two pence for a foot-soldier. However they did not fully understand what this weird fellow, who they all knew as the Hermit of Pendragon, was teaching them – or, indeed, why.

Harcla and Ketel left the place by the river and walked their horses to where Uther stood. They had last seen him three weeks before, outside the gates of Pendragon Castle. His appearance had much changed in this time and they saw, as they approached, that although he had allowed his hair to remain long it was now tied at the back with a long strip of braided leather, and his beard had been neatly trimmed. His dress, too, was more compliant with modern custom for over a quilted jerkin he displayed a brilliant red short tunic and on his legs a dark burnet hose; also he had dispensed with sandals and now wore soft leather boots.

'My lord Andreas,' he said to Harcla, a broad smile upon his face.

'Well met again, Richard le Bret,' Harcla replied.

Uther's face changed and his eyes, opening in astonishment first, then clouded and became obscure. 'I have not heard my own name spoken these ten years,' he said. 'There is a strangeness to the sound.'

'Clifford has told me about Flanders,' Harcla said. 'Others remember, even though you may try to forget.'

As Harcla and Uther were speaking Ketel came forward to examine a short bow that lay on the grass by the hazel wand; this was one of

Uther's new designs. He stood the bow upright against his body for a moment. It was no more than four feet in length and light, almost slender, in his hand.

'I do not pretend,' said Uther, walking across, 'that they will be as durable as the heavier and longer bows we are more used to.'

Ketel weighed the bow in the palm of his hand. 'The balance is perfect,' he said.

'Of course,' laughed Uther. 'What was expected?'

'What about its range?' Ketel asked.

'They will not be deadly accurate beyond say, eighty yards – less than a half of what would be good with a long bow.' He saw Ketel looking at Harcla questioningly; there was doubt in his eyes.

'Their overall range, of course, is much further,' he said. 'But, Ketel, please do not forget the battles my lord plans to fight will not be classic encounters over two or three hundred yards, with beautifully precise emplacements of horse and foot; with grand knights on war horses, lordly by lance and shield, and the archer on foot, loosing over his own men half of the time! No, no! Robert the Bruce will destroy thee if he is fought in that manner.'

Uther's voice had risen. The urgency of his speech reminded Harcla of that day outside the gates of Pendragon, when he thought he was dealing with a lunatic.

'Listen to me!' Uther urged. 'This weapon is for skirmishing; for riding and shooting, and escaping! This is not a clumsy warfare; it is for skillful, adventurous men. And these ponies are good,' he continued, waving an arm behind him. 'Small, yes; but swift and hardy. Perforce, their riders can only be gently armed – the weight, thou seest. And certainly, the ponies themselves will not be covered, or armoured. It has its dangers, but, Christ, we shall be fast!'

As Harcla listened he found it impossible not to be infected with Uther's enthusiasm. 'By God, he's right!' he said to himself. 'This is how we should fight Bruce.'

'Come, Uther,' he said, 'if that is what I should still call you?'

'As thou wishest.'

'Well - Uther, then. Where have you been sleeping, my friend, since your arrival?'

'In Kirkby, my lord, with the priest. Or rather, with his pigs; I was given a duty.'

'That is finished with. Come up to Hartley when the day's exercise is complete and I shall find you quarters. Dine with us tonight.'

144

Uther bowed his assent and turned to his company of riders. These young men, having collected all the flights they could find, had approached the three men closely as they talked.

'Is that my lord Andreas?' whispered one to a friend as they stood at the back of the group.

'Of course, can you not tell? He has the imprint of a flower on his cheek when he smiles. Look!'

'Ahh! How could such a thing be?'

'No one knows. It is a great secret.'

Ketel appeared at their side. 'What are you two young conspirators at?' he asked them.

'Nothing, Ketel,' replied the knowledgeable one. 'But it is our greatest wish to ride with you and my lord.

Ketel frowned. 'You shall have to prove yourselves first,' he said sternly. 'What are your names?'

'Thomas of Howgill,' said the first who had spoken.

'And I'm Patrick of Blande, at your service Ketel,' said the other.

'Very well, Thomas, and Patrick. Not everyone is chosen, you know. You must earn the honour.'

'Thank you, Ketel,' they said. 'We shall.'

Ketel smiled and ran to catch Harcla who had left Uther and was riding up the track towards the gleaming walls of the castle.

The Lady Sarah de Harcla sat with her friend Emma la Fraunceise in her solar on the second floor of the great house. Its tall windows overlooked the western wall of the bailey and the river far below. On the pasture in between, Uther's company practiced their manoeuvres and the occasional shouts of men and the whinnying of the ponies travelled to them through the open window. The sun, dropping from its heights, cast bright beams into the room.

'It is so good to have you with us, Emma,' Sarah said. 'Life is ordinarily so dreary!'

Emma pulled her face a little. 'I am pleased to be here,' she said. 'But, can we not do something tomorrow? Perhaps we could visit the lady Idonea at Pendragon; I hear she is not well. And besides the air will be good for us.'

'My father would not allow it – at least not without half an army to guard us. He has become most protective since that Scots' raid last November.'

'I did not know they had attacked Hartley,' Emma said. 'I thought your brother headed them off.'

'Well, he did,' replied Sarah. 'You should know anyway; your uncle Sir Richard was there too.'

'He doesn't tell me much. Besides he was angry with me. I had determined to ride with them.'

'Emma, you are incorrigible.'

'It seemed common sense to me,' said Emma fiercely. 'Our numbers were few; and anyway, I can fight as well as a man - well, most men. Andreas has said so.'

'And how does he know? On what occasion did you earn his praise?'

But Emma was silent and would not answer.

Sarah got up then and walked to the window. Outside, Uther's men charged towards the straw target. She watched them idly.

'Anyway,' she said, 'tomorrow I must sit down with Sir Michael's reeve to discuss the household expenses. I seem to have assumed the role of lady of the house since my mother died. Look at this bunch of keys I must carry around with me: one for every storeroom and building in the whole castle! My poor shoulders are drooping under their weight!'

'Sarah, my true friend,' said Emma, laughing freely, 'you should not be so grave.'

'I have to be,' Sarah replied, acting the older sister. 'My father trusts me to be responsible, you know; and also, in a way, I suppose I am preparing for my wifely duties.' Sarah raised her eyes and smiled secretly.

'Ahh!' grinned Emma happily. 'When is it to be?'

'I am so excited,' her friend said, rushing the words as they embraced. 'We hope to be married in the autumn, after this horrible invasion.'

'Sarah, I am so happy for you. Robert de Leyburne is a very lucky man; and I have told Andreas to tell him so!'

'Emma, you shouldn't!'

'Why not? It's true, isn't it?'

The two young women stood in the sunlight by the window and, laughing, embraced again. Their hair intermingled - the thick waves of one and the plaited auburn of the other. They parted then and gazed out beyond the bailey walls. A solitary horseman appeared out of the sharp defile two hundred yards below the castle. The rider urged his horse to a canter on the rising ground; its hooves kicked up a spray of dust and loose stones from the baked surface of the road. Further off, another detached himself from the group of warriors to follow.

The first horseman rode bareheaded and was now almost at the gates. He looked up, grinning, to shout something to the troopers on the walls.

The men laughed and called back: 'And you, my lord, are welcome also.' The guards at the gate pulled the great doors open.

'Andreas,' Emma whispered, and she grasped Sarah's hand.

'My brother,' said Sarah.

'My love,' said Emma.

~ 21 ~

NEWS OF WAR

K etel rode up alongside Harcla and together they entered the sunlight of the bailey. They walked their horses past a ragged man, condemned by some small felony; he knelt upon the ground facing the wall with his hands trapped above his head in a wooden finger-pillory. He raised his eyes piteously to beg release.

'Drunk again, Barty?' Ketel called down to him as they passed. 'Or was it brawling this time?'

'Neither, I swear.'

'You swear too much,' said Ketel, riding on. The man Barty lowered his head sadly in contrition. Some children of the village, running behind Harcla and Ketel, stooped to pick up stones from the flinty ground and these they hurled at the defenceless man.

Two boys ran out from the stabling to take the horses; they stared up with rounded eyes at the young lord returned. They thought he was almost unrecognisable. Harcla's horse pulled back its head and, spitting, bared its teeth.

'Be careful, boy,' Harcla said. 'He bites.' He jumped down, tapped the stallion's head with the palm of his hand and threw the reins across.

'Where is James, my lord?' asked one.

Harcla turned his head. 'He has been delayed,' he answered, and he walked toward the open doorway of the house.

The boys hesitated and Ketel, glancing across, motioned them to be silent. 'Do not worry,' he said then as Harcla disappeared into the keep. 'James was hurt during a skirmish in the marches: In the back, by a spear-thrust. But he is getting better; he rests at Roxburgh Castle.'

The stable boys were agog. 'Roxburgh Castle? In Scotland?'

'Yes, Roxburgh is in Scotland, alright,' Ketel answered.

'How goes the war there?' they asked then.

'The war?' Ketel laughed in grim amusement. 'I cannot answer. It does not seem like a war; it is more like a hunt, or rather, like a stalking of deer – mostly we are the deer. But sometimes we hunt too, we hunted well seven days ago.'

Ketel's great yearning to tell the story of the ride into the borders and the taking of the Liddesdale Pele overwhelmed him and, in the shade of the stable buildings, while the boys washed and brushed the horses, he lay back on some sheaves of hay and luxuriated in the recounting of it. By the time he had done, half a dozen men of Hartley garrison together with Uther's fledgling band of horse archers had surrounded him and they all stood listening, in rapt attention.

Thomas of Howgill and Patrick of Blande, the two young riders Ketel had spoken to in the field below, sat before him on the ground, entranced.

'But, Ketel,' Patrick said at one point. 'How did my lord Andreas know the Scots would not open the gates of the tower and ride you all down? They would have destroyed you.'

'Ahh! Patrick,' Ketel replied. 'He did not know; and neither did we, I tell you. He guessed they would not, and upon that he based his strategy.'

'Strategy?' said Patrick again. 'No! That is a cold word. It was glorious!'

'It was glorious,' said Ketel, and his blood rose at the thinking of it.

'It was strategy,' Uther said, interrupting. He stood at the edge of the group around Ketel. 'A clever subterfuge,' he went on, raising his voice so that all could hear him. 'Dost thou think the tower would have been taken otherwise?'

'It was strategic and glorious,' said Ketel, a little put out. 'It is a pity, Uther, you were not there.'

'I know,' Uther replied. 'But we shall be with you soon, and then to see warfare, glorious or strategic, call it what thou wishest.'

The young riders cheered zealously but the men of the garrison, the pike and staff men, were not quite as certain of their own impatience for the September levy.

As Ketel's narrative unfolded before his animated audience in the stable, Harcla related a less colourful version to Sir Michael, who was resting in his apartments. Harcla thought his father was failing; his hands and head displayed a persistent tremor, as though he were permanently answering in the negative. Frequently his gaze would wander around the room and his eyes seldom alighted on his son's face. Harcla was unsure whether he had comprehended his story or not. Sir Michael made no mention of James other than to ask again why Andreas had not brought him home.

Harcla looked in dismay and rose to go.

'This packet arrived for you,' Sir Michael said then. 'Two days ago;

it is from Clifford. We did not realise else you were coming.'

Harcla forbore to say he had written from Wark eleven days since. 'Thank you, my lord,' he said though, and he opened the letter.

To Sir Andreas de Harcla, Captain in the West Marches, at the Castle of Harcla in Westmorland.

Written this day August 6, the feast of Saint Xystus II, Pope, at Wark Castle in Northumberland.

Andreas Salve,
I salute you.
The knights and men at arms of your Liddesdale force are returned to Wark. I have asked Fraunceise to form a single company from the remnants of your troop and that of Strickland (he is still in Carlisle with his vallet and he lost two men besides at Liddesdale).

Fraunceise took them out yesterday on a three day mission to Roxburgh and the borders. I tell you this so that you may know they intend to collect your brother James from there, if he is fit to ride.

Lucy has organised the manning of the Liddesdale Pele and he is now in garrison at Carlisle. Castre's thirty foot, I gather, were indispensable to us in the attack and I have written to thank him for the part they played in that success. (De Harcla's mouth hardened at this; he thought Lucy must have corresponded cleverly with Clifford. 'I am not as sharp as Gaveston thinks me,' he said to himself.)

Also, a packet has arrived from your contact, which I opened in your absence. He is unhappy at some discovery but wishes to be "sure of his ground"; we may have more news by the time of your return.

I would be pleased if that event were within, say eight days, the vigil of the Assumption. I trust you recover well and enjoy, during your convalescence, the companionship of friends and cousins.

Harcla was smiling as he put the letter down. He looked across to his father, dozing in his chair. 'My lord,' he said, shaking him gently by the shoulder. 'My lord, Clifford says James is safe.'

Sir Michael opened his eyes. 'Thank you, Andreas,' he murmured.

Harcla got up from his seat and quitted the apartment.

He walked out to the hay fields behind the castle. The afternoon sun was hot upon his back and he stopped to strip off his jerkin. Hartley Beck ran in the steep fall of land away to his left and, in front of him, beyond the meadows and bathed in light, stood a low wooded hill. The upper branches of its trees, birches, alder and rowans, swayed in the gentle breeze and the rich greenness of them turned from dark to light as the leaves rolled like waves in the air.

Harcla trod the path toward the meadows. They were part of the estate lands of Hartley and a number of villagers, supervised by Sir Michael's reeve Godfrid, were hard at work there stacking the freshly made hay onto carts, which then trundled the half-mile or so down to the castle. Godfrid had taken advantage of the fine spell of weather by ordering a cut of grass five days before, and now, nicely wilted and scattered, the hay was being gathered up to provide winter feed for the cattle and horses of the manor.

Godfrid saw Harcla's figure approach; he was facing the sun and he raised a hand to shield his eyes. It took a few moments for him to recognise his young lord for Harcla's tunic was edged bright in the sun and the linen folds of it billowed in the movements of air his passage made.

'Is that you, my lord?' Godfrid called out, walking to meet him.

'Greetings, Godfrid,' Harcla said smiling. 'How goes the work?'

'Well enough, my lord, well enough. But how goes your work?'

'Well enough, Godfrid,' he answered, and they both laughed.

A laden cart, pulled by a couple of oxen, rumbled toward them. 'Take that load to the abbe Thomas in Kirkby,' Godfrid ordered. The driver nodded his head, pleased for the longer journey.

'My lord,' the reeve said, turning to Harcla, 'It is good that you are home for I need to speak with you on matters affecting the manor. Sir Michael, your father.....'

'Yes, yes I think I know,' Harcla interrupted. 'But not today, if you please, my friend. Will tomorrow do?'

'I am with my lady Sarah in the morning,' Godfrid said.

'On similar matters?'

'Well, those concerning the household.'

'Good. We can discuss all at one sitting,' Harcla said, and he looked up to see the supple action of the sunlight through trees. 'And now I must bid you adieu.'

Godfrid bowed and watched Harcla as he strode away towards the wooded hill.

Emma la Fraunceise waited for him there.

She had watched his leaving of the castle from Sarah's high window and, guessing his destination, had run there by another path. She stood amid the first of the trees a little out of breath and her breast heaved. She leaned against the trunk of a tall rowan and her eyes sought him as she glimpsed out from behind it.

There was a fire of passion about Emma which, when lit, was impossible to douse. The object of this fire was Andreas and whenever she gazed upon him she thought the love that flooded her to explode her heart.

He walked into the wood and Emma la Fraunceise moved toward him. He saw her then and he stopped, gazing upon her silently. He saw the soft light of the sun in her eyes and the fullness of her beauty. He drank her in.

Emma sat down upon the coarse grass at the foot of the rowan tree and rested her back against it. 'Come, Andreas, and sit by me,' she said.

Her hair fell in waves about her shoulders and, smiling like Andromache, she spoke again: 'I thought you were never coming home.'

'It was always my wish to,' he answered, 'and here I am.'

'Yes, Andreas, here you are,' she said with some satisfaction. 'With me; and I am not inclined to let you go again.'

Harcla crouched to the ground and smiled back. 'Ah, but you must, my lady,' he said. 'Lord Clifford expects me at Wark.'

Emma pulled a face. 'Wark! Wark!' she said. 'It is all we hear of! What is this place that exercises such a fascination?'

'It does not fascinate,' Harcla replied simply. 'It is the site of our summer headquarters, that is all.'

'Is that all? There are other pleasures there no doubt. Perhaps I should go with you and discover for myself.'

Harcla gazed at her and smiled again. The short rays of the star upon his cheek defined themselves in the sunlight and Emma's eyes were fixed there, as though in lament; an involuntary movement of her hand hid her own face.

'I should teach you to handle a knife more adroitly,' he said cruelly. 'Or perhaps I should ask Ketel to; he is the master technician, after all. And then I should not be scarred but dead.'

Emma's eyes filled with tears. 'You know my sorrow,' she said, 'and when people speak of it and ask how could such a thing be, and I know it was me! Andreas, it is unbearable!'

'My dearest love,' he said, brushing her tears with his fingers, 'forgive me. My face is for you to behold, as yours is mine – for aught else I care not.' He brought his hand to her arm, caressing the soft wool of her gown, and his fingers slid to hers among the cinquefoil in the grass.

'I love you,' Emma said, raising her free hand to his face.

152

Harcla looked upon the golden bed of cinquefoil that surrounded her and he was unmanned. 'I do not know how to answer, my lady,' he said quietly.

'But you should, Andreas!' she said, recovering her spirits. 'Are you slow of mind? Talk to me!'

'There is some good news,' said Harcla discursively. 'Although Clifford awaits my return he does not expect it for six days.'

'Well,' she cried happily, letting go for a moment, 'that is almost time undreamt of. An eternity.'

'A heavenly one,' Harcla said, kneeling before her, 'if it be with you.'

'Ah! That is better, my love,' she whispered. 'You are almost become a poet. Come, enthral me.'

~ 22 ~

TWO MEETINGS

THE next morning Harcla woke early. He pushed open the shutter of his window and looked out to the rising fells in the east. The bright disc of the sun soared above the long sharp ridges of the fells and made the morning break into life. Ketel, though, retained his slumbers and snored peacefully; Harcla stepped over him and walked lightly, quick with life, into the Great Hall.

He knew she would be there. She was standing by the fireplace, gazing into the last of the glowing embers. The folds of her long blue gown twirled as she turned to meet him and the movement made a scattering of the light dust of ash on the floor.

She coughed into the air and brought her hand to her mouth.

'Emma,' he said. 'My love, come with me.'

He led her through the outer rooms of the castle and into the bailey. He took her hand as they walked; he was staggered at the coolness of it. They stopped then and she turned to him, her hips swaying against his.

One of the boys from the stable brought two horses forward.

'Would you like to ride, my lady?' Harcla asked her.

She looked down to her feet and the awkward length of her robe. They both laughed.

'Emma,' he said, with great deference. 'You can lift it, can you not?'

'Surely,' she answered, 'but place your hands here, my lord, if you please.'

His hands formed a stirrup for her beside the horse and, raising her skirts, she leapt upon its back.

'Where are we going?' she asked, as they rode down the hill toward the river.

'Secret,' he replied, laughing again. 'But come, follow me if you can!'

He kicked his horse up the steep track to the great church and raced past it and out to the fields beyond. They followed the green road out to Winton Field and then turned to their left through a small wood that led them to the banks of the Eden once again.

154

They paused at the water's edge, by the ford, and looked up to the rippling stream where the Smardale beck ran into the bigger river; the surface of a great pool swirled there. They walked their horses to the middle of the river.

'I used to swim here when I was a boy,' he said.

'Do not allow my presence to deter you now,' Emma replied. 'But it is too cold for me.'

Harcla rode on to the far bank and jumped to the ground. He stripped quickly, ran to the raised edge and plunged into the clear pool. The rising sun caught the high arcs of water that rose and fell in his wake and they glistened momentarily, like shafts of coloured light through a prism.

The water was indeed cold and Harcla felt, in the darkness of the water, the muscles of his arms and legs tightening as he swam. He surfaced, breathing quickly and pushed for the shore.

'Andreas!' he heard Emma shout. 'You are mad. Come out!'

He thought indeed she spoke the truth and he scrambled up the bank, gripping the tussocks of grass. 'Emma!' he shouted over to her. 'That has cooled me!'

He dried himself with his burnet hose, which he then placed on the saddle of his horse to dry; he threw his tunic over his head and sat to pull on his boots.

Emma walked toward him. 'I hope it has not cooled your ardour also,' she said laughing.

He took her hand. 'Temporarily,' he answered. 'But come, Emma, walk with me.'

They tied the horses to a branch of an old rowan at the foot of the ford and followed the river northwards. The valley opened out here from the close presence of the fells and the rough pasture of the uplands had given way to gentler meadows and ripening fields of oats.

After a little while they became aware of a rising, warbling sound that began to fill the air as they walked; it was the shrill twittering and crying of birds, dozens of them, as they flew fluttering about the far bank of sand.

Emma gasped.

'What singing!' she cried, holding her ears. 'What birds are these?'

'They are known as riparia,' Harcla said. 'They have dug their nest-holes in the steep bank yonder. Can you see?'

He pointed to the vertical edge of sand.

'Yes,' she cried in delight, 'there are multitudes.'

'They are feeding their young,' Harcla said.

Some of the birds, flashing a brilliant white as they swooped in the air, dropped their wings and soared above the running water.

'Look!' said Emma. 'They glory in their flight.' She watched entranced. 'But what is riparia?' she asked him.

'The word means "those that live by the banks of rivers",' he answered.

'I should like to be riparia,' said Emma, gazing upon their freedom.

'You are,' Harcla said, 'and more beautiful because you are sentient.'

She clung to him then and kissed him. 'My love, my love,' she whispered. 'Are you mine?'

'I live for you,' he said.

In Durham, on the evening of the same day, Peter Claxton closed the door to the Chapter House quietly behind him. He watched his secretary Sylvester walk quickly across the lawn and through the outer archway. The dean followed him down the steep track leading to the city.

Sylvester's long canonical robe marked him out easily as he moved among others on the road. He passed two novitiates panting their way up the hill, and he stopped for a few moments, chatting with them. The dean halted behind the corner of a town house and waited for him to continue his journey.

After a little while Sylvester waved a goodbye to his young friends and strode on into the heart of the city. He crossed some busy streets and turned right into a dirty lane toward the river. It was quieter here, the only sound the squawking of gulls as they circled above the water.

A series of timber wharves had been built out from the bank, and, lying alongside these, the long cargo boats for carrying grain to the northern garrisons were at their moorings; they moved slightly in the tidal swell of the river.

In the shadows of a storehouse by the most distant wharf, one hundred yards away, a solitary cloaked horseman stood. Dusk was falling and heavy clouds gathered on the eastern skyline. Sylvester looked up from the muddy pools at his feet and saw the rider raise his arm in a salute; he withdrew a packet from his robe and hurried to meet him.

Peter Claxton, wanting to doubt his eyes until this last moment, accepted now, as he watched, that his trusted secretary was a traitor. The calamity of this conviction broke like the hastening storm in his brain and he ran forward, his sandals squelching in the muddy path.

He shouted out.

Sylvester, now thirty yards from the cloaked rider, turned to face the dean. His eyes were so full of anguish and guilt that Peter Claxton, as he approached, felt his heart soften and he reached out a hand to him.

'Sylvester,' he said, 'what are you doing?'

The canon's involuntary reaction to this discovery of his sin became masked now by a look that was mostly fearful. He glanced quickly behind him; he saw the rider nudge his horse into a slow walk toward them.

'I am a warrior too,' Sylvester cried out as he faced the dean once more. 'This is my way.'

'But, Sylvester!' said Claxton, aghast. 'You are acting the traitor.'

'Traitor? I am no traitor,' Sylvester said, gritting his teeth, 'I serve my king; as does my brother.'

The dean gazed on his secretary in great confusion. 'Your brother? And who is your brother?' he asked.

The rain began suddenly, in big heavy drops, and these fell and became a stream running down their faces.

Sylvester laughed wildly in the rain. 'You do not know my name, do you, Claxton?' he barked out, pushing the sodden strands of hair from his eyes.

The dean shook his head and then reached out purposefully to grab the packet, but Sylvester stepped back and raised it above his head; they wrestled clumsily, like boys.

'My name, you fool,' Sylvester shouted into his ear, 'is Randolph!'

The cloaked rider came up quickly. He snatched the packet from his conspirator's outstretched hand and with his other hand he withdrew a knife from his belt. He leant down to the dean, who was still held awkwardly in Sylvester's arms as if they were embracing, and he plunged it deep into his back.

Peter Claxton fell to the wet ground, an awful disbelief etched into the gaze of his dying eyes.

'You, Sylvester, are the fool,' said the rider hoarsely. 'Else I need not have killed him. Now throw him in the river and be gone.' He kicked his horse hard and galloped up the lane and out of sight.

Sylvester stood as though his life too had emptied itself and he gazed down at the body at his feet. He began to cry, like a child lost in the world, and his tears mingled with the rain upon his cheeks.

~ 23 ~

WINE FROM SPAIN

Harcla returned to Wark on the appointed day; as he rode, with Ketel, into the bailey of the castle, Henry of Appleby ran out to tell him that Lord Clifford desired an immediate interview.

'You carry on, Ketel,' Harcla said smiling, 'and renew old acquaintances; the others of our company will be eager for news of home.'

When Harcla entered Clifford's apartment he saw his friend pacing the room.

'Sit down, Andreas,' the earl said quietly.

Harcla walked over to the high window, to his favourite seat. His hand brushed along the shoulder of the chair and he saw the small horizontal tears in the dark sindon cloth.

'A body was fished out of the Wear at Durham four days ago,' Clifford said abruptly. 'It was Monseigneur the Dean, your brother's friend.'

The shock made Harcla shift forward in his seat. 'Drowned?' he asked quickly, as though he feared a worse death.

'No, not drowned, Andreas. He was knifed first.'

'Jesu!'

Clifford moved over to the table and poured two cups of wine from the flagon that stood there; he thrust one into Harcla's hand. 'I was greatly troubled by his last letter,' Clifford said, sitting down. 'It smelled of danger. You were not here and I should have sent Leyburne to him.'

Harcla was silent, staring at the wall behind the earl's head.

'There is more,' Clifford went on. 'His secretary, a white canon by the name of Sylvester, had been found hanged in his cell a few hours earlier.'

Harcla listened intently and his friend continued. 'Apparently, he had not appeared for matins and a search was made.'

'I met this man,' Harcla said. 'And this was suicide?'

'Almost certainly. The door was bolted from the inside; they had to break it to enter.'

'My God!'

'There can be no doubt that he was the informant. The Dean must have surprised him and his messenger at a rendezvous by the river.'

'Peter should not have gone,' Harcla said.

'No, of course he shouldn't! Damn fool of a priest! God's blood, what a messy business! The archbishop is making enquiries into the whole affair; I suppose I had better go to him and explain our involvement.'

Clifford paused and watched Harcla, whose gaze now was fixed on the white clouds as they moved slowly in the upper air.

'He must have been overcome with remorse,' Harcla said, 'and then took his own life.'

'There is yet one more piece of the jigsaw,' Clifford went on. 'It transpires that Sylvester's family name is Randolph; he was brother to the earl of Moray, a nephew of Bruce himself! Is it not incredible?'

'I imagine Sylvester believed he served his true king.'

'I imagine he did!' Clifford said sarcastically. 'But at least we have solved our riddle.'

'And the solution come with the deaths of two priests.'

'There were other deaths, Andreas,' he said. 'Do not forget our convoys and garrisons in Scotland. Well, there should be no more errant reports. Christ! Of course, Sylvester must have been responsible for the great garrison at Liddesdale.'

'Yes, and I thought Antoigne had deliberately misled you about that.'

Clifford looked across to Harcla. 'Harcla,' he replied seriously, 'a private enmity is one thing – but do not let such issues cloud your judgement; that is a dangerous road.' Clifford was annoyed and thought his lieutenant in need of this reproach.

'Yes, my lord,' Harcla answered, as though in admission, yet there remained some nagging doubt.

The two men drank in silence and Clifford filled their cups.

'I feel a responsibility for this death,' said Harcla with sadness. 'He was a good man.'

'I shall write to Henry for you Andreas, if you wish.'

'Thank you Robert, but no, I should write.'

'As you please,' said the earl. 'And yes, I am sorry too. But we have snared our prey and finished him – which was our intent.' He looked to the empty flagon and called for Henry. 'Have you eaten, Harcla?'

'No, my lord.'

'Then dine with me,' Clifford cried. 'And come, don't slouch. Drink your wine! Henry! Henry!'

Under Henry's supervision the kitchens of Robert le Ros, the warden of the castle, treated them well and the two men dined privately on larks roasted in butter and coriander, a sweet fruit pie made of cream, eggs and dates within a hot pastry and a broiled salmon which they ate with warmed oat cakes, all washed down with a second quart of Bordeaux.

A couple of hours later, after the third, Clifford pushed back his chair and rose unsteadily to his feet. 'I have a special wine for you to savour now,' he said thickly, moving toward the window-space with an exaggerated care.

Harcla watched him as he walked, affecting a ridiculously high stepping action, as though he were wading through a river. Clifford's return journey to their table seemed to take longer, perhaps he was against the current, and he carried in both hands a large beautifully shaped silver flagon; he had left this by the window so that the wine within it might catch the last of the warmth of the sun. 'Drinking temperature, Harcla,' the earl said, with great seriousness, 'is an important consideration, too often neglected.'

He placed the flagon, almost indeed a ewer, with absurd care, upon the table, and plunged a finger into the dark liquid. 'Blood heat,' he announced with satisfaction and poured the wine.

Harcla, in a warm and ambrosial state himself, regarded these ministrations with a silent hilarity that he struggled to check.

'Wine should be savoured,' Clifford said disingenuously. He raised the cup to his nostrils in order to enjoy the aroma of the wine, and he swirled it, a little too eagerly, for some sloshed out and the drops of it fell from the tip of his nose.

'What you are about to drink,' the earl said, wiping his face unperturbed, 'is a wonderful example, it is indeed the superior, the best example, the best I ever tasted of Garnacha!'

Harcla's fight against his mirth collapsed and he laughed freely, and very happily; the only sounds from him were great gurgles of laughter. 'Garna..what?' he gasped out, pushing the tears from his eyes. 'I have never heard of it; but, Robert, it is very good indeed! Ha ha ha.'

The earl drank off his cup and smacked his lips, forgetful of his own advice; he watched his young lieutenant in unrestrained laughter, holding his sides, almost in pain.

Clifford re-filled their cups and he began to laugh too.

'Ha Ha Ha,' Clifford laughed back.

It seemed to Harcla then that he was the luckiest of men; the luck that made him Clifford's friend, almost a son. Who else would have trusted him so? And what amazing fortune that he and Emma lived in the world!

He knew that life was good.

Henry and Ketel, standing behind the door, overheard the great hilarity and shook their heads.

Harcla, ready to share confidences, sat back in great ease. He thought of their conversation on the road to Boroughbridge, and his prickly defensiveness then. Was that in another life, he wondered?

He said: 'Robert, I wish to marry.'

'Marry!' Clifford exclaimed; he spilled more of his wine and he brushed the drops from his tunic. 'Marry who? Or do you need to say?'

'My lady Emma la Frraunceise,' Harcla admitted.

'Ahh! Our lovely Emma!' said Clifford, his eyes glazing over. 'I should introduce myself, should I not? And if she is as beautiful as her mother Alice then you have a great prize!'

Harcla considered this comparison in silence. Clifford, for his part, felt ancient precious secrets bubbling unstoppably onto his lips. He poured the wine incautiously.

'Alice was my love, Andreas,' he said, the words rushing out. 'Did you know that?'

'I did not, my lord,' replied he, wondering at the connection but plunging anyway into his own question. 'I wanted to ask you about a living.'

'What do you mean? You do not have a living.'

'Precisely so, my lord, but I shall need one.'

'Well, Hartley will, on your father's death, pass to John and his heirs; and even if he die childless, then it will be Henry's. Andreas, you must seek your own way.'

'I know that well enough. But what can I look towards?'

Clifford, in a paternal love, rose to his feet. 'There are manors I can bestow Andreas, at the blessing of the king.' Clifford paused and rubbed his chin; he swayed a little. 'Pendragon may be vacant soon,' he said.

'Win your victories,' the earl continued, 'and the king, like a pet cow, will feed from your hand.' He reached for his wine and rambled on, 'for that is what he is, after all – a bloody queen not a king, and easily led by whoever holds the halter. Christ, it makes me sick! I should have joined Bruce when I had the chance; would you have come with me, Harcla? God's blood! The north would be ours, we would be unstoppable!'

This was too much for Harcla; his brain swirled and he closed his eyes.

Clifford brought himself up and tried to clear his head; he looked at his lieutenant, asleep in the chair, his head nodding on his chest. The cup of wine, held between Harcla's two hands, was balanced on his belly.

Clifford took the cup and drank it off. 'Bah! These young ones cannot drink,' he muttered happily to himself. 'Even this one!' He sat back pleasurably, his mind in a haze, and he fell into a deep sodden sleep.

~ 24 ~

THE GREAT MARCH

September of the year began dry and warm, an extension of the late hot summer. The fields of oats and wheat were tall and full and the people, with one eye fixed on the eastern skies, spoke with a guarded confidence of the harvest to come. The barns and field-houses of the country, if they were like those of Hartley, would be already filled with a heavy crop of hay for the stock to grow fat on in the winter, and if the wheat were cut as bountifully as the grass then food for men and women would also be plentiful, as they looked to the bleak months that lay beyond this mellow bliss of autumn.

It was the time of year too when troubled captains of war were forced to embark upon their late campaigns; for, as autumn turned to winter, there would be no growth of grass for the horses and no fresh game that the fighting men of their armies might hunt. This was also their last chance to march; an army, by design, must travel and the roads it travelled, where they existed at all in this northern kingdom, would deteriorate badly as the storms and blizzards of winter began.

Edward of England was conscious of these things and full of hope when, on September 23, near the town of Selkirk, he looked out on the dry autumn road and the waving fields of corn beside it. The road led down to the great river Tweed and the border with Scotland and the walls of his newly erected tower there shone white in the sunshine; from its tall ramparts the Plantagenet banner of three lions flew.

When Edward rode into Selkirk at the forefront of his army such was its size that the last columns of it were a distance of four miles behind him; Clifford's two hundred Westmorland levies had been placed here and among them was the core of his summer force from Wark.

The camp was well established by the time the rearguard marched through the town and down to the meadows alongside the Ettrick Water. Ketel and Harcla looked upon the huge array of tents and bivouacs of the army as they rode along and they saw, in the evening sunlight, the bright banners of the earls and knights hoisted on tall poles and fluttering in the air. The great standard of the king soared above all by a large tented pavilion close to the town.

As they rode through the meadow they passed a banner displaying the three hungry pike of Lucy. Sir Antoigne himself was in conversation with one of his lieutenants and he looked up, nodding a greeting. His man, Threlkeld, followed his master's gaze and raised his head too and then scowled as he recognised our friends; he muttered something under his breath and Antoigne laughed, spreading his feet surely on the grass.

'I hope, Harcla,' Lucy called out with a smile, like the mocking Achilles, 'that you are recovered after our exertions at Liddesdale.'

Harcla's face hardened. 'Our exertions, Antoigne?' he said laconically. 'I had forgotten you were there; a simple mistake.'

Lucy's face coloured immediately and he brought himself up. 'By Christ, Harcla,' cried he, stung into indiscretions, 'I could have made it much worse for you!'

Harcla, shocked at this admission, halted, pulling sharply on the reins, and he looked down upon him. 'Have a care, Antoigne,' he said bleakly, 'for I care not for thee at all.' He wheeled his horse about and rode on.

Lucy shouted after him: 'We should meet this campaign, in the lists. The king is thinking of a tourney at Biggar. Can you fight without a woman at your elbow?'

Threlkeld sniggered.

Harcla turned to Ketel. 'Christ!' he said. 'I should kill that snake before his venom become fatal.'

They rode on through the camp, through the busy noises of men and horses and beasts for slaughter. Everywhere the knights' vallets were unsaddling the war-horses, throwing off the linen covers and brushing down their glistening flanks. There were soldiers erecting tents, feeding fires, polishing shields and waxing swords and daggers; messengers raced between the pavilions of the great lords.

Other men, dark haired and swarthy, stood in the long grass by the riverbank; some of them lounged at their ease, dipping their toes in the running water. They spoke together in Welsh and were handling long bows as though they were natural extensions of their arms. A couple of targets had been erected at this lower end of the field and these were prickly with feathered flights, like the upright backs of hedgehogs. These men, strangers to the northern militia, laughed among themselves and shouted guttural bravos as each arrow thudded into the straw.

Amid this great activity were the sounds of many snarling dogs, the mewling of sheep and the lowing of cattle.

Ketel pointed to a clear area of land, marked out by four stakes and

164

with Clifford's crest flying between them; it was a good site, on flat land, away from the trees. Henry of Appleby was sitting upon the grass in the centre of this space. His back rested on the flagstaff and to this were tethered a dozen fat lambs; they bleated mildly and chewed on the grass by his feet. Henry seemed to be sleeping in spite of this, and the louder noises around him.

'You make a poor guardsman, Henry,' said Harcla, riding up.

'My lord!' Henry cried, starting at once. 'You have arrived at last! I have spent these two hours watching your place; and no easy job, I promise you!'

'Tell the truth, Henry,' Ketel said, laughing. 'You were asleep, were you not? Guarding nothing but these lambs, and they are tethered!'

Henry would have laughed with his friend but he coloured a little because of Harcla's presence. 'My lord,' he said, abashed.

Harcla pointed to the sheep. 'These are our supper, are they?'

'Sir Robert has acquired them in your behalf certainly.'

'Well, you must thank him for me,' Harcla replied. 'Henry, what is this news of a tourney?'

'Yes, my lord, it appears the king thought it good that his knights rediscover their martial prowess. Some are grown rusty, I know my lord Robert believes so too.'

'That may well be. Thank you, Henry, for keeping our placement.'

'Please, my lord, Sir Robert asked me to tell you that he is at the pavilion, in council with the king. He will speak with you later this evening.'

'Good!' Harcla cried. 'The world is brighter already! Eh, Ketel?' He issued his orders regarding the making of their encampment and then threw himself upon the grass by the river, studying the Welsh bowmen at their play.

He stretched out and cradled his head on his inter-locked hands; after a while his gaze wandered, rising through the trees to the blue of sky beyond them. In the west, behind a low ridge of fells, one half of the sun was still visible – a semi-circular disc so bright his eyes could not rest upon it. But its light transformed the branches and leaves into golden things that yet retained their greenness, like slender stems of fruit, and what danced there, as they swayed in the evening air, was the image of the woman he loved.

Of Harcla's summer force at Wark, two – John de Harcla and Richard la Fraunceise – now held commands of their own companies, under

Castre and Clifford respectively; among the others James, recently recovered from the wound he received at Horsley Pele, Ketel, Conan and Alexander rode with him as before. These men were considered hardened warriors by Uther's young troop of twelve horsemen, whose average age was about eighteen years; they had joined Harcla at Wark on the Nativity of the Virgin, along with the many thousands of others who rode and marched to the great muster of Edward's army.

The castles and manor-houses of the English borderlands were now cleared, almost entirely, of their fighting men; and this was done so that Edward might lead his ten thousand into Scotland. The mood though among the knights of the army, their men-at-arms and multitudes of foot-soldiers was blithe; laughter and good humour ran through the thick line of the marching host like a benign contagion. Even Clifford, accounted the great pessimist, could not help but think that perhaps he had been wrong as he looked out on the fantastic power gathering at Wark - the two thousand knights, brilliant and deadly in the sun, and the ranks upon ranks, an infinite number it seemed, of the foot – their long pikes thrust over their many shoulders – the whole army looked like an enormous glittering, scaly snake.

And now, having reached Selkirk, the king summoned Clifford and his greater captains to conference, to be followed by a supper later in the evening. The issue at hand was one of direction – which road into Scotland should the army follow in order to take Robert the Bruce?

Discovering the movements of the Scottish king was proving difficult for no two reports were alike; one piece of intelligence put him at Stirling, a second at Linlithgow and a third at Dunbarton on the Clyde. Edward could not understand this disparity and began to doubt the integrity of his scouts.

His policy so far had been an agreeable one in tracking the line of his border strongholds along the Tweed – they made for safe and comfortable resting places. But now he was at a crossing of roads, he must break northward or continue confidently the line of march westward through the Ettrick Forest to the Lothians; the forest and the lands around it were well-known as wild and lawless places, the haunt of Bruce's bands of irregular cavalry, his independents – to Edward's mind, of course, these men were mere outlaws and beneath consideration.

The generals of the king's army, seated pleasurably around his high table, debated the alternatives with light hearts. No one could truly say which road would take them to Bruce more speedily, but they were all happy in the belief of inevitable success; it was simply a matter of patience, time would bring its reward. The king himself seemed determined on the western road and the town of Biggar for his next headquarters.

Only Clifford argued strongly, and he spoke for the northern route; it was less hazardous, he said, not knowing what might be encountered in the west.

'Ah, my lord!' the king replied. 'You misdoubt my strategy. Turning north now would spoil our chances. What if Bruce lies westward, in Clydesdale? It would be easy for him to take us unaware.'

'He could do that anyway,' Clifford reasoned, 'no matter where he be.'

Edward showed some signs of impatience with his Lord of the Marches, his fingers tapped upon the table and his stare was harsh. 'Sir Robert,' he said crossly, and glancing at Gaveston for support, 'you are becoming known as a purveyor of gloom. Do not ruin our supper with this cheerless talk. Bruce is afeared and we shall soon destroy him.'

Several knights, sitting at the tables close by, stopped their chatter and turned their heads the better to hear the king's rebuke.

'God's glory!' Edward continued, more loudly now. 'You have been pestering me these three years to mount this campaign – and the moment we embark upon it you urge restraint. I fail to understand you.'

This argument was hard to resist and Clifford fell silent.

Gaveston smiled secretly then and executed his revenge for Harcla's clever remarks at their first meeting. He turned to the King. 'Perhaps, sire,' he said with relish, 'some few of Clifford's esteemed company might ride ahead for us, the better to procure more accurate intelligence.'

Edward laughed. 'Excellent, my dear Piers!' replied he, patting Gaveston's shoulder. 'You solve two problems in the one throw!' The king glanced across to Clifford. 'Well, my lord earl,' he said, 'what say you to that?'

'I await your commands, sire.'

'Good! Then see to it.' The King laughed again and turned away.

Clifford bowed his head. Those nearest to him dropped their glance and he, companionless, looked around the lower tables where eighty picked knights of the army sat at their leisure; they were joking among themselves and talking light-heartedly, probably recounting tales of the earlier Scottish wars. The age of most, he saw, was not more than thirty years; and I grow old, he thought to himself, wondering what he should prize.

Some of these knights would not have met for a long time; it was four

167

years since an English army had marched this far north and twelve years for one of this size – the time of the ride to victory at Falkirk in 1298. The final reckoning had come at last, they were saying to one another. All were merry, and fearless in their strength.

Clifford's melancholy gaze fell further out, to the younger knights. He saw Harcla at one of the long trestles, almost opposite Lucy; their vallets, Ketel and Threlkeld, stood and stared at each other above their masters' heads, across the wide board. The two knights were conversing with friends among them and each did not look upon the other. Clifford frowned at this but then thought to himself that they were, after all, as unlike as the fox to the wolf.

Fraunceise was seated at Harcla's right and waited on by Conan. He was speaking clearly, as was his wont, in a voice that carried easily over the lower tables. The general conversation had drifted into discussions of women and Fraunceise, always eager to display his lettered education, discoursed happily on the independent nature of the women of Troy in ancient times.

'There was a young girl,' Sir Richard related, 'whose name was Cresside, and renowned for her beauty. Her uncle and guardian, a vile unscrupulous man, upbraided her for knowing her own mind too well, for she would not accept his choices of a husband. These men did not please her, for various good reasons; one was too old, another ugly and a third over much like Ganymede.'

'Ganymede?' Antoigne interrupted. 'Who or what was Ganymede?'

'A catamite,' answered Fraunceise.

'Ahh!'

Sir Richard smiled and went on, 'The uncle rose in a mad temper and shouted at her: "You are such a woman! One knows not at what ward you lie." Cresside replied, and hark to this! "Upon my back, to defend my belly; upon my wit, to defend my wiles; upon my secrecy, to defend mine honesty; my mask, to defend my beauty: and at all these wards I lie, at a thousand watches."'

Fraunceise sat back. 'Quelle femme!' he said admiringly of his young heroine.

Musgrave leaned over to Lucy and whispered: 'Why must we listen to this trash?'

Lucy put his cup upon the board and glanced across to Fraunceise. 'Are you, in fact, discussing your own niece?' he asked neutrally. 'I do not know her but some of my men have had the pleasure.'

Musgrave cackled into his wine and behind him, Threlkeld's face darkened.

John de Harcla, with Alexander at his back, muttered something about Sir Richard's love of melodrama. Kelleth remained silent but glanced across to Conan, then his eyes slid toward Threlkeld. He watched Threlkeld's hand move slowly, nervously toward his belt. The eyes of Lucy's lieutenant were rancorous and betrayed his mind for it turned on the humiliation at Crosby two years before.

'Of course,' Fraunceise continued blithely, 'Trojan women, famous for their beauty, were also warlike. It was not unknown for them to aid their warriors in battle; but fighting with a woman must present some difficulties. It depends, I'm sure, on the nature of one's attachment to the female.' He looked around at his audience. 'If those sentiments are of an affectionate leaning then one's actions must be hampered by an over-protectiveness.'

John de Harcla shook his head and Lucy smiled as he sipped his wine.

'Well, take my niece then...' Fraunceise said carelessly.

'Christ!' Harcla broke in. 'Richard, that's enough.'

Fraunceise, disturbed in his philosophies, turned across all unaware.

'Have you had the pleasure, Harcla?' Antoigne said salaciously. Threlkeld smirked, staring at Ketel in the silence.

Harcla's blood rushed to his face and he coloured as he rose from the table; but his voice as he spoke was steady. 'Be good enough to follow me outside, Lucy,' he said quietly. 'We should not disturb our friends.'

Harcla, accompanied by Ketel, walked to the doorway; the canvas folds of it ruffled a little in the evening air and Harcla's hair brushed against them as he stooped to quit the pavilion. He nodded to the trooper on duty there and strode towards the river.

'At last!' Ketel said to his master as they walked down the hill. 'I wondered how much you would take.'

Harcla said nothing.

A minute later Lucy and Threlkeld also left their places at the table and followed the two men outside.

Twilight had come and the small fires of the camp burned brightly; the smells of charred meat and its burnt fat hovered in the heavy air about the fires, and the enlightened air around them was thick with moths and midges from the river; they were as dark clouds in miniature circling the heat of many little suns.

When Ketel and Harcla reached the long grass by the river, beyond the last of the fires, they turned and looked back to these oases of light and saw the figures of two others moving towards them.

Harcla undid the clasp of his cloak and Ketel caught it as it fell from his shoulders; he withdrew his sword, the one Uther had forged for him, and swung it in the slow-moving air, flexing the muscles of his wrist. The sword was lighter, much narrower at the hilt and flattening to a sharper point, like an elongated dagger.

'Parry too often, my lord, and it will splinter,' said Ketel depreciatingly. 'It has no solidity – do not defend too much.'

Harcla nodded his thanks. 'I do not intend to,' he answered.

Lucy appeared out of the hazes of light and stopped five or six yards from his enemies. He looked around him. 'It grows dark, Harcla,' he said.

'It matters not to me.'

'Perhaps we should await the morning.'

'I have waited long enough.'

'I only wish to see you the better,' Lucy's voice grated out, 'as you grovel.' He smoothly produced his broad sword and held it out straight, the line of sight along its length to enter Harcla's throat.

'Your speech is distasteful, Antoigne, like rotten meat in my mouth.'

'Oh, you are so proud!' Lucy spat out, 'I puke at your arrogance. Who are you anyway? Upstart! Worm of manure! – you and the miserable band of peasants which admires your every step.' His hatred poured out of him, unfastened by the darkness. 'I puke on you and that thin wench, who puts me in mind of a skinned cat....

'Shut thy mouth,' Harcla answered, sick in his stomach. 'Blood will settle this.' He waved his sword at Threlkeld who had stepped forward, loosening the long dagger at his belt. 'And keep your man back, for he is a cur too. Is he your bastard brother? He carries the same reptilian traits.'

Threlkeld, maddened and lacking any cogent thought, lunged at Harcla; Lucy was incensed as he saw this breach of the etiquette of combat and shouted at him to stay back but Ketel's knife had already flown from his hand and, spinning in the firelight, it sank into Threlkeld's breast.

Lucy's man fell back in the grass with his sword arm still outstretched as he attempted to rise.

'I have another delivery for you, should you wish,' Ketel shouted, and he pulled out the second of his three daggers.

Harcla glanced upon Threlkeld sitting in the grass as though at his ease, but with the four inch hilt protruding incongruously from his jerkin.

Lucy leapt forward with a terrible cry on his lips, his heavy sword was high above his head, and he swept it down and across to hew at Harcla's neck. Harcla watched the blade as it clove the air toward him; he waited interminably and then stepped lightly to his left, dropping to his haunches and deflecting the thick edge of it into the ground; Lucy made a loud grunting sound with the effort.

Ketel caught a movement in the corner of his eye and he looked round and saw another figure, that of the earl of Westmorland, emerge from the haze of firelight and walk towards them in the water meadows. 'Holy Jesus!' he muttered.

Clifford was yelling at them as he approached. 'Harcla! Lucy! Pardieu! What are you at?' In a violent rage he threw himself between the two knights, parting them roughly with the edge of his sword.

'Christ in heaven!' he bawled, looking around him quickly. 'Fools! You bring disgrace upon me as well as upon yourselves.' His eyes fell to the ground where he saw Threlkeld, grey in the face and panting. 'Ketel, help that man. My God.....is he dying? Get away from here. Return to your tents; I shall speak to you both later.'

The two knights, in complete silence, sheathed their swords, drew their cloaks about them and walked away.

Clifford seethed as he watched them go. 'And this is how I am repaid,' he said to himself.

Ketel was forced to help Threlkeld up the hill alone; the vallets slipped and staggered in the dewy grass, with one arm around the other's shoulder as though they were born friends stumbling home from a boosy supper.

~ 25 ~

ETTRICK FOREST

THE small group of men rode slowly in the forest. It was the evening of their third day from Selkirk; the weather had turned these last days and the cool easterly wind brought light rains that slanted in upon their backs. When the clouds lifted and the rain stopped they took down their hoods but large drops fell in streams from the dying leaves above them, where they had lain; this seemed itself like a heavier rain and it soaked them.

They rode in single file and Harcla was the foremost; he raised his arm for what seemed to the company the twentieth time that day and called a halt. He pulled out Ambrose's chart from his jerkin and studied it wearily from the saddle. Ketel peered over his shoulder.

Behind these two the whispers of the men grew until Uther rode alongside them and asked: 'Where are we, my lord?'

Harcla looked at him sharply. 'God in Heaven!' he barked out. 'Do you think me omniscient? And tell those men there to stop their bleating.' He jerked a finger behind him, adding: 'Christ! They crow like old women!'

They were stopped in a clearing of the forest; the path they had followed thus far became three before them and Harcla pondered his route. The huge beech and oak towered above, allowing partial glimpses of the heavy grey sky. On the ground the many dead leaves, like fragments of yellowing parchments, lay upon others of lost autumns and were stacked in moist layers on the floor of the forest.

The horses' hooves, as they had trudged through the westward path, had trodden on mulch – flattened by the steps of previous horses. The onward road was the same while those paths to the left and right were untouched and knee high in rotting leaves.

'We must travel on,' Harcla said finally. 'Come, it cannot be far now. This forest must end!'

He was looking for the township of Biggar and planned to rest there that night in the abbey of Saint Mary. The company had passed the last two nights in the open and all were anxious to avoid a third. At Biggar Harcla was ordered to split his company in two, sending Uther and four troopers southward, to sweep the country in a wide loop before rejoining the army at Treskeir or Kirkord. Harcla and his own party were to ride on into Clydesdale as far as Renfrew, taking as long as it may.

If either group learned of any news of Bruce, his army, or any gatherings of men led by Randolph, Edward de Bruce or Douglas then a rider was to be sent back to report the intelligence to Gaveston and the king. It was anticipated that in this manner some five or six of the company of ten would, at different times, be hurrying to the safety of the army as it made its laborious snail-like way through the Lothians.

This plan was Clifford's, at the command of the King, and he informed Harcla of it late in the evening of the twenty-third, after he had surprised his protégées in their duel.

'So that you may know where we shall be,' the earl had said,' the King plans to rest at Treskeir on the twenty-eighth, Kirkord on the twenty-ninth and arrive in Biggar on the thirtieth.

'We shall despatch riders as we march along our western road; they will scout just two or three miles ahead of the army. But you, Harcla, will always be several days before us – your reports therefore are of great importance, without them the army marches blind.' He stopped for a moment. 'Do not forget this,' he added, 'as you have forgotten other things.'

Clifford waited for Harcla to answer, but his lieutenant looked down at his feet, and did not attempt to make any excuses, or blame honour, but he could not see how he might have acted differently; he knew anyhow that Clifford would have done the very same.

'Do you hear me, Harcla?' the earl asked crossly. Clifford tapped the hilt of his sword impatiently and he said, as though still betrayed: 'Now get out of my sight!'

Harcla kicked his horse into a walk and Ketel, glancing over his shoulder, caught the eyes of Conan, Alexander and James as they raised their sodden heads. Ketel smiled. 'We are nearly there,' he said to them quietly.

Uther fell back to his four troopers, two of whom were our young friends Thomas of Howgill and Patrick of Blande. 'We are nearly there,' he said in a loud whisper. 'Patience! You are soldiers now.'

'Quiet!' Harcla called out over his shoulder. 'Good God! Give me peace!' They rode on in a silence heightened by the separate dripping of the rain and the wet swishing of branches in their wake.

They reached the haven of Saint Mary's at Biggar one hour later as night fell. The company was offered an outlying dormitory of the abbey, a part of which was already occupied by a small party of white friars. Harcla accepted the room happily and his men hurried to its shelter and the warmth of its fire. Thomas and Patrick, being youngest, were given the duty of the horses.

The others stripped themselves of their soaked gear and threw it upon wooden racks suspended from the roof beams above the hearth. They stood naked in front of the fire delighting in its heat; the steam rose from their bodies and clothes and soon the dormitory seemed like the sauna room of a Roman bathhouse.

When they were again clothed one of the friars came across and spoke to Harcla as he sat in an ingle, staring out into the darkness.

'You have travelled far, my son?' asked he in a deep Lowland accent.

Harcla looked up to him. 'We left the King at Selkirk three days ago,' he answered.

'The King?' questioned the friar, and his eyes smiled mischievously. 'Do you mean Robert or Edward?'

'Father, I should not need to answer that.'

'No, of course, forgive me. You mean Edward, naturally; besides Robert the Bruce is at Dunbarton – or at least he was two days ago – and now he is to break north to Stirling.'

Harcla was astonished at this barrage of information. 'Should you be telling me this?' he asked.

'Ahh! My son, the whole world knows it.'

'The whole world may but King Edward does not.'

'People say he is simple; perhaps they are right, after all. Speaking for myself, I have never met him.'

'Have you met King Robert?' de Harcla asked, intrigued.

'Indeed I have. And there is a man of different mettle altogether.' The friar's eyes glazed over in rapture, as though he witnessed a beatific vision. 'He is not as other men,' he said. 'His gaze is unanswerable! His eyes are glints of steel.' He looked down suddenly as Harcla raised his head to listen the better.

'They are not unlike your own, my son,' he said at last, 'although he does not carry your blemish. Is it a flower or a star?'

'And should I know? You are the one gazing upon it.'

The friar laughed. 'You are not like most English we see,' he said. 'Where are you from, child?'

'A place called Hartley, many miles from here.'

'Hartley? Hartley?' the friar pondered slowly. 'I have heard that name. Is it your own?' he asked once more.

'It is.'

'Are you Andreas?'

'I am.'

He laughed again. 'May Mary bless my soul! Andreas de Harcla!'

Ketel, as was his duty, was sitting close by, and as he heard these words he came up to stand by his master.

'My lords Edward and Randolph have spoken of your worth,' the friar said. 'King Robert would wish to meet you, I know.'

'Father,' Harcla replied, 'you should take more care in what you say to the world.'

'I am a simple priest, nothing more. You should pity my rustic speech – if I have offended please forgive me.'

Harcla laughed in turn. 'You are a clever man; well-chosen for your role, I guess. Give King Robert my greetings. I admire him but I am not his man.'

'At least not yet,' returned the friar quietly and he walked away, pulling at the white folds of his robe.

Ketel watched him go and then turned to Harcla. 'He presumes much, that man of God,' he said.

Harcla smiled at his guardian. 'I thought you placed all trust in priests, Ketel.'

'Not in priests entirely, my lord; in God, yes. There is over much of politics in priests, I think.'

'Are you become a philosopher?' Harcla laughed, 'like my lord Fraunceise. He will be pleased to have such a diligent pupil!'

'Ha! My lord,' replied Ketel, pulling a face. 'I hope I am never so wearisome!'

They both laughed again and Ketel was turning to the others by the fire when Harcla, made frank by the friendliness of their banter, called him back. 'But that priest, Ketel, in politics or no, offered a choice – now which road would you travel?'

'Road?' Ketel answered simply, 'It matters not the road; the journeying itself is an end to me.'

Harcla was greatly struck at this. 'I love thee much, my friend,' he said, 'perhaps the greatest, apart from one other – which, by her sex, is made different.'

Ketel, honoured and confounded by this speech, gazed into the spaces by the roof beams, where their cloaks hung. 'I have told you before, my lord,' he said distinctly, 'I walk your road and always shall.

The others also – I tell you this truthfully.'

   'The others?'

   'Yes, all! Even Fraunceise and your brothers, and lately Uther too.'

   'Ketel, you do not know what you are saying!'

   'With respect, my lord. We have all talked of this; all of us together.' He laughed, a little self-consciously. 'We ride with you.'

   And this time Ketel did move away, leaving Harcla by the window-space to resume his long staring into the mirk of the night.

26

THE WESTWARD ROAD

As dawn broke James de Harcla rose, breakfasted quickly and gathered his pack together. He was to ride back to Edward's army with the news the Scots friar had told Harcla of.

'Do not tarry, James,' Harcla said to him as he made ready to depart. 'Go first to Treskeir; if Clifford is not there then ride on to Selkirk. You will carry no written message, in case.....' he paused unhappily. 'Good God! You know why. You have memorised what I said to you?'

'Yes, Andreas. I have it etched in my mind.'

'Ride fast, little brother.'

'Do not worry,' James replied smiling. 'I shall be like the wind.'

Harcla smiled in turn and waved as his brother rode out from the abbey and down the muddy track they had travelled the day before. He considered then his father's anxiety and wondered if James were naturally unlucky, an unfortunate trait in a warrior; he began to think he should not have sent him.

As the morning drew on the cold rain came again and the others of the company sighed as they left the warmth of their dormitory. It was a parting of ways for them too and Uther, conscious of Harcla's longer road, said that one of his men should ride with him.

'We shall be back with the King in two days at most,' he said. 'But thou, my lord, journey unknown ways.'

Each man had put on his waxed over-cloak and the horses, trampling in the mud outside the stabling, twitched their heads in the rain.

'Take Thomas,' Uther said.

Harcla nodded and glanced across to Howgill; he was smiling beneath his hood, from where wiry tufts of hair escaped.

'Very well, Uther,' Harcla said. 'As you say, I may need more riders.'

They looked out to the rounded hills in the south, the tops of them swathed in mist. 'Are you sure of your route, Uther?' Harcla asked him.

'Of course,' answered he. 'At least, I am surer than thou must be of thine. Take care, my lord; Clifford should not have sent thee.'

Harcla laughed, thinking only such a one as Uther would dare say that. 'The task would fall on someone,' he said. 'I am happy enough – and besides, who is there else to trust?'

They said their farewells then and Uther and his three rode off. They would travel as far south as Moffat before turning northeast to rejoin Edward's army on its trail through the valley of the Tweed.

Harcla's company turned westward. The Scots friar, who had stood watching them by a doorway of the abbey, shouted out a farewell as they rode away. Harcla waved an arm in reply; he felt young, confused as to the placings of trust.

In these upper reaches of the Clyde the river meandered greatly and the small group forded it three times that morning; thereafter they were able to follow its course more closely and in the afternoon the widening river was always visible down to their right through banks of trees.

By their fewer number Harcla had been forced to alter his favoured riding formation of a solid chevron; it now resembled the inverted symbol of the female – himself in front, Ketel directly behind and in the third rank Conan, Thomas and Alexander. Ketel's bow was ready strung and he carried the length of it crosswise upon the pommel of his saddle.

They had skirted the town of Lanark some two hours after leaving Biggar and were now riding easy ground where Ambrose's map showed a castle named Craignethan lying a couple of miles above the line of the river, where a smaller stream joined it.

They crossed this stream, about the size of the Eden at Hartley, and just beyond it a track came into their road, coming down from the round hills to their left. They halted there and watched a man approach them; he was driving a cart laden with hay.

'Pax tecum,' Harcla called out to him.

'Dia's Muire dhuit!' the man replied. His face was dirty and eaten with smallpox.

Harcla was perplexed and he turned to the others. 'Does anyone have Gaelic?' he asked them, wishing that Uther was with them still.

They shook their heads; but then Howgill spoke up. 'I have a little, my lord,' he said.

'Bravo, Thomas! Ask him if Craignethan is near here.'

The young trooper rode forward and spoke quietly with the Scot; this man nodded his head at Thomas' questions and smiled, trying to please.

'Ambrose's genius is wonderful!' Harcla said to himself, finding thus that Craignethan was indeed close by, lying in a fold of the hills.

To one question the hay-driver answered 'Randolphus' – this was clear to Harcla as he listened; and to the next he said 'Dha chead gca-paill'.

'God's blood!' Harcla cried as Thomas translated for him. 'Randolph and two hundred riders!'

Howgill returned to the group as the Scot, all smiles and obeisances, went his way. 'The hay he carries is part of a quantity for Randolph's horses,' Thomas said. 'They ride east at dawn.'

'East?' Harcla queried. 'Are you sure?'

'That is what he said, Andreas.' Thomas bit his lip and Harcla wondered at this informality.

Conan and Alexander joked together. 'We can always travel up to Craignethan and ask their intentions,' Conan said, grinning.

'Be careful, my friend,' replied Alexander, 'do not tempt the fates.' And they glanced at Harcla, their eyes creasing in smiles.

'Do you think me that incautious?' he asked them.

'Well, my lord, Randolph would no doubt tell you,' they answered easily, 'and perhaps offer us a quart of his Bordeaux as he spoke of his plans!'

'Ha!' Harcla exclaimed.

'We should not mention Mallerstang or Liddesdale, of course,' Ketel interjected.

'No, we would not wish to appear overly superior,' said Alexander.

Everyone laughed; Thomas looked at their faces, he felt a pride swelling within him and he was glad to laugh too. The horses moved lightly in the wet road, dancing with the sound of the laughter.

Harcla turned to the four men remaining to him. 'One of us must go back,' he said. He looked at Kelleth. 'Alexander, you go.'

'Thank you, my lord,' Kelleth said, nudging his unwilling horse out from the dance of the others.

'Kirkord first,' Harcla said to him. 'If they are not there, then Treskeir. Tell Clifford he must expect a raid from Randolph within one or two days. Do not be overtaken.'

Alexander wheeled his horse and galloped away.

'Farewell!' his friends shouted after him.

With Kelleth gone Harcla led his smaller company upstream and looked for a crossing-place. The road they had travelled thus far was like to be, he thought, over busy for their purpose and he determined to ride westward by the unbeaten ways on the north bank of the Clyde.

He placed Ambrose's map in a deep pocket of his pack, like an old friend who has outlived his usefulness, for Craignethan sat upon its very western edge; they had reached the limits of their knowledge and whatever lay before them was uncharted.

After a short distance they came upon a stretch of the river that ran fast and shallow, splashing over rounded pebbles in little waves, and they walked their horses across the river here and clambered up its far side. Around this place the valley softened and opened out becoming rich pasture and water meadows that were perhaps half a mile wide; they saw the small black cattle of the country still grazing there. Above them, to their right, a series of wooded escarpments rose, cliff by cliff, and lay in beautiful colours cast by the sun and falling upon the autumn trees.

Harcla sent Ketel to act as scout one hundred yards ahead and they rode steadily until the sun began to sink more quickly toward the west, where the river, as big as the Solway at Carlisle, would run into the sea.

Harcla was about to ask Conan to search for a night-stopping place, away from the Clyde and further to their right, under the escarpment, when he saw Ketel's arm rise and fall in two deliberate movements.

'Get down!' he said quickly to Conan and Thomas. 'The horses too.'

They dismounted hurriedly and pulled the horses to the ground. Harcla looked up through the thick greenery of grass and brush shading the bank; he saw the place where Ketel had been – a tall willow sweeping down to the water – and on the opposite edge, riding east on the track they had recently quitted, a body of horsemen clattering into view.

'How many are they, my lord?' whispered Conan as he wriggled up to Harcla.

'Forty or fifty,' answered he. 'But I do not think they are for us.' He paused then and thought of the friar at Biggar, but he dismissed this. 'They are on their way to Randolph, I guess.'

They lay there quietly in the damp evening grass and watched the riders trot gently along the road. All would have been well but Thomas' pony, not liking its prone position, whinnied loudly then and kicked at the air. Harcla looked behind him and saw Thomas lying on the ground and struggling with the reins as the horse tried to rise. Conan squirmed back in the grass to aid him but it was too late and some few of the Scots riders, as they came abreast of the straining horse, began to point and shout out to their leader.

'Jesu!' Harcla muttered and he turned again to watch the Scots. The knight at their head had stopped and was staring directly at the melee of men and horses across the river; Harcla saw it was Soulis.

Thomas was standing now, desperately holding the bridle as his pony reared and bellowed in front of him. Soulis and a dozen of his men were sliding down to the river. Ketel reappeared, as if by magic, and was riding back to Harcla.

Harcla shouted above the growing noise. 'Howgill, for Christ's sake!' he called. 'Mount your horse!'

Conan was already mounted and stringing his bow. Ketel rode up and, as he did, loosed two or three arrows into the Scots as they waded through the water. This slowed them a little and one was hurt; they began to shout themselves and they urged their horses on.

Harcla turned to Conan. 'Listen!' he said quickly. 'We should separate anyway – after this; but Conan, you must now go back too. Tell Clifford there is Soulis and a further fifty. Do you understand?'

'Yes, my lord.'

A flight of arrows, loosed by the Scots on the far bank, fell among them.

'We shall be killed!' Conan shouted, his eyes wide in a great fear. 'Christ! We are finished.'

'Get away, Conan,' Harcla said to him. He swung upon his own horse and watched Ketel come riding up; he heard Ketel's cry of sudden pain as an arrow thudded into his groin and embedded itself, through his leg, in the leather of his saddle. Ketel halted, wrenched the shaft out from him and flung it upon the ground; his face, as Harcla gazed upon it, became white, as though emptied of blood. In that moment his horse reared up, hurt itself and Ketel almost fell.

'Dear Jesu!' Harcla whispered, the courage ebbing from him.

The upper part of Ketel's leg was streaming with what seemed the whole of his blood and it ran down the flanks of his horse; the dark smell unhinged its mind and it stamped the ground, and then, as though becoming aware of its own pain it kicked out its rear legs, from its rump a grey arrow shaft stuck up in the air like an obscene finger.

'Ketel!' Harcla shouted. 'Go with Conan.'

Ketel's eyes lifted from the struggles with his horse; there were many kinds of pain there. 'I cannot,' he said.

'Go!' Harcla insisted, 'and God go with you.'

'My lord, my lord!' he begged, swooning.

Conan of Askham summoned his strength amid the falling arrows and rode close to his friend. 'Come, Ketel,' he said, looking fiercely upon him. 'We must go.' They touched their hands together, in token of friendship, and Conan kicked their horses hard and they leapt away.

Ketel cast a last imploring glance behind him. 'Andreas,' he called; but Harcla, sundered himself, had already turned to Howgill.

Another flight of arrows whistled in the darkening air; Soulis climbed from the river.

Thomas had calmed his pony and he and Harcla dug in their spurs and wheeled away toward the sinking sun, but Harcla was hit by the fall of an arrow as he turned; he knew it was there, sticking in his back through his cloak and jerkin and held upright by the chain mail of his hauberk.

The pain suffused him and he thought he would fall. 'We are finished,' he murmured, as his senses drifted. He felt young, weak.

'I know you, Harcla,' Soulis shouted out, laughing. 'By Christ, I know you!'

Harcla roused himself and glanced back over his shoulder. Behind Soulis he saw Conan and Ketel disappear in a hollow of the land; they were riding as though bound together, for Conan had locked Ketel's near arm within his own that he would not fall.

'Where is Strickland?' Soulis yelled out to Harcla.

Harcla, in a haze, had forgotten he was Walter's friend. 'Still in bed, as far as I know,' he called back, but grimacing as the hurt within him grew.

'Ha, ha, ha,' Soulis laughed again. 'I knew this war would be too much for him.' The rest of his words were lost in the wind rushing past Harcla's ears.

'It is too much for me!' Harcla whispered to himself, gazing on the flying ground beneath his feet; and he glanced across at Thomas as though seeing him for the first time, he was unhooded now, a familiar determined set to the corner of his mouth as he leant forward in the saddle, urging his pony to greater speeds.

27

THE SCOTS CONFER

hen John de Soulis had stopped laughing at Harcla's desperate retreat from the river he turned his company, forbearing to give chase, and rode on to the castle of Craignethan pleased with his work – for Soulis was a knight better suited to those earlier days when there was still something of a rough sanctity in its calling.

He told his story to Thomas Randolph the earl of Moray as he sat by the comfort of the fire in the great hall. Randolph was in good humour; he had left his uncle Robert the king at Dunbarton the day before with orders to harass Edward's army wherever he saw fit – to do the greatest damage in speedy targeted strikes. These orders were pleasing to him for they gave the opportunity to display his own prowess. Randolph was a good general, perhaps the best that Bruce had gathered to him these last two or three years.

He eagerly awaited the time when his first attack should be; but Bruce's captain was sorry that Harcla was away from the army and he puckered his brow at Soulis' news and said, 'You must return the way you came and find him again.'

'You mean Harcla, my lord?' queried Soulis.

'Of course.'

Soulis looked troubled. 'Have I done wrong, my lord?' he asked him.

'I do not know as yet,' Randolph replied thoughtfully, rubbing his shoulder. 'But I want to ask him about the suicide of my brother Sylvester. Our intelligence from Durham, as you know, dried up about two months ago and then at our messenger's next rendezvous we discovered why.'

Soulis sat in silence but thinking irreverently that Sylvester had always been highly strung; he smiled inwardly at his joke, considering Randolph far too grave – as though he carried a greater weight than Bruce himself.

Randolph looked up to him. 'Besides,' he went on, 'King Robert would wish the matter of Harcla tidied, one way or the other.'

'But the king, I think, is no longer at Dunbarton and Harcla can do no damage.'

'Well, John, he has taken his five hundred to Kirkintilloch alright; but

Harcla is dangerous, wounded or no, and we should be certain of his whereabouts.'

Soulis saw the truth of this and nodded his head. 'But,' he mused, 'I do not think he will turn without Clifford.'

The two men looked at each other for a few moments then Randolph spoke again. 'I shall go ahead with our two hundred as planned. Edward's army is so strung out I can attack wherever I may choose. I shall strike at dawn next day but one, probably near Treskeir, and then again the following night, wherever they halt before Biggar.'

Randolph's eyes, as he spoke, became brighter, shining darkly like amethyst; Soulis was aware that his uncomplicated manner hid an inner excitement which, like that of all great leaders, transmitted itself unseen to others.

'John,' Randolph went on, 'you must send a messenger to ride quickly to the king at Kirkintilloch with this news of Harcla; you ride west too, but more carefully with say, two dozen horsemen.'

'Two dozen, my lord?' Soulis queried.

'Yes, by God, two dozen and once you have found him, hold him and send again to the king. He must not escape us this time.'

Soulis was about to quit the hall when he thought of the other matter. 'What are we to do with Harcla's rider,' he asked, 'the man Kelleth?'

'Ha!' Randolph replied in great amusement. 'I laugh to think how easy we took him. The young fool! – he attacked us; my scouts could not believe it. But he has told us nothing, other than his name and lord – and he must have been the bearer of some news for Clifford.'

'Harcla cannot be aware of the king's movements, or yours, come to that.'

'That may be, John,' said Randolph dismissively, 'and it probably makes no difference anyway; the English are impotent.'

'But what are we to do with him?'

Randolph thought awhile and the dark light in his eyes gleamed a little. 'Cut out his tongue and release him,' he said. 'Keep the pony.'

'My lord?' questioned Soulis, thinking he had mis-heard.

'You heard me alright, John. Let it be done and Harcla may know my wrath; he killed my brother – what is the useless speech of one his churls to that?'

'Very good, my lord,' said Soulis, his face ashen, and he walked off to attend to his men.

The following morning, the twenty-eighth, Thomas Randolph rode east toward Treskeir with some two hundred and forty light horsemen. They rattled out from the gateway of Craignethan with much noise and laughter; Randolph waved an arm to Soulis, standing above the gate-house.

'Ride well!' Soulis shouted down to him.

Randolph smiled. 'Come, lads!' he called to his men, above the clatter, 'we go to hunt the English!'

The wild cheering rose higher in the morning air and they disappeared behind a fold of the many small hills of that country.

Soulis turned toward the keep; he had one more task to perform before he rode west in search of Harcla. He spoke to one of the guards. 'Bring the man Kelleth to me,' he ordered. 'I shall be down below.'

Soulis ran down the stairway to the open ground of the bailey; the men of his company were already mounted and ready to depart. Mauchline, the troubadour of Jedburgh, the man who had attempted to skewer Harcla to the oaken gates of the Liddesdale tower, held Kelleth's horse, ready saddled.

'Who is this for, my lord?' he asked.

'It's owner,' Soulis replied, for he had determined the course he should take and was certain all would come right; he swung up to his own horse, easy in his mind. Alexander walked into the bailey flanked by two guards of the castle.

'Come, Kelleth,' Soulis called across to him. 'Mount your pony; now is your chance to ride with real horsemen!'

Alexander looked up at him in confusion. 'Where are you taking me, my lord?' he asked.

'Ha! To find your lord, boy.'

Kelleth eyed Soulis doubtfully.

'Come, I thought you would be pleased.'

Harcla's man wondered what were Soulis' plans, but he was happy enough to quit Craignethan and he thought too he may find a chance to redeem himself; of his close escape from a mutilation too horrible to contemplate he had, as yet, no idea and thus did not realise, no matter what Soulis meant by his disobedience, how greatly he was beholden.

He jumped up to his pony and caught the gaze of Mauchline; the two young men looked upon each other expressionlessly, remembering Liddesdale

'Watch him well, Mauchline,' Soulis said and he ordered his band to move out. 'We ride west!' he cried.

~ 28 ~

TRESKEIR

THE two men approached the fire; they had seen its light over the last few minutes, glimmering through the trees of the wood, and it made them glad. They rode a single horse and one of them, the foremost, was only held upright by the strength of the other's left arm – it encompassed him and clasped him firmly to the other's chest.

This other, the second man, grasped the reins in his right hand and kicked the horse into a trot. 'Not far now, my friend,' he said quietly.

The first man did not reply; once more he had fainted and his head lolled forward on to his breast.

At first Conan had staunched the blood from Ketel's groin with wrappings of linen but every few hours, as they rode, the wound opened up afresh and soaked the cloths. In the morning, after spending the night-time hours beneath the shelter of a beech tree, Ketel became very weak and unable to ride; he had fallen and it was then that Conan pulled him up to his own horse. They had ridden steadily all day with Ketel's wounded horse tied behind them; Conan, nearing exhaustion, prayed that they were close by Treskeir.

The firelight they had seen shone brighter now although the track they followed led them slightly to the left, toward the Tweed. 'Christ!' said Conan to himself, 'I never wish to see another bloody river.'

Ketel mumbled something incoherently.

'Stay, my friend,' Conan said.

His mind turned on the way of things – on how the simple and true always became complex and false. Not false, perhaps, but mixed; a cup of sweet and bitter with many layers blurred within it, and therefore uncertain of its purpose.

He pulled Ketel's body closer to him and in his tiredness smiled; some things remain simple, he thought, and he pushed their horse on. The dark branches of many trees leant together in arcs and the two men rode a natural avenue that filled with the old leaves falling in their passage.

'Halt!' a voice called out from the mirk ahead. 'Qui va la?'

Conan laughed in recognition. 'Is that you, my lord?' he shouted.

Richard la Fraunceise of Maulds Meaburn rode forward with half a dozen troopers at his heel. 'Conan?' he asked, peering into the gloom.

'Yes, my lord,' replied he, offering up his thanks, 'but Ketel is hurt.'

Fraunceise looked upon the ragged men of Harcla's company. 'By God, Conan!' he exclaimed. 'I do believe you are more dead than alive!'

'Please, my lord,' Conan urged.

'Come then,' Fraunceise said quickly. 'Follow me; we shall go to Clifford. James de Harcla is with him.'

'Good!' answered Conan. 'I am glad for that.' He stirred his memory and, as though by a great effort, he said, 'And Alexander too?'

'Kelleth?' Fraunceise queried. 'No, he is not here. Why, should he be?'

Conan fell silent, staring through the wet darkness of the trees. He was very tired, Ketel's body a dead weight within the circle of his arm. He felt hungry.

'Yes,' he said at last, 'he should.'

The mind of Fraunceise worked in strange patterns and it was some moments before he thought to speak of Harcla himself. 'What of my lord Andreas?' he asked then.

'I do not know,' Conan answered. 'I think he was hit.'

Fraunceise was incredulous. 'Harcla? Hit?' he cried. 'Impossible! But who is with him?'

'Howgill.'

'Who? For Christ's sake, who else?'

'He is one of Uther's men,' said Conan wearily. 'There is no one else left.'

Fraunceise stared at Conan and then at Ketel hunched formlessly in front of him; for a few seconds his face portrayed such utter astonishment that Conan, had he cared to, would have laughed.

The company rode on for about a mile and, coming to the edge of the wood, followed a track by a long field of oats. Looking ahead to the water meadows, Conan saw the lights of the army, a great number of fires burning in the night; and then an even greater number it seemed, rising in a straggled line away eastward over the hills..

Fraunceise followed his gaze. 'That is the road to Selkirk,' he said, to turn Conan's thoughts. 'We occupy the country, much good that it does us.'

When they arrived at Clifford's quarters, a steading to the east of Treskeir, Henry of Appleby told Fraunceise that his master was away in the great house, in conference with the king.

'You had best go there straightaway,' Fraunceise told Conan. 'Henry will guide you; and we will see to Ketel.' He shouted for Clifford's physician and began to wonder then what had occurred in those wastelands away to the west.

It seemed to Conan that he had been sleeping for only a few moments when he awoke to a cacophony of wild shouting. In reality he had slept long and dawn was only an hour away. He heard the cries more clearly as his senses came to him; they told of attack and calls to arms.

He jumped to his feet, stumbling on the tussocks of grass that formed the floor of the tent and he accidentally kicked against the prone figure of Ketel beside him.

'Be careful, you fat oaf!' Ketel growled. 'Do you not know I am dangerously wounded?'

Conan laughed at this. 'You recover well, Ketel,' he replied, and he rushed out of the doorway with the six or seven others who shared their quarters. He recognised some of these sleepy-eyed men and they all stared out into the half-light where all was disorder and chaos; dozens of others, only part dressed, scurried madly to and fro searching for pikes and spears and bows. Conan heard the whinnying of horses in the darkness to his right; in a makeshift paddock of small fencing the horses belonging to this company ran and reared.

Strange riders on wiry ponies were urging them to break the fence and then shepherd them away toward the trees. The Scots glanced about them quickly as they worked and Conan, who had gathered half a dozen men and run to the paddock with torches, gazed on their weird painted faces glowing in the light; they were fearsome, small and hard like goblins, and men quailed.

'Who leads us?' Conan called to those nearest to him.

'Sir Richard,' said one.

'Sir Richard?' queried Conan. 'Fraunceise is not here; he is on guard elsewhere'

'No, no,' returned the other. 'Sir Richard de Musgrave.'

'Then one of you had better go to him,' Conan said flatly, 'and tell him his horses are reived.' As he spoke the Scots riders broke the paddock and rode off with twenty horses, hullooing loudly.

Conan could hear the heavy metallic thudding of combat away to his left and he ran a hundred yards up the hill toward this sound of clashing swords on shields and pikes. Lights were lit within some of the wagons lining the road as he sped past them and these cast eerie shadows on the grass and upon the lightning bolts that were yet more of Randolph's painted riders as they flew down from the rounded hills.

Bruce's captain had chosen his place well; this part of the rear of Edward's army had camped a straggling one to two miles east of Treskeir and it lay in a dip of land covered by trees that looked south to the rising ground and north to the Tweed behind it. Randolph's men wreaked havoc for about twenty minutes and then retired to the forest, counting their spoils and their booty.

When Musgrave appeared on the scene of the attack all he could do was count his dead, his lost horses and the quantities of food and grain stolen from the now burning wagons. These lit up the night sky in spiralling orange and yellow flames, much fiercer than the camp-fires they leapt above, and seemed to Conan as he gazed upon them some sort of token of the wilder, bloodier encounters to come.

He heard the thudding of heavy cavalry approaching and he turned toward the road. It was Clifford and his knights; they rode up wildly in the flashing shadows and the earl called to him.

'Where is Musgrave?'

Conan pointed to the burning baggage-train. 'Over there, my lord,' he replied.

Clifford rode forward a pace or two and shouted for Musgrave. A solitary figure emerged from the unnatural light of the fires.

'Well, Sir Richard?' Clifford said.

'It was the Scots,' Musgrave answered.

'By God, Sir Richard!' the earl exclaimed. 'I hardly expected anyone else. What happened?'

'They killed our guards on the hill above and surprised us. There was nothing we could do.'

'How many were they?'

Musgrave was nonplussed. 'I do not know, my lord,' he said.

'Guess.'

The knight looked around him helplessly.

'With your permission, my lord,' Conan interposed.

'Speak, Conan.'

'Our report was correct, my lord. I would say two hundred.'

'And their leader?'

'Again, my lord, as we thought. It was Randolph.'

Clifford's face hardened. 'How many sentries were posted, Musgrave?' he asked coldly.

Musgrave sweated. 'Six, my lord.'

'Six! Christ's blood! You were at the council were you not, when Conan gave his news?'

'Yes, my lord.'

'Yes, my lord,' said Clifford, mimicking him. 'And we agreed to double the watch, did we not?'

'Yes, my lord.'

The earl was exasperated. 'Then tell me, my lord,' he barked, 'what is the point of securing intelligence of the enemy if we do not act upon it?' Clifford did not wait for his knight to answer but continued. 'God in heaven, Musgrave, there are men out there,' he said, pointing to the west, 'risking their lives that the king, and you, for Christ's sake, may sleep easy in your poxy beds!'

Lord Clifford was beside himself with rage and he wondered too what had possessed him to send his lieutenant on that perilous road to the wastelands. Conan had spoken well at the council; his words made all the more effective by his still dirty riding gear and obvious fatigue. Alexander of Kelleth was lost and Harcla himself deep in the west and alone, or almost so. By God, it could not be countenanced!

Clifford's self-recrimination was blasted on Musgrave. 'You, Sir!' he shouted to him. 'Take your company, follow the enemy's trail and discover their head-quarters.'

'My lord earl,' Musgrave replied. 'I have no horse, half of my foot are dead or wounded, and I need to make an account of the lost wagons and other animals.'

Clifford was rendered speechless by this refusal; although knights were largely autonomous in their actions, there was an accepted code of conduct, of deference to authority, which Musgrave, in the face of danger, seemed willing to ignore.

Uther Pendragon, safely returned from Moffat, had ridden up with Clifford's men and he stood with his horse close by. 'My lord Clifford,' he said, 'this is a task for me. My horsemen from Hartley will ride for you!'

'And I!' said Conan.

'And I!' said Ketel, who had limped up the road from his bed.

Clifford's laughter rang out in the clean air and the light from the dawn sky behind him eclipsed the dying fires of Musgrave's sentry posts and the smouldering wagons. He fully realised their motive and he smiled, almost enviously.

'Then go, my friends,' he said, 'and find your lord.'

THE SEARCH FOR HARCLA

hen Harcla had glanced across at his young companion in the flight from the river, such was the shock that he thought his sight was failing him and that his brain, in its leave-taking, conjured up precious images.

And now, two days later, when he opened his eyes for the first time since that ride and gazed again upon that face, he wondered if he dreamt still, existing in some blissful state prepared by God for those close to death.

He lay in a high-sided wooden bedstead and covered with a bright green blanket thrown with yellows and dark reds. His hands grasped the sides and he attempted to rise; but he could not and he fell back panting. He stretched his body and in the moving realised he lay naked, the pain awoke too and he felt it keenly, remembering the arrow that had pierced him.

He was warm though and with that thought his eyes took in the glowing hearth set in one wall and further away the light from a window that cascaded into the chamber and fell upon the unhooded face of his companion; it was held a little to one side, a small smile hovering on the lips.

Harcla gazed upon the thick waves of hair, shortened now, almost cropped. His eyes drifted again and saw the whitewashed walls and the rough plaster about the timbers; they were perfectly bare but for a simple cross of Christ nailed to the near wall.

'I am in a monk's cell,' he thought. He raised a hand to his forehead and touched there the dried flakes of oil of chrism. 'They have anointed me,' he said.

The face of his companion spoke, and it was like the music of Andromache to him. 'Sleep again, Andreas. You will be well. Forget all else.'

He closed his eyes and reached to hold the hand that lay by his on the blanket; it was like searching for cinquefoil in the grass of a meadow, and he remembered this and slept.

On that afternoon of the twenty-ninth, as Harcla slept and Uther's company, with Conan and Ketel, rode in search of him, Edward's huge army continued its westward march. Some of the younger knights were growing impatient and Randolph's lightning dawn raid had served to infuriate them; they sat astride their huge war-horses, as heavily armoured as themselves, and began to sense their uselessness. 'What use can we be,' they said to one another, 'if Bruce will fight in that manner?'

Musgrave heard these words and rode stolidly on; he was still stationed to the rear but now, of course, since the raid, with a much lesser burden of care. Clifford glared at him whenever he passed him by.

They were halfway to Kirkord and climbing away gently from the great river when Fraunceise rode down from the front of the army and fell in beside Clifford; the two men smiled and slowed their horses to a walk.

'How goes it, Richard?' Clifford asked in greeting.

'Well enough,' replied he, 'but I have some news from home.' Fraunceise paused and Clifford looked across to him.

'Well spit it out, can't you?'

'It appears all is not as it seems,' Fraunceise said.

'By God, Richard!' Clifford exclaimed. 'I have enough without your long-winded riddles. Speak plainly!'

Fraunceise's face took on a look it often did, that of miscomprehension mixed with a mild surprise. 'Well, my lord,' he said, 'Thomas of Howgill, supposedly Harcla's last remaining companion, is, at this very moment, sitting by his mother's hearth – probably consuming great bowls of hot porridge!'

'What! What!' Clifford spluttered, choking on his words. 'You push me too far. Christ! Is this one of your jokes?'

'My lord,' said Fraunceise solemnly, 'you have not heard the funny part as yet.'

'Who, then, is with him? I presume it is no ghost?'

'Robert, I fear it is my niece; she has disappeared from home.'

'What! Emma! It is impossible!'

'I fear not. Howgill has confessed to a deception; she has bewitched him. Also, it seems the lady Isabel, my wife, thought her at Hartley with the lady Sarah, and Sarah, in turn, thought her at home with Isabel.'

'Good God!'

Emma la Fraunceise got up from her place by the side of Harcla, left the room and went in search of the abbess. Emma may have been impetuous by nature but she was also capable of cogent thought; and in the hours and days of Harcla's delirium she had time enough to consider their situation.

She was amazed too at her own duplicity, and although a little cha-
grined at her vainglory was secretly pleased at the success of the elaborate deception. Patrick of Blande had been party to the affair, inevitably,
but would say nothing; she had known both young men, Thomas and
Patrick, since childhood and, whereby she was mesmeric, they could not
refuse her.

However, the more she had thought of her predicament the less she
was encouraged; a young woman in a mad escape from desperate enemies intent on murdering her, one hundred miles from home, or so she
guessed, and now sheltering with her wounded lover in an obscure nun-
nery she had never heard of, and, worst of all, Harcla himself raving in a
fever.

She had cried in her dreams the first night, frightened at the strangeness of his and despairing of his return to hers; but she felt instinctively
that once he recovered, and she had complete trust of this, all would yet
be well.

Richard le Bret, the man also known as Uther, the hermit of
Pendragon, halted his company and looked around him. They were
stopped beneath the brow of a small hill, a mile to the north of the Clyde;
the hill, though small, was long and shaped like the belly of a woman and
along its lower ridge a line of hawthorn ran, bare now and shrunken
against the coming winter.

It was the last day of the month, the third since they left Clifford and
the army at Treskeir. They had ridden steadily west, coming eventually
to the ford below Craignethan; Conan and Ketel glanced across at one
another here and their mouths hardened. They saw again the wooded
escarpments of the country, duller now without the sheen of beauty the
sun had given them the time before.

Once they had passed this place Uther and his men, as they rode
along, began to make enquiries of Harcla at various steadings and
manor-houses.

'Has anyone seen,' they would ask, 'two horsemen riding west? One
on a dark charger, the other a bay.'

The answer was always the same, always in the negative. After a day
of this Uther had become disenchanted. 'We are on a fool's errand,' he
muttered to himself. 'He could be anywhere in this damned country.'

At one large house nearby, as the rest of the company waited, Conan
asked the usual question, but the tenant, standing in his yard, did not

reply immediately, but looked up at him oddly.

'Have you seen them?' Conan repeated.

At length the man answered. 'No, I have not,' he said. Conan was about to turn away when the man continued, 'But you are not the first to ask.'

Conan wheeled his horse about on the muddy gravel. 'Explain yourself, if you please,' he said.

The stranger smiled and told him what he knew.

A few minutes later Conan rejoined the group and related his story to Uther. 'A Scots party, perhaps two dozen riders, are scouring the land also,' he said. 'They were here yesterday asking of two horsemen westward bound.'

'Sang Real!' Uther exclaimed. 'My lord Andreas is a coveted being!'

Conan could not help chuckling a little; even now he found the Irish warrior's language difficult to fathom.

'It must be Soulis,' Ketel said. 'If Randolph is away by Treskeir.'

'We should press forward,' said Uther.

But Ketel frowned. 'Wait, Uther,' he said to him, 'we are not thinking clearly – if we were to ask at every house we should still be asking at Christmas!'

'Yes,' Uther replied, 'then what dost thou propose?'

'Listen, Uther!' continued Ketel. 'My lord would not beg shelter incautiously, wounded or no, in case he put himself in the hands of his enemies.'

'Agreed.'

'Good! So at what place would there be the least likelihood of that?'

'Ahh!' Conan cried, smiling. 'A place of God; an abbey, or a convent.'

'Bravo, Conan! Do you agree, Uther?' he asked, turning to him.

'Yes, yes. It is worth trying.' Uther thought awhile. 'We must assume anyway, they continued their path down Clydesdale. How far are we now from Craignethan?'

'Say, fifteen miles,' Ketel replied.

'And Soulis made his attack in the late afternoon?'

'Yes, Uther.'

'Very good. They must have stopped somewhere that night – and that place can be no more than what? – five miles further to the west, even if they rode like the wind.'

The others of the company brightened, hearing this lively debate, and they jostled their horses in their eagerness.

'I used to know this country,' Uther murmured, rubbing his cheek. 'Christ! A bloody convent! The Carmelites have a place a mile or two from the north bank of the Clyde. It was pointed out to me once, years ago, from the towers of Buittle Castle, from the other side of the river.

'What are Carmelites?' Conan asked.

Ketel looked at him scornfully. 'You are not only a fat oaf,' he said, 'but also an ignorant one. They are white friars of Our Lady of Mount Carmel.'

'White friars?' said Conan quickly, thinking of Biggar.

'Yes. Nuns too, I think.'

'Ha! Ketel!' Uther said. 'You become more like your tutor my lord Fraunceise.'

Ketel snorted and Conan laughed.

'Come, my friends,' called Uther. 'Ten minutes ride will do us.'

The company formed together and broke into a fast gallop, heading for the long rounded hill and its spiky chaplet of hawthorn, two miles distant in the rising ground to the northwest.

The religious house of Our Lady of Mount Carmel lay sheltered in a stretch of fertile land that fell southwest with the stream of Calder Water. It was shielded from the wild winds of that country by a series of long-ridged hills that ran in an elongated arc around and above it and the narrow valley thus formed then opened out to become gentle uplands as it approached the banks of the great river.

From a flat ridge beneath the northerly line of hills, just two hundred yards above the priory and convent buildings, the knight Soulis and his company had made a little camp. Earlier that morning enquiries had been made down below and now Soulis was a happy man as he gazed the quarter-mile or so across the valley to the southern hills, their distinctive line of stunted hawthorn following the ridge as it fell to the river.

As Randolph had ordered, Soulis dispatched a rider with his news to King Robert at Kirkintilloch. The message read:

Sire, my lord the earl of Moray tells me you are desirous of ascertaining the whereabouts of a certain knight, Andreas de Harcla of Westmorland. I am pleased to be able to tell your majesty that he rests at the convent of Our Lady by the Calder Water in Clydesdale. He is accompanied by one other, a religieuse, which fact I do not comprehend.

Howsoever, here he shall stay until such time as I am aware of your pleasure.

Soulis expected his reply directly, for Kirkintilloch was only a couple of hours distant, and then, once this affair was concluded, he could happily join with Randolph in the harrowing of Edward's army down by Biggar – by all accounts as easy a task as squeezing the juice from ripe fruit.

He thought of winning some ransoms. 'Ha, ha, ha!' he laughed gleefully. 'How wonderful it would be if Walter de Strickland were to fall into my path!' But any prize will suffice, of course. Even Harcla!'

The Scots knight considered for a while in silence. 'Harcla's stock has risen in recent months,' he reflected. 'He might be worth five or six hundred marks! Whew!' Soulis smacked his lips together and chuckled loudly.

Mauchline, hearing this merriment, looked up from the ground where he sat with Alexander of Kelleth. 'My lord?' he said.

'Mauchline,' Soulis said to him, turning all eventualities in his mind, 'both roads – from the convent and the priory – are guarded, are they not?'

'Yes, my lord,' answered he. 'Six men at each, just beyond the gates.'

'Good, good! We have him now.' Another thought struck him and he turned to Kelleth. 'There was no woman with your company, was there?' he asked. 'Or nun?'

'A woman?' Alexander replied, puzzled. 'No, my lord.'

'Mmm, well he has found one at all events; perhaps he has turned magician.'

Kelleth smiled secretly. 'Whatever he may be,' he said, 'you will never take him!'

'Be quiet, boy!' Soulis retorted, disturbed in his happy reverie and suddenly angry, 'or, by God I will carry out your punishment.'

Soulis walked away toward the higher ground and it was then that Alexander, through Mauchline, learnt of his intended fate; he went white, sat back in the faded heather and was silent. He looked down at his hands and saw that they were shaking violently. 'I must get out of this,' he whispered to himself.

Mauchline, perhaps discomfited by Kelleth's weakness, got to his feet and looked away across the valley; but he stiffened suddenly as he stared. 'My lord! My lord!' he shouted urgently, pointing to the southern ridge of hawthorn. 'My lord, quickly!'

Soulis strode down the slope to where Mauchline stood, with his arm outstretched. He creased his eyes and saw, etched in a beautiful line before the jagged thorn trees, twelve armed riders; they were dark silhouettes, clear against the sky, their upright spears like thick spikes that glinted.

'Blood of Christ!' Soulis cried. 'Blood of Christ! Mauchline, can you make out their crest?'

The singer of Jedburgh shielded his eyes with the flat of his hand and gazed to the motionless line of men. 'Cross gules,' he said flatly.

'Yes, yes. What else?'

As Soulis spoke, asking his question, one of the riders across the little valley, it was Ketel, pushed his horse forward a pace and lifted his bright target high into the air above his head.

'Martlet, I think,' said Mauchline. 'Upper right quarter.'

The face of Soulis hardened and he swore, but Kelleth's spirits soared within him.

~ 30 ~

THE END OF SOME THINGS

Harcla opened his eyes; he saw Emma's gaze resting on him and he smiled.

'You return to me,' she said.

He smiled again and looked to the window-space; the early morning light was bright with the promise of sun and, through the open shutter, cool air, fragrant like fell water, flooded the cell. 'The weather will change again,' he said, sitting up. 'We should go.'

He swung his legs to the floor; his head swam for an instant as he stood upright and then, looking down to the bedstead with its fine cloths in disarray, he thought it as like to a coffin, narrow and tall-sided. He shivered and reached for his clothing. The tunic, jerkin and hose had been neatly pressed and lay by a chair; his sword, the one Uther had forged for him, stood in its scabbard at an angle of the wall and beside it his pack, travel-stained and battered – within it, he knew, was a small leather bag containing ten silver marks, Ambrose's precious but now useless chart and also, in a secret place, Emma's letter, the one he had received at Wark. He smiled at this and showed it to her.

'See,' he said, 'how well creased it is.'

She laughed with him, handling the paper. 'How prim I was!' she said, reading.

'We were young then,' he said.

He moved to the window and drank in the air, like life returning, and Emma told him then of the last moments of their ride from Soulis, how they had come upon this place and of the great kindness of the abbess; and lastly that he, Harcla, had been unconscious for three days.

Emma looked away from him unhappily, for, after all this, there was a small disquiet troubling her; Harcla mis-read her thought and asked: 'What story then did you give?'

'Oh! It's not that, Andreas,' she answered slowly, 'But, well…. I said that I was your sister, a postulant nun; that we were journeying to Carlisle and got caught up in the warfare ravaging the country.' She stopped and looked across to him as he smiled. 'Was that good enough, Andreas?' she said.

Harcla's eyes creased in smiles and the short lines of the scar upon his cheek lay like furrows. 'More than good, Emma,' he answered her. 'You are my delight and my strength – and without thee, it is certain, I should be alone, lost and, like as not, dead.'

'In truth I thought I had lost you,' she said.

'But you have not,' he said softly, 'nor I you. Be certain of our strength, Emma, and no harm can touch us.'

After the dawn mass for Michael, the great archangel, he walked with her in the kitchen garden and then, before their breakfast, they went to the stabling to see that the horses were well-cared for and fit to ride.

The heavy animal smells were all around, and the intense rich breathing of the horses; his dark stallion nuzzled his hand. 'We must leave this morning, Emma,' he said again as they stood together in the darkness. 'You had best tell your friend the abbess.'

It was in this way that Emma was walking away from Harcla and toward the door when it burst open and six men, armed with swords and daggers, rushed into the ground of the stabling, almost falling as the door gave way.

Harcla spun on his heels and, pulling his hand from the stallion's head, he reached for his sword and swept it into the air. 'Come back to me, Emma!' he shouted, moving lithely to the Scots.

These men stood for a second and then two of them darted along the far wall, like imps, following Emma as she ran back to Harcla. The others walked ahead carefully and called out to him. 'Surrender, my lord,' they said.

Harcla grimaced and did not bother to reply. He stepped forward yet Emma was still not close enough to gain his shelter. 'Leave the woman,' he shouted to the two closing on her.

But Emma had turned, withdrawing her own dagger, and she lunged at one who then fell back with a gash to his arm but the other, in that small space, thrust his sword at her and it pierced her side.

'Andreas!' she cried.

Harcla forgot the four before him and he swung fiercely to his left, to the one who had hurt her. He caught the Scot squarely in the back as this man had leant forward in the act of attacking her and the sword ripped through his flesh to the bone and severed the spine; the man whimpered and crumpled to the floor.

Harcla straightened again with Emma now safely behind him; she gasped a little and held her side, a darkening patch blemishing the grey of her tunic. Harcla faced the four; they moved warily, encircling him, but his blood was surging and, deciding the man on his extreme right was weak and fearful, he went for him first.

But as he did he saw another figure emerge into the half-light of the open doorway. 'Jesu!' he muttered. 'Yet more?'

But this last was one of his own, it was Ketel come down from the hill and he, unhappy of a long sword fight, withdrew from his belt one dagger after another, three in all. He threw them singly in the air and they spun brightly into the necks and throats of those menacing his lord; they staggered and fell, dropping their useless arms and what words they shouted in their despair were gurgled and not to be understood. The fourth man Harcla killed himself by a long thrust into his heart; he looked on the ragged corpses in the straw and Emma sobbed hysterically at the sight.

'God's blood!' Harcla cried. 'Ketel! I am glad you are for me.'

'There are more of them, my lord' Ketel said quickly, 'riding down from the hills. We must get away.'

'How many are we?' Harcla asked; and he glanced at Emma, leaning against the timber of the horses' stalls.

'With Uther, twelve.'

'Good! We can kill more of them.' Harcla's eyes, like Ketel's, were wide, dilated, impenetrable. He ran from the stable to gather their packs from the dormitory and as he passed Ketel he told him to mount Emma's bay himself and place her on his own dark stallion. 'She will ride better with me,' he said.

Emma was sick as Ketel helped her up to Harcla's charger. She looked at him then, her eyes full, and he was moved to pity. 'My lady,' he said to her gently, 'be strong. Mount the horse.'

Harcla returned and leapt astride his horse in front of Emma who flung her arms around him.

Ketel called from the doorway. 'Christ!' he said, 'Uther had better come now!' He watched Soulis' company careering down from the northern hill.

Harcla, Emma and Ketel rode into the open spaces of the convent garden, trampling the onions and leeks, and on the ridge above Soulis they saw, in glorious splendour, the great banner of Bruce unfurled. King Robert himself, surrounded by thirty of his personal bodyguard, stood in his armour, bright in the sun like a rock.

Harcla and Ketel gazed at this vision for a second. 'Good God!' Harcla exclaimed, 'is the war here?' And they galloped for the broken ground to the south. They saw that Soulis was cutting off their retreat and Uther seemed slow in bringing down his horsemen from the southern heights.

But then the shout began, begun by Conan and echoing through the stunted hawthorn hill. 'Harcla! Harcla! Harcla!' And at last they moved, sweeping down in a great arc.

Harcla saw them come. 'Christ!' he yelled to Ketel as they rode. 'They are fast!'

Uther led them and as they raced onwards he half-turned in the saddle, urging them to greater speeds. Their bows were ready strung and as they rode they fitted their arrows from the quivers at their backs. The ponies, guided thus only by the pressure of their riders' knees, flew along the turf and cast behind them cascading clods of dark earth.

Robert the Bruce watched from his hilltop. 'What men he has!' he said.

Soulis' band had reached the flat ground of the convent and was joined by the group of six from the eastern gate – those from the west failed to appear. Soulis saw the two horses carrying the three fugitives emerge from the shelter of the stabling and heard the shouts of encouragement from the King's men up above. He was astounded at this, seeing the banner and Bruce himself, steady in the bright morning.

'Take him, Sir John!' the king shouted down to him.

Soulis called his company together, to ride in a tight phalanx. 'We want triumph' he said to them and he looked around for Kelleth. 'Where are you, boy?' he shouted.

Mauchline and some of the others in the next rank had surrounded him. 'Here, my lord,' Alexander answered.

'Good! Stay by me; I may need your voice!'

Soulis lifted his eyes and saw Harcla, Ketel and the other breaking wildly away from him; and he marked, at the very edge of his sight, the riders of Hartley cutting in from the right where the slope was easiest. They were now fifty yards distant and closing rapidly.

'Armes! Armes! Armes!' Soulis cried, and his men lowered their spears to the horizontal and brought up their dark targets. Kelleth rode in the centre, weaponless, gazing with unbelief at his friends hurtling toward him with looks of death in their eyes.

At thirty yards he heard the order from Uther, a great bellow that rose above the clatter and thud of the horses. 'Loose!' he roared, and his eyes were fixed on the enemy. 'For Christ's sake! Loose now!'

Three terrible barrages of grey-flighted arrows, each only three seconds apart in time, ripped into Soulis' company; he could not have expected this and his face betrayed his horror. The English did not dismount to shoot, they did not even slow but loosed from the saddle, as they flew across his line of ride, the three flights apiece.

Soulis' charger, an arrow in its chest, buckled and threw him to the ground where he rolled and then did not move. Six others of his riders lay sprawled on the grass, their ponies galloping off in fright, and some were standing or running back to the hill, leaving their horses to writhe in their torment.

Mauchline ran to Soulis and Kelleth, finding his voice after an age, shouted to Conan as he and the rest of Uther's men rode in to finish the destruction.

'Conan!' Alexander cried. 'Conan, my friend!'

Conan turned to the sound and his jaw dropped in astonishment; Uther came up, looking all around him. 'Well met, man!' he said. 'But hurry, we must go. Look!' He pointed to Bruce's men who were picking their way downwards, in the wake of Soulis' fallen company, toward the valley floor.

Kelleth scrambled up behind Conan and they rode to join Harcla at the foot of the southern hill.

'Harcla!' the King shouted. He and his bodyguard had reached level ground and were riding toward him at an easy canter.

Harcla brought up his horse, reins in his left hand, sword in his right and Emma behind him. Uther and his men reformed in a single line with Harcla in their centre; immobile and silent, as though sculpted in granite, they faced the Scottish king.

'Harcla!' the king shouted again, and his voice was like steel.

Uther wiped the sweat from his forehead and watched the steady approach. 'We must go, my lord,' he said quietly. 'They are too many.'

'By the Christ, Harcla! Have you no voice?'

'Yes, my lord,' answered he at last. The line of Harcla's horses stamped the ground and snorted into the air.

'I wish to talk with you,' the king said.

In that instant the memories of many things sped through Harcla's mind: Jedburgh, Liddesdale, the friar at Biggar, Peter Claxton, Clifford - Emma. He looked at those around him and he decided. 'There is no time, my lord,' he called back. 'We must go!'

And Harcla, not waiting for more, turned his horse. King Robert raised his arm and halted his men, where Soulis had fallen. He watched Harcla's company clamber up the southern hill to the hawthorn ridge. 'I must have that man,' he said to himself.

Once they had gained the hilltop Harcla's company paused, looking down to the convent in its little valley and the gathering of riders there and the dead men in the long grass.

'Why did Bruce not come?' Uther asked.

Harcla shook his head but Conan said, 'We are too good for them!'

Ketel laughed. 'And what do you think, Alexander, eh?'

'Kelleth is still uncertain who he should be fighting for. Ha, ha, ha!'

They jostled him and poked him in the chest, making fun of his silence as he gazed distraught at the rider he supposed to be Thomas of Howgill.

But then all eyes were on Harcla. 'Where to now, my lord?' they asked him.

'Christ's mercy!' Harcla exclaimed. 'Home! Where else?'

And the others laughed and spurred their horses to the south. Harcla's smile was wide with happiness; Emma sat close behind him and he felt her arms tighten her hold of him. The warmth of her breath on his neck and cheek was like wine and he heard the soft lilt of her voice in his ear.

'The day grows dark, Andreas,' she whispered. 'Take me home.'

EPILOGUE

inter came quickly that year and with the storms and blizzards Edward's great army melted away. The king rode with Gaveston and the rest of the household to his stronghold of Berwick and rested there until Epiphany, ignoring the correspondence of his lords ordinaires, Hereford and Pembroke.

Emma la Fraunceise weakened badly and did not recover from her wound. On the second day of the journey home she died in Harcla's arms and, forsaking all, he carried her body to Maulds Meaburn and buried her there. Fraunceise, of course, and Clifford too, attended her requiem and the earl wept bitter tears at the graveside. He did not go to the King at Berwick but wintered at Appleby and found solace betimes in his Spanish wine, of which he had great quantity. Harcla's sister, the lady Sarah, was stricken by grief and she did not marry at that time.

Of the others, Conan returned to Askham and Alexander to Kelleth – for months he spoke little and when he did people said his voice had lost its lightness. Antoigne de Lucy persisted his malignant way and Musgrave his stupid one. Uther continued in Harcla's service; he had grown tired, he said, of his cave beneath the stone image of Saint Thomas and there was nowhere else he might go, even if he wished it.

Ketel too stayed at Hartley with his master who had become quiet and strangely idle and, as November turned to December and the great snowfalls came, the world slowed and there was nothing much to be done anyway.

ACKNOWLEDGMENTS

I would like to thank the staff of the Record Office at Carlisle Castle for the practical assistance and unfailing courtesy they rendered me. I spent some time there reading Joseph Bain's *Calendar of Documents Relating to Scotland*, the *Calendars of Patent* and *Close Rolls* of Edward II, Nicholson and Burns' *History of the Antiquities of Cumberland and Westmorland*, Aymer's *Foedera* and the *Transactions of the Cumberland and Westmorland Antiquarian and Archaeological Society*, in particular article viii in volume xxix of the new series which is entitled Sir Andrew de Harcla, Earl of Carlisle. In addition I would like to thank English Heritage and the staff at Carlisle Castle.

For those with an interest in the period Sir Arthur Bryant's *The Age of Chivalry* is a very readable history while Colm McNamee's *The Wars of the Bruces* provides gripping detail of the extraordinary family de Bruce.

For Harcla's role in the development of tactical warfare see J.E. Morris, *Mounted Infantry in Mediaeval Warfare*, in the Transactions of the Royal Historical Society, 3rd series volume vii, and also T. F. Tout's *The Tactics of the Battle of Boroughbridge* in volume xix of the English Historical Review.

Other books from Hayloft Publishing

A Riot of Thorn & Leaf by Dulcie Matthews
(£7.95, ISBN 0 9540711 0 7)

A Country Doctor by Dawn Robertson
(£2.25, ISBN 0 9523282 32)

Military Mountaineering by Retd. Major Bronco Lane
(Hardback, £25.95, ISBN 0 9523282 1 6)
(Paperback, £17.95, ISBN 0 9523282 6 7)

Yows & Cows by Mike Sanderson
(£7.95, ISBN 0 9523282 0 8)

Riding the Stang by Dawn Robertson
(£9.99, ISBN 0 9523282 2 4)

Secrets and Legends of Old Westmorland
by Peter Koronka and Dawn Robertson
(Hardback, £17.95, ISBN 0 9523282 4 0)
(Paperback, £11.95, ISBN 0 9523282 9 1)

The Irish Influence by Harold Slight
(£4.95, 0 9523282 5 9)

You can order any of the above books by writing to:

Hayloft Publishing, Great Skerrygill, South Stainmore,
Kirkby Stephen, Cumbria, CA17 4EU.

Please enclose a cheque plus £2 for UK postage & packing.
Tel. (017683) 42300
For more information see: www.hayloft.org.uk